OTHER BOOKS BY LIZA WIELAND

Land of Enchantment

Quickening

A Watch of Nightingales

Near Alcatraz

Bombshell

You Can Sleep While I Drive

Discovering America

The Names of the Lost

PARIS, 7 A.M.

LIZA WIELAND

SIMON & SCHUSTER

NEW YORK   LONDON   TORONTO   SYDNEY   NEW DELHI

Simon & Schuster
1230 Avenue of the Americas
New York, NY 10020

First Simon & Schuster hardcover edition June 2019

For information about special discounts for bulk purchases, please contact Simon & Schuster Special Sales at 1-866-506-1949 or business@simonandschuster.com.

The Simon & Schuster Speakers Bureau can bring authors to your live event. For more information or to book an event, contact the Simon & Schuster Speakers Bureau at 1-866-248-3049 or visit our website at www.simonspeakers.com.

Interior design by Carly Loman

Manufactured in the United States of America

1   3   5   7   9   10   8   6   4   2

Library of Congress Cataloging-in-Publication Data is available.

ISBN 978-1-5011-9721-5
ISBN 978-1-5011-9723-9 (ebook)

For Judy Whichard

On the twenty-fifth [of June, 1937], they took the ferry from Dover to Calais and drove to Paris through Beauvais. Elizabeth's journal breaks off at this point, and the three women's specific activities for the first three weeks in Paris are unknown.

BRETT C. MILLIER, *Elizabeth Bishop: Life and the Memory of It*

E lizabeth dreams of babies, that they are connected to her body, but not to her flesh. They are attached to her clothing by buttons and zippers and snaps and something like cockleburs that will later be invented and called Velcro. Double-sided tape, staples (not through the flesh), and large paper clips. Babies ride in her pockets. Two of them, very still, rest on top of her hair, under her hat. In the dream, she worries not so much that they will hurt her or be hurt, but that they are thirsty. Maybe she should be concerned about their mothers, but she isn't. She wonders if they could all have the same mother. She doesn't even think about their fathers, though she is, in the peculiar atmosphere of dreams, aware that she is thinking about them. She tries to look at their faces, but they squirm and twist away. All the babies are dressed or swaddled in bright colors, electrifying patterns, a yellow Star of David over their wildly beating hearts. There will be no hiding these babies, and Elizabeth is vaguely worried about this. But not for their safety, only that she will have to explain her voracious baby love, this immodesty of babies, this glut, this selfishness. *Why do you have so many?* someone will surely ask. What she thinks but will not say is, *Because I can. Because no one will have suspected this of me.*

And so after she wakes in the morning, after breakfast, Elizabeth says to Clara, Yes. Yes, I will help you smuggle these children out of Dieppe and south to Paris. And she decides she won't say or think anything more about Ernst vom Rath and his Polish lover or Sigrid and her marriage of convenience. She won't be afraid of what comes next, and she'll try to stop rushing here and there like a sandpiper and settle down somewhere and finish a book of poems.

And she decides, too, that she will never tell Sigrid or Louise or Margaret. She will leave it completely out of her letters to Miss Moore, to Frani Blough, to everyone. If the story of her life is ever written, this episode will not appear, although she suspects some clever sleuth will uncover it, but not for years after she's dead, a half century or maybe longer, after everyone else is dead, too.

Except for these babies, who will have grown up perhaps knowing that two women saved them. Or maybe just one woman: Clara. They will tell their own children: the Countess Clara Longworth de Chambrun singlehandedly brought us from the north of France to a convent in Paris, thus saving our lives.

The crises of our lives do not come, I think, accurately dated; they crop up unexpected and out of turn and somehow or other arrange themselves according to a calendar we cannot control.

ELIZABETH BISHOP, "Dimensions for a Novel"

GEOGRAPHY I

1930

If you can remember a dream and write it down quickly, without translating, you've got the poem. You've got the landscapes and populations: alder and aspen and poplar and birch. A lake, a wood, the sea. Pheasants and reindeer. A moose. A lark, a gull, rainbow trout, mackerel. A horned owl. The silly somnambulist brook babbling all night. An old woman and a child. An old man covered with glittering fish scales.

An all-night bus ride over precipitous hills, a heeling sailboat, its mast a slash against the sky, trains tunneling blindly through sycamore and willow, a fire raging in the village, terrible thirst.

See? The dreams are poems. And the way to bring on the dreaming is to eat cheese before bed. The worst cheese you can get your hands on, limburger or blue. Cheese with a long, irregular history.

This was a crazy notion to bring to college, but you have to bring something, don't you? You have to bring a certain kind of habit, or a story, or, because this is Vassar in 1930, a family name. Some girls bring the story of a mysterious past, a deep wound, a lost love, a dead brother. Other girls bring Rockefeller, Kennedy, Roosevelt. They bring smoking cigarettes and drinking whiskey and promiscuity (there's a kind of habit), which some girls wear like—write it!—a habit. This is a wonderful notion, the nun and the prostitute together at last, as they probably secretly wish they could have been all along. Elizabeth laughs about it privately, nervously, alone in her head.

Her roommate, Margaret Miller, has brought a gorgeous alto and a talent for painting. She's brought New York, which she calls *The City*, as if there were only that one, ever and always. And cigarettes, a bottle of gin stashed at the back of her wardrobe, a silver flask engraved with her mother's initials. Margaret has brought a new idea of horizon, not a vista but an angle, not a river but a tunnel, a park and not a field. She will paint angles and tunnels and parks until (write it!) disaster makes this impossible, and then she will curate exhibitions of paintings and write piercing, gemlike essays about the beauty of madwomen in nineteenth-century art.

The cheese, meanwhile, occupies a low bookshelf. Most nights, Elizabeth carves a small slice and eats it with bread brought from the dining hall.

And sure enough, the dreams arrive—though that seems the wrong word for dreams, but really it isn't. They arrive like passengers out of the air or off the sea, having crossed a vast expanse of some other element. Elizabeth's father, eighteen years dead. In her dreams, he's driving a large green car. Her mother, at a high window of the state hospital in Dartmouth, Nova Scotia, signaling for something Elizabeth can't understand, her expression fierce and threatening. A teacher she loves disappearing into a maze of school corridors.

A Dutch bricklayer setting fire to the Reichstag. A two-year-old boy dressed in a brown shirt, a swastika wound round his arm like a bandage. His sister's mouth opened wide to scream something no one will ever hear because she is gassed and then burnt to ashes. All these people trailing poems behind them like too-large overcoats. And Elizabeth is the seamstress: make the coat fit better, close the seams, move the snaps, stitch up the ragged hem.

* * *

Elizabeth, Margaret says toward the end of October. I'm not sure these are poems. They're more like strange little stories. But I am sure that cheese stinks.

I know, Elizabeth says, but it has a noble purpose.

Which is what, for heaven's sake? If you want to have peculiar dreams, try this. Margaret holds out the silver flask.

Just . . . without a glass?

Just.

Elizabeth takes a long swallow, coughs.

Oh, she says when she can speak. It's like drinking perfume.

How would you know that? Margaret says.

I quaff the stuff for breakfast, of course!

Margaret lies down on her bed, and Elizabeth sits below her, on the floor, her back against the bed frame.

So, Margaret begins. About men.

Were we talking about men?

If we weren't, we should be.

I wish I knew some men the way you do, Elizabeth says.

And what way is that?

To feel comfortable around them. Natural.

Maybe I can help. Give you a lesson or two.

Start now.

Margaret sits up, shifts the pillow behind her back. Elizabeth turns to watch, thinking this will be part of the lesson, how to move one's body, the choreography. Margaret looks like a queen riding on a barge. What poem is that? *A pearl garland winds her head: / She leaneth on a velvet bed.* Margaret as the Lady of Shalott. When Elizabeth turns back, she sees herself and Margaret in the mirror across the room, leg and leg and arm and arm and so on, halves of heads.

Halves of thoughts, too. It seems to do strange things, this drink. It's exhilarating.

First, Margaret says, boys—men—they want two things that are contradictory. They want bad and good. They want prostitute and wife.

Prostitute and *nun,* Elizabeth says.

Margaret smiles, which makes her entire face seem to glow. Such dark beauty, Elizabeth thinks, like my mother. In some photographs, she looks like someone's powdered her face with ashes.

That's the spirit! Margaret says. And not only do you have to know how to be both, you have to know when.

Must take some mind reading.

Which is really just imagination. Which you have loads of, obviously.

Margaret leans forward to rest the flask on Elizabeth's shoulder. This helps, she says.

Helps us or them?

Both, Margaret says. She watches Elizabeth unscrew the cap on the flask. Not so much this time.

Elizabeth takes a tiny sip, a drop. Suddenly, she feels terribly thirsty. A memory crackles out of nowhere, a fire.

Much better, she says. Almost tastes good.

So it's a math problem, Margaret says. Which do they want, and when. Probability. Gambling.

What if you guess wrong?

Then you move on.

Moving on. That must be the real secret to it.

Down the hall, a door opens and music pours out. How have they not heard it before now, the phonograph in Hallie's room? She is trying to learn the Mozart sonata that way, by listening. Miss Pierce tells them it will help, to listen, but it's still no substitute for fingers on the keys, hours alone in the practice room, making the notes crash and break on your own.

Margaret is talking about a boy named Jerome, someone she knows from Greenwich, her childhood. Elizabeth gazes up at her, drinks in the calm assurance of Margaret's voice, the confiding tone, the privacy. College can be so awfully public, even places that are supposed to be private: library carrels, bathroom stalls.

Jerome was in her cousin's class. Now at college in *The City.* Columbia. He is bound to have friends. Elizabeth listens to the sounds of the words, the hard-soft-hard *c*'s like a mediocre report card: college, city, Columbia, country. The music of it soothes.

She turns to look out the window, rubs her cheek against the nubby pattern of the quilt on Margaret's bed, takes some vague and unexpected comfort in the fabric. A light from the dorm room above theirs illuminates the branches of an oak tree outside, two raised arms, a child asking her mother to be picked up, pressed to a shoulder. She hears a child's voice say the words. *Hold me. I'm thirsty.* Margaret is talking about men. The tree is asking to be gathered up, held aloft. An impossible request: the roots run too deep, too wide, scrabbling under this dormitory, beyond, halfway across campus.

Elizabeth reaches for the flask, takes a longer swallow, then another.

Margaret says she thinks of painting seascapes as if light and water were holding an interview. And they are both nervous.

Margaret and Elizabeth have gone to Wellfleet, in a car borrowed from Fannie Borden, the college librarian, to stay in Miss Borden's summer cottage. They find the place just as Miss Borden had described it, small and windtight, despite its many windows, set closer to the water than its neighbors. Margaret wants to paint outside, at the edge of the surf. She tries for half an hour, but it's too cold, so she sets up her easel just inside the door. Salt air has smeared the glass to a grainy blear that's like melted sugar. The winter sun tries to make the waves courageous, Margaret declares, but by midafternoon, the sea has lost its nerve completely. It lies flat and gray, the same shade as the sky.

Margaret has been painting since dawn, working on three canvases. One is mostly shoreline, sand, and grasses, a path toward the water, and, at the top, a ruffle of cresting waves. Another is copied (loosely) from a photograph of the harbor. The third is their actual view, with a lone sailboat disappearing off to the left.

Doesn't your arm get tired? Elizabeth asks.

Only if I stop, Margaret tells her.

Elizabeth envies this focus and concentration. She's done nothing these six hours except read and make boiled egg sandwiches for lunch. Margaret doesn't even sit down to eat.

I wish I could be as dedicated as you are, Margaret.

To what?

Anything.

You're dedicated to feeding us.

Elizabeth sets her book (Augustine's *Confessions*) facedown, splayed open on the sofa, shifts, stretches, crosses the room to stand beside Margaret. There hasn't been a boat all day, she says.

I know, Margaret says. This is the ghost ship.

That might appear at any moment.

So I'm ready for it.

Should we try a walk? Or is it still too cold?

Margaret shakes her head. Let me work at this another hour or so. Then we can try. Pull that chair over here beside me so you can have the view, too.

My view is watching you misinterpret the view.

Very funny, but you should have this one.

Still holding the paintbrush, Margaret drags the armchair into position beside her easel. She takes Elizabeth's shoulders, turns her around.

Now go get that juicy book and sit, she says.

It's hard not to keep looking. Even this weak wind keeps the water moving. Or is it the tide, really, rolling underneath? These three soft elements conspiring to make something sharp, the points of diamonds, a hard thin line of coast. This morning, Margaret had said the sunlight made the water look like a case of knives. It was true: knives rolling at them like chariot wheels, vicious. There was a fable in that somewhere, a little story, a scrap of history. *The Assyrian came down like a wolf on the fold.* This is nice, she thinks. Right here. Beside Margaret.

Why don't you paint the ship on fire? she says.

Don't give instructions, Elizabeth.

Sorry.

And then paint sailors swimming around the ship, Elizabeth imagines saying. How ironic! All that water and still the ship goes down. One man left on deck, the captain. No. The boy who swabs the decks, who's come to love his decks so much he can't bear to lose them. He's waiting for someone to come and tell him to abandon ship. His father. No one ever arrives.

Your imagination is so loud, Margaret says. Let's put it to better use.

She opens her paint box, which is olive green and artfully spattered, rummages to the bottom, finds a child's watercolor kit, tears a sheet of watercolor paper from her pad, sets them on the table beside her.

Get a glass of water, she says. *You* paint the burning ship.

I can't paint, Elizabeth says.

If you can see, you can paint. And sometimes even if you can't see. Monet, for instance.

The scene comes to Elizabeth from memory: a flat gray sea, and beyond it blue cliffs with caves made into lacework, like pictures she's seen of the Alhambra. A red sun, a ship already burnt but not sunk, held still, arrived at its destination maybe and then caught fire, charred masts like the bitter remains of a forest. If you make little *v v v*'s in the sky, that could be birds.

Elizabeth is aware of not having raised her head once in three-quarters of an hour or so (she doesn't have a watch—the clock is behind them, on the kitchen wall, heard but not seen, like a bad child).

Margaret glances down at Elizabeth's painting, sighs. Oh, Elizabeth, she says. You have to *look* at the scene. The colors are too runny. Here. Mix this in.

She presses a blob of white pigment from a tube. With a few, quick strokes, she's done something wonderful to Elizabeth's painting. Crystallized it. Let in the light.

All right, Elizabeth says. She stands, walks around to the other side of the table so that she is facing away from the sea.

I'll do this view now, she says.

It's the kitchen: a high, rickety table and the stool beside it, the icebox, the pie safe, the extension cord running from one side of the room to the other, tacked up to the ceiling in the middle. The closed door. In the summer, it would be open, and from here you could see climbing roses, the yellow ones. Make it July then. Make it *that* July, the last one.

Years ago. Back from her first stay in the sanatorium, Elizabeth's mother has flung open the door to get the scent of roses. Gertrude Bishop has been awake all night, roaming through the small house, then walking down to the shore and back. Each time she leaves, Elizabeth tries to hold her breath until she hears the screen door open again, the sound of it like inhalation. If she can't breathe, maybe her mother will come back and stay home for good.

Elizabeth paints the door half off its hinges; the round yellow roses open wide like babies' faces, crowd outside, peering in.

Much better, Margaret says. Even if everything looks like it's going to fall apart.

That's how I see it.

Use the white the way I showed you.

Elizabeth swirls a tiny crescent moon of white into the table, the ceiling, the roses.

That is really something, she says. It's like what salt does for food.

I never thought of it like that, Margaret says, but you're right. You could be a painter. But if you expect me to try being a writer . . . Well, don't.

No. You're a painter forever.

After dinner, they put on their coats and walk out to the water's edge, stand in the beam of moonlight, arms linked, close together for warmth. Elizabeth wears a hat, but Margaret does not, and so her long hair blows back and becomes part of the darkness, as if Margaret's white face is carved out of the night, like George Washington on Mount Rushmore, those photographs in the newspaper.

I wish we didn't have to go back tomorrow, Elizabeth says.

Well, we do, Margaret says. But if we get up early, we can have most of the day here. I don't mind driving in the dark.

You'll have to go slow then. Remember, it's not our car.

Everyone else will already be home by then, Margaret says. She shivers violently, and Elizabeth presses in closer.

Home, Margaret says. That's a funny word for college.

Elizabeth sighs. It's a funny word, period, she says.

The train from Great Village, Nova Scotia, to Halifax passes one hundred yards to the north of the psychiatric hospital in Dartmouth. Only it doesn't pass. It stops. And then continues. All right. So far, so good. Exhale. But no, the stop must be acknowledged. Maybe three minutes. Completely excruciating. The hospital comes into view before the stop, so there is enough time to remember, to change your mind, close the book, stand, wrestle the luggage.

Enough time to ask for help, to hear the dark-suited businessman say, You must have come a long ways, miss.

Not really, not a long ways, Elizabeth thinks. Only about thirty miles, but there's the bay in between, shadowed blue, full of invisible fish, water pinched between the thumb and forefinger of land. From a distance or without spectacles, the names of bayside towns run in the water like schools of fish: Scots Bay, Spencer's Island, Parrsboro, Tennycape. Even a town called Economy, with its very own point.

I was on my way to college, Elizabeth says, but I thought I'd visit my mother.

Oh? Is she in Dartmouth now? (So proceeds the imaginary conversation.)

Yes. Now and forever. Fourteen years. Since I was five.

That's a long time. She must love for you to stop in to see her.

Yes. She must.

There is no businessman. There is only the stopping, an eternity wedged into three minutes, the doors crashing open, station noise as real as passengers rushing in, then the real passengers themselves, boxes and bags, arctics and overcoats, hats and gloves, eyes searching for an empty seat.

And always this fear: that one of the women embarking from Dartmouth, journeying to Halifax, will be her mother. Elizabeth's mother, Gertrude Bishop, on the train by accident, escaped, still in her slippers and hospital gown (small blue flowers on white cotton) peeping from beneath her coat. She's stowing away to Halifax to see a specialist, or the tax man, or her imaginary accuser, or her husband, dead these eighteen years.

Or maybe she's escaped with clear purpose. Maybe she's come out of the brain fog long enough to understand that this is the time of year her only child, Elizabeth, would be leaving Great Village and traveling south to school. Late summer, the warmest days, all the hospital windows open, a bowl of ripening peaches like mottled suns on the table in the common room. The peaches send the message: Elizabeth is on the train. You can find her. See her. Talk to her. Take back that thing you said about wanting to kill her. Touch her round little face. Don't be afraid. Gaze into those eyes that stare and stare and never miss a thing.

Margaret passes Elizabeth the bottle. Canadian whiskey, doubly smuggled (across Lake Ontario, out of Manhattan), sweet enough to drink like this, without ice, water, a glass.

Let's run away, Margaret says.

Elizabeth thinks, I am away. And then the idea begins to interest her, the possibility of *farther* away. A long road that curves out of sight.

Not forever, Margaret says, as if she thinks Elizabeth might refuse to go. Just to get out of Poughkeepsie for a few days.

Elizabeth crosses to the wardrobe, conscious of her body making the motions of departure.

Let me get into my uniform, she says, laughing.

It's how the girls at Vassar refer to Elizabeth's navy peacoat. But it's practically the only one on campus, so how can that be a uniform? There are a great many fur coats walking around the college, a troop of foxes, a sleuth of bears. Margaret's is mink.

We'll need money, Elizabeth says.

I've got a little, Margaret says, and you've got less.

Half inside their coats, they take up their handbags, rummage for bills and change. Almost eleven dollars.

This is January, the second term just beginning, but not yet fallen with its full weight. A girl can still rise up into her coat and drift out into the dark, float onto the bus, which carries her to the railway station, all of it quickly, nearly silently, like a perfect escape. Miraculous. Elizabeth is still not quite used to this freedom, the fact that you could walk out at night without an older person running after you, puzzled or fearful or angry.

The last train south is about to leave, and so they hurry aboard without tickets. Margaret says they can buy them from the conductor. Going where? Elizabeth wants to know, but Margaret doesn't answer. They slide into seats. The train gathers its wits and seems to lean forward, pulling itself slowly into the winter darkness. The electric lights flicker, dim, darken, and the train stalls. Elizabeth feels a suffocating disappointment and then rising fear that Miss Pierce or Miss Lockwood will rush aboard the train, drag them away by their collars.

Margaret swears quietly, a whisper. After all that, she says.

Inside the car, in the pitch black, time seems to stall, too. Complete stillness, like a spell broken. Elizabeth wonders if this is what death feels like, this disenchantment.

Then it's over. The lights flash on, and the whole train hums, jolts to life. Margaret and Elizabeth watch their own faces in the train windows, the night mirror. Bridgeport, Margaret says, looking into her own eyes.

You have a plan, I take it, Elizabeth says.

Yes, I do. My mother has a house on Jennings Beach. She hardly ever goes there. It's closed for the winter, but I know where the key is. There's a huge fireplace and lots of wood. Or we could turn on the radiators.

The conductor appears beside their seats, calling for tickets. When Margaret asks to buy them, he seems so completely flustered and put out that Elizabeth believes he might let them ride for free. He leaves them to find a ticket book. The name on his coat is Balfour. Elizabeth wants to ask if it's his first or last name, but then he's gone, disappeared into the darkened end of the car. Margaret's face shines with a kind of grim delight, like the moon. This is how people look when they are contemplating a problem they know will get worse instead of better.

Here's the thing, Margaret says. We have to change trains at Harlem. I'm fairly sure there won't be a train out until morning.

We'll have to call your mother then, Elizabeth says. Or we could hitchhike.

You're out of your mind.

I know.

Do you think this is a crazy thing we're doing? Margaret says. Or dangerous?

I'd like to do more dangerous things than this.

You *think* you would.

No, really.

Like what?

I don't know yet.

The conductor lurches seat to seat announcing that the club car will close in fifteen minutes. How about coffee? Margaret says. Elizabeth nods; Margaret stands and moves up the aisle. She glances back once and winks, but Elizabeth isn't sure what this is supposed to mean.

When Margaret has grappled her way forward and disappeared, Elizabeth wonders if she might be alone in the car. No sounds drift up from the other seats, no shifting, breathing, turning pages. She contemplates the possibility that Margaret might not come back, for whatever reason. Alone on a train, at night, with no money, not a single penny. Maybe the conductor will let her stay on, ride back to Poughkeepsie. Or she can call Miss Swain, the English professor who seems to understand her. Miss Swain will arrange the passage back or drive down to Bridgeport. She will burst into the train station and laugh in that fierce, defiant way she has. On the ride back, in her car, she will speak calmly, quietly. She will even find a way to praise this folly. I think you might be doomed to be a poet, Miss Swain said once, last term. *Doomed.* What a word. But Elizabeth likes the sound, the emptiness of those twin *o*'s, like the wail of a ghost.

The door at the far end of the car crashes open, and Margaret strides forward carrying two paper cups of coffee. She moves as if speed and balance are the same, or as if she is trying to outrun someone. Her smile is electric, almost vicious. She eases into the seat, hands Elizabeth one of the paper cups.

Taste it, she whispers.

Elizabeth recognizes the scent even before she brings the cup to her lips.

A man in the club car, Margaret says. He paid. He said it was *an investment.* But he's getting off before Harlem. I think it's brandy.

They sip the coffee, waiting for the man from the club car to come for the return on his investment. But no one passes through except for the conductor, who smiles at them as if they are a terrific force he has subdued.

By Irvington, snow has begun to fall.

Let's get off here and take a taxi, Margaret says.

Elizabeth and Margaret leave the train at Irvington, but there are no taxis. They follow signs to Route 9, where Margaret believes there will be traffic headed toward New York. Wind swirls them into near blindness. The snow comes harder, angling at them, into their faces. Trucks zoom past. Elizabeth's coat is soaked through. She feels entombed in ice, numb.

It's two in the morning, she yells into the wind. Who's going to be out at this hour?

We must look pretty bad if even trucks won't take us, Margaret says.

Like drowned rats. No one would stop in this weather anyway.

Then, for a long stretch, fifteen or twenty minutes, no vehicles pass. They trudge on, southeast. We'll meet daylight, Elizabeth thinks, and then someone will take pity on us. They hear a vehicle slow behind them.

Hello, girls, the driver calls. We've been looking for you.

Oh no, Margaret whispers as the car slides into view beside them. Elizabeth wants to laugh. Policemen, but also a roaring heater. Warm air blasts out the window, along with the scents of coffee and doughnuts. Margaret opens the rear door, climbs in. Elizabeth follows.

Who called you? Margaret says. My mother? The college?

The two officers glance at each other. The college? the driver says. That's a good one. We'll just go down to the station now and have a chat about that jacket.

At first they don't understand, Margaret and Elizabeth, why Elizabeth's pea jacket is so interesting, or why it's so funny when they say they've come from Vassar on the train, that they've been riding all night, that Margaret's mother might be telephoned, or that, far more simple, someone might find them transportation to a locked house in Jennings Beach. It seems like a riotous game, around and around, and they keep playing, now with two more policemen because the station is warm, the coffee is hot, and outside is a raging snowstorm. Elizabeth begins to feel she might be dreaming: the train with its windows like dark mirrors, the brandy supplied by a sinister gentleman, the arrival in snow, the post road whitely obscured, these four men so profoundly entertained by her jacket, their inevitable questions.

What you got in the pockets, miss?

The coat pockets? Elizabeth says.

For a moment she thinks the men might try to find out for themselves, stick their hands in on top of hers, which are now nervously fingering scraps of paper. What's written on them? She can't remember, and so she draws them out, turns them over under the light.

Of course. Her notes from Greek class. Also a little magazine, *Breezy Stories,* a volume called *The Imitation of Christ.*

What's all this? the police sergeant wants to know. He passes the Greek notes to the others. Can you read this? I think it's Italian. Are you nuns?

At that big convent over in Poughkeepsie, Margaret says.

Aw for pity's sake! the sergeant says. Let's call your mother then!

Margaret tells him the number, and he dials. After Margaret's mother answers and he explains, he has to hold the receiver away from his ear. Mrs. Miller does not sound the least bit sleepy when she tells the sergeant that yes, they are college students and she will be there as soon as possible to fetch them.

The police lead them out into the station lobby. The first two pull on their coats and disappear into the night. The others drift away, down the hall. Elizabeth hears music from a radio.

Opera, Margaret says. Not what you'd guess around here.

I wish I had some of that coffee from the train, Elizabeth says.

Mrs. Miller appears a half hour later, imperious, impeccably groomed. She looks quickly at Margaret and Elizabeth, then strides into the sergeant's office without knocking.

How could you, gentlemen? Mrs. Miller says. You should be ashamed of yourselves.

We got a call, ma'am. Two women up from the City, out looking for . . . You know. A good time.

These are girls, Mrs. Miller says. Obviously.

I can see that now.

Take your eyes out of the gutter then.

Yes ma'am. Sorry for the trouble.

Mrs. Miller herds them out of the police station and to her car. Margaret, she says, you sit up here with me and tell me where you were going. Elizabeth, you may want to stretch out in the back there, get a little sleep.

She drives them on to Jennings Beach, worrying all the way to the coast that the radiators in the house won't work fast enough and Margaret will catch a cold.

Elizabeth, she says, finally, gently. We will get you a new coat, a nice one. That jacket does look like you got it off a sailor. You don't want to be mistaken for something you're not, do you?

No.

That happens all the time, though, Margaret says.

To Elizabeth? her mother asks.

To everyone.

Elizabeth wants to leap into the front seat and hug Margaret.

The sky seems to be pulsing and streaked with chartreuse. How is it that the sky's tuned green? Elizabeth says, but Margaret and Mrs. Miller can't see it.

You're bleary-eyed, Mrs. Miller says.

It's an apology. She isn't angry, not even slightly put out. Elizabeth marvels at this, a mother who will do anything, travel in the dark of night—in a blizzard!—to rescue a whimsical daughter. Inside the house, Mrs. Miller pulls sheets and blankets out of the tops of closets, then makes up beds for the three of them. The house is enormous, four stories. They will be sleeping on different floors, in the warmest rooms, which are stacked on top of one another, next to the hot water pipe, Mrs. Miller tells them, as she's handing out toothbrushes and towels.

Now sleep as long as you like, she says to Elizabeth. Rest from your adventure.

Elizabeth's is the middle room of the three. Margaret is above. She hears Mrs. Miller climb the stairs and close the door. She does not come down before Elizabeth falls asleep. Elizabeth hears whispering, tears, and endearments, which weave indistinctly into her dreams.

Elizabeth and her own mother are on a train. Hooded figures move up and down the aisle, vague, foreboding. Something or someone has been forgotten, left behind. Elizabeth and her mother are trying to get over this loss, past it, move on, look ahead. They choose forward-facing seats for this very reason. But Elizabeth is afraid her mother will recall the forgotten object or person and become agitated. She has only just succeeded in calming her mother after some previous disturbance. The train moves along an unfamiliar coastline. She wishes her mother would listen to the roar and retreat of the ocean. Can you hear it? she asks her mother. Just try to listen. Try to make the waves like your breathing, in and out.

When Elizabeth wakes, the bedroom has darkened. The window is a navy blue square the color of her peacoat. She swims toward consciousness sideways, feeling like a boat being hauled from water that is cold, dark, deep, flowing, and flown. These are the words in her head, not exactly words, more like sensations, or—oddly—*knowledge.* Information. The house is perfectly still, and her body is held inside it, cocooned. The ocean breakers make the sound of the word: *in. for. MA. tion.* She would like to stay here forever, buried inside these quilts and blankets, paint, plaster, wood. She can pretend to be asleep for some time longer in this empty space, this perfection of nowhere. Here, the indignities of college life are kept at bay. The whole landscape of college is scaffolds and pillories, stocks and bonds, glass houses, and stones lying around everywhere. These notions, like wolves, drift in from the darkened edges of her mind. The music classes. What is it about musical composition that she can't seem to master? The mathematics of it, probably. She is an orderly person. Everyone says so. Or maybe it's because she can't see the notes, the dynamics, the harmonics, the way you can see a bird or a fish or a boat or a star. But you can hear it. So why isn't hearing as good as seeing?

Slowly, daylight brightens the window. Footsteps above: Margaret must be getting out of bed, preparing for whatever will come next. She might ask her mother to drive them back to school. But Mrs. Miller has probably already offered. She's planned her day around the end of this adventure, the smiling delivery in Poughkeepsie: Look who I found! I rescued them and brought them back to you. She'll whisper to her friend the Vassar president, Henry Noble MacCracken, Don't be so careless, Hank. I pay you to keep an eye on them.

My girls, she says when Margaret and Elizabeth appear in the kitchen.

My girls! What a lovely pair of words!

That was quite the night, you two! Now let's have something to eat, and then I'll take you back to the convent.

Margaret is right. She is not writing poems. They are not anything except impractical. One must have a job, a title (even *assistant* is enough), an office to go to every day. She discovers a shelf of medical textbooks in the library and cultivates a special fondness for *Gray's Anatomy,* the body inside out. When she mentions this prospective future to Margaret, the disbelief is both oceanic and, for nearly a half hour, strangely mute. Then Margaret struggles for language. *Sputter* is what she's doing. *Scrabble.*

Why? Margaret asks finally.

Her first impulse is to say, *Why not?* Outside the window, the green perfection of Vassar is a taunt. Orderly, narrow walkways, blooming hedges, maples and sycamores in exuberant leaf, all by design, perfectly timed.

It's a calling, she says.

It's a terrible idea. You don't even study the sciences. You like literature and music and French.

The French had some very famous medical people.

That's not a good reason, Margaret says. She stares out the window, then bends to look for something in the bookcase.

The Curies were French, Elizabeth says.

It's about your mother, isn't it?

How could that be?

You want to cure her.

How could I cure her now?

Elizabeth turns away, to her dresser, and begins to rearrange the lipsticks, the bottles of perfume Mrs. Miller gives her every December and February, Christmas and birthday. Arpège, Vol de Nuit, Tabu, Joy.

You want to have cured her, Margaret says gently.

I don't think anyone could have done that.

Someone might have been able to.

If they had, they would have done it. She picks up a lipstick that looks like a shell casing. But, she says, I think you hit the nail on the head.

Which nail?

My mother.

Elizabeth knows Margaret is right. She can't do anything about her mother.

But I want to be useful. Miss Peebles says I should apply to Cornell medical school to study pediatrics.

You could be a teacher.

I couldn't. I don't have that kind of patience.

And you don't think caring for children will require patience? And most of them will be sick. It will be so sad all the time. Hour after hour, in your office, a little person who feels bad and mostly can't tell you why. And the frantic mothers. Begging you to just *do* something.

I know. But poems aren't terribly useful either. But I'm beginning to think stories might be, a little more anyway. Or novels. The energy to write a big, fat thing like *The Golden Bowl*. I'd be pleased with myself.

That's more your calling.

And what's yours? Oh, I don't even know why I'm bothering to ask. Maybe just to hear you say what everybody else assumes.

Obviously, Margaret says, my calling is a house in Greenwich and children, dinners and diapers and an unhealthy interest in tidiness and order. I mean—just look at this room!

The strew of clothing seems almost designed to create an effect— the rainbow of blouses hung from every imaginable hook, desk chairs and bedposts, picture frames, scarves veiling the lamps. Piles of color broken by the white expanse of blankets and pillows. Like a village in winter, a blur of life and color clustered beside and between snowy fields. Farther away, a border of water, the dark wood floor. Their boots are boats. The desks are wild floating islands, mountainous with books, with flotillas of pencils and pens cruising about the shallows.

We'll clean later, Margaret. Just say it out loud.

An art critic.

That's not it. Too practical. You'd go mad.

All right. A painter. I'm sure you're shocked.

Certainly far worse than a writer. We can be foolish together then.

I don't think foolish is a requirement. Just rich husbands.

Please, Margaret. What would your mother say?

I'm kidding, Elizabeth. You know that, don't you?

The college librarian, Miss Fannie Borden, dips into her water glass like a heron, as if she can swallow only a few drops at a time. Their waiter stands at a respectful distance, eyeing her.

The bicycle is a riddle, she says. She speaks quickly, in a whisper with a creak to it.

Elizabeth and Margaret wait. Elizabeth fiddles with the matchbook on the table. A big red *A* for Alex's. A scarlet *A*. She wonders if the management realizes.

If you take off the chain, Miss Borden says, the number of moving parts and overall complexity are significantly reduced. A direct-drive free-wheeled hub joins the crank arm axis with the rear wheel axis, shortening the wheel base and minimizing the design. The ride is nimble. And that, girls, is why my bicycle has no chain.

It's a physics problem, not a riddle, Elizabeth says.

Elizabeth! Margaret says. Don't be rude.

As you wish, Miss Bishop. I stand corrected. In any case, it's lovely of you to have invited me to lunch. I should confess I was somewhat concerned.

Elizabeth looks at Margaret: relief starting to cloud over. They admire Miss Borden—she's an original—but perhaps asking her to lunch was a bit impulsive.

Miss Borden glances around the restaurant to see if anyone is paying attention. Almost everyone is. Miss Borden is, in Margaret's words, *politely notorious.* It's a compliment.

Concerned, Miss Borden continues, because the term is not quite ended. It may be *inappropriate,* as they say here. But I think not. Certain other students might hope to improve their grades, but you two are such excellent bibliographers, I needn't worry.

It never crossed my mind, Margaret says.

And others, Miss Borden says, might be interested in stories about my family.

Families are a puzzle, Elizabeth says.

There is a rhyme about Miss Borden, Elizabeth knows. *Fannie Borden in the stacks, hiding from her auntie's axe.* First-year girls assumed Elizabeth had invented it. Every year's graduating class tries to compose the next two lines, which are always lurid or obscene.

Miss Borden dabs at her lips with a napkin, then folds it on the table beside her coffee cup. Indeed, she says. But here we are. And so, quite *inappropriately,* I have a gift for each of you.

She bends to her enormous bag, on the floor beside her chair. Her spine curves beneath the fabric of her dress, as if the vertebrae were softer than bone, held together by elastic bands. She produces two books, one large, the size of a Spanish-language dictionary, the other much smaller.

Actually not gifts, she says. Loans.

You're a librarian, after all, Elizabeth says.

Miss Borden smiles. You are too clever by half, Miss Bishop. I admire that. Here, Margaret. *Modern Painting* is for you.

The Mather, Margaret says. I've been looking for it.

Miss Borden nods once slowly, like a benevolent queen.

Margaret opens the book. Pages of glossy plates attract all the light in the room and reflect it back. Each page is a beacon.

And Elizabeth? What have you been looking for?

The Marianne Moore?

This is my personal copy, Miss Borden says, handing over the small volume. Treat it kindly.

Elizabeth can barely speak, but manages to say of course she will.

I have known Marianne since she was a child, Miss Borden says. She had fierce red hair and addressed us all by the names of the animals she thought we resembled. I can introduce you to her if you'd like.

The New York Public Library. Third floor. Outside the reading room. The bench on the right. These were the coordinates, as if Miss Marianne Moore were a kind of geometry. As Elizabeth approaches, the stern-looking woman in the turban, blue the color of dragonflies, stares for a moment. A slash of yellow sunlight falls on her coat and pocketbook. Then she stands and walks away. Golden dust motes, like tiny bees, swirl over the empty bench. Elizabeth has worried for weeks that this is exactly how their meeting would begin and end: Miss Moore would take her measure and not like what she saw. Miss Borden said sometimes Miss Moore meets her devotees in Grand Central Station because of its infinite escape routes. The dust clumps as if it might coalesce into a person. Inside the reading room, someone, a man, coughs violently. Down the hall, a door closes, the echoes a shudder of glass shifting inside a frame. Footsteps on the stairs behind her. Don't! Elizabeth tells herself. Don't be discovered weeping in the New York Public Library. She hears a rapid-fire whispering, like Miss Borden's.

Miss Bishop? Is that you? I'm very sorry to be late.

Elizabeth turns, sighs, swallows back her tears. For the smallest increment of time, she thinks she might embrace Marianne Moore. Instead, she watches Miss Moore see *her*, take in her sealskin jacket, white gloves, pearl earrings. She has the distinct impression Miss

Moore's X-ray vision can locate the tiny notebook in her purse, read the questions closed in there, waiting shyly to be asked. She notes Miss Moore's braided hair, red streaked with white, coiled around her head in a style her own mother might have worn (the thought pierces), her pinkish eyebrows, eyes pale as cloudy sky.

Shall we sit? Miss Moore says.

Later, Elizabeth will remember a delicious blur of subjects, names, and words. Hopkins, Crane, Stevens, the circus, *Hound & Horn*, Herbert, Crashaw, strangest animals I have ever known. *Good for you* is an insulting expression. Do you research *for* a poem, or do you research and then the poem arrives? Tattooing: Is it for good luck or to show possession?

Margaret Mead. In some cultures, the females look after one another in many different ways. Elizabeth wonders what this can possibly mean. And then she knows. She blushes, though she is quite sure Miss Moore is simply being factual.

Impersonal. Miss Moore is neutral, measured, despite the fascinating, speedy talk. She looks a bit like Mickey Rooney.

Elizabeth believes that nothing more unlikely than this meeting has ever happened in her entire life. She has the sensation that everyone in the New York Public Library is leaning closer to listen. The books, too, all of them, inching forward, imperceptibly, to the edges of their shelves.

I must be going now, Miss Moore says. You'll send me some poems, Miss Bishop?

Yes, Elizabeth says. Yes, of course. That would be kind of you. To read them, I mean.

Miss Moore reaches into the pocket of her overcoat, draws out a scrap of paper and a pencil stub, writes out the address in Brooklyn.

I live with my mother, she says. I expect you know that. She's an excellent reader of poetry. A strict grammarian. A veritable cudgel.

She hands the paper to Elizabeth. One or two at a time, please, she says. Poems, that is. No more.

Of course, Elizabeth says. Thank you very much.

Don't thank me yet, Miss Moore says. Maybe in twenty or thirty years. We shall see.

At first, at Barbara Chesney's house in Pittsfield, Elizabeth doesn't notice the crutches. The room is mostly in shadow—or rather it is filled with firelight that transforms and disembodies and amplifies. The crutches are behind Robert Seaver's chair, in a corner, next to the door. But she believes they are a pair of fishing rods. So Elizabeth is drawn to this young man immediately because he must love to fish and maybe sail, as she does. She is already composing an invitation to Wellfleet when she moves between him and the fire and discovers the truth.

There is an empty chair, so Elizabeth swallows the sailing invitation and sits down.

Barbara has been telling me we should meet, Robert says.

That was the very first sentence, she will recall later. The death knell. She glances across the room, locates Robert's sister—another Elizabeth—staring at them, her face vacant and sad, as if she already knows what will happen.

Why? Elizabeth says, and immediately the question sounds cruel, as if she were asking, *Why on earth? How absurd!* She wishes she'd said something neutral, like Miss Moore would. I'm not really a neutral person, she says out loud, as if Robert can follow her thoughts.

I know, Robert says calmly, smiling. I suspect that's why Barbara thought we might be friends. Because I'm not a neutral person either, and we're both rather literary.

Oh? Are you a writer?

No, but I'm what every writer needs. A reader.

Robert lifts both hands, palms up, the gesture for *Look: empty.*

What do you read? Elizabeth says.

I read everything. But I have to confess I think it's all downhill from Shakespeare.

I came to the same conclusion last year. Then I thought I should talk myself out of it, or I'd end up not being able to write anything of my own. Then I read Hopkins, and I felt better.

You're a poet.

Doomed to be a poet, as one of my professors put it.

I would say that's a better doom than most.

I'm leaning toward fiction now. Stories. Maybe a novel.

A few couples have risen from the circle to dance. The singer is Ruth Etting: "I'm Good for Nothing but Love." Their bodies make grotesque shapes in the firelight, and Elizabeth feels attracted and re-pulsed at the same time. She half wishes she had the nerve to do it, just stand up without much deliberation and match her body to the music, let the sound of it move through her. And yet, she tells herself, glancing up at the ceiling, around the walls of the room, I'd be making *that,* those terrible shapes and gestures. She knows Robert is watching her. She hears him sigh, a quick *ohhhh* of breath, and feels the same sound gathering in her lungs, her chest.

I don't dance, Robert whispers, inclining his head toward the crutches. Polio. When I was thirteen. Elizabeth murmurs that she's sorry, and Robert gives a little shrug. It's caused me to concentrate on other things. Other aspects of life.

Intensity, Elizabeth says, and Robert nods.

He's looking at her with something like amazement. She likes being on the receiving end of such a gaze. Girls at school stare at her like that, but the expression is usually clouded by something else—

envy maybe, or an indeterminate sort of mistrust. Like looking at a puzzle one can never solve.

Elizabeth rides the train to Pittsfield about once a month, usually when Robert's parents are away. Robert's sister plays chaperone, and Elizabeth senses the same sort of amazement from her. This wonder might be a genetic trait, like their dimples or their blue eyes. Or maybe his sister's look of wonder is more like suspension, waiting to see what Elizabeth might do or say next. She knows his sister keeps a journal, and she longs to read about herself, about these visits. She sees the journal lying on the desk in the bedroom, in plain view, a light blue notebook with gold edging. Robert's sister has gone for a walk, and Robert is downstairs resting. She hears his gentle snoring (like everything else about him, soft, tender, alluring that way). It would be so easy. But how could you invade someone's privacy like that? It was the worst sort of betrayal. If anyone were to read what she'd written, without her consent, it would feel like a mortal wound, the kind you could never get over.

She closes the door to the bedroom, makes her way down to the small sitting room, watches Robert sleep. He is a very expressive sleeper. It's almost as if his dreams are printed on his forehead, his cheekbones, engraved into the corners of his mouth. She leans back in the armchair, closes her eyes. He can tell her about his dreams later, if he wants to. She won't peer into them on her own.

In a little while, Robert's sister comes in. The creaking of the front door wakes Robert. He blinks once, smiles at Elizabeth, and then he says it: Let's go out for a walk so I can tell you what I was dreaming.

A small lake stretches behind the house. After the polio episode, Robert's father installed a walkway paved with moonstones, and a bench.

So you won't have to go far to see something beautiful, was how he'd explained it to his son. Robert gestures for Elizabeth to sit first. He lowers himself off the crutches and stows them under the bench. He takes Elizabeth's hands, grips them as if the details of his dreams will be revealed through his fingers.

I don't know if I was awake or asleep, he begins. But I dreamed I gave you this. He lets go of her hands and reaches into his vest pocket. You're supposed to unpin it from yourself first, he says, but that seems like too much extra business.

Elizabeth feels a whirling storm in her head. She wants to think about what this means, but there doesn't seem to be time. She likes Robert enormously, his literary talk, his rapt attention, his courage. That could be enough for a pin. She instructs herself not to look beyond this minute right here in front of her, the lake, the touch of Robert's hand and its inverse, the cold edge of the fraternity pin, now pressing into the center of her palm.

The class is called Contemporary Press. The course description: *Students will read the newspaper and talk about current events.* Elizabeth hates it, but she cannot seem to stop herself from going, believing she will eventually ease into Miss Lockwood's method. Elizabeth hopes the twice-weekly idiocy of it will pare away some roughness in her own character, maybe crack the shell of her loneliness. But week after week this paring and cracking does not happen, and then it is too late. She must stay in the class or withdraw and waste that much of her tuition.

It's awful, she tells Margaret. She encourages us to lump everything together, to think about the big picture. I hate the big picture. You only look at the big picture if you can't see very well.

And Miss Lockwood's eternal, infernal search for *consensus.* Elizabeth realizes she hates the word itself, the way it half rhymes with *nonsense.* Miss Lockwood is happy only when everyone in the room is nodding and smiling and congratulating herself for thinking the same as the girl sitting at the next desk over.

So she says nothing. Sometimes she shakes her head and disagrees, but mostly she watches the sun slide out of the window behind Miss Lockwood's nodding head. The class begins at four o'clock, and it's winter term, and so for three months, the afternoon darkens with disapproval every Tuesday and Thursday. Elizabeth wants to point this out. See? The sun goes down on your big picture.

One day, in late March, Miss Lockwood asks the class to list the qualities of the typical businessman, and Elizabeth can no longer contain herself. She starts to laugh, at first a little, broken sighing, but then she just gives in to it, listening to herself at the same time, marveling at the happy sound. As if she's just been given a gift. She puts her face in her hands, hears the laughter amplified. The pencil scratching beside her stops. Desks creak, and then the room goes eerily silent. Elizabeth is aware of Miss Lockwood's footsteps, really a sort of heaving glide. She feels the breathing presence of Miss Lockwood right in front of her.

Miss Bishop? Are you not quite yourself today?

The question makes Elizabeth laugh harder, a completely indelicate snort, like a pig. No, no, she thinks, just the opposite. Finally I am myself. I've never been more myself.

Quite, she manages to whisper. The laughter has gotten completely away from her now, washing into hysteria and then a shimmering fearlessness.

Well, do share with us your . . . , Miss Lockwood begins, but she can't seem to hold on to language.

All right, Elizabeth says.

She can hardly believe she is going to continue—if only she can stop laughing. It's like jumping off the highest diving board: you just go. She lowers her hands. Miss Lockwood stands only a foot away, glaring, enraged. Elizabeth fixes her eyes on an imaginary, invisible object near the ceiling.

Who cares about the typical businessman? she says. In what way is he interesting? In what way is the typical anything interesting?

Miss Lockwood takes a step back, moves her body to suggest a kind of inflation. She is intrigued. She is a raft filling with air.

Good enough, she says, a different menace in her voice. Ladies? Miss Bishop has asked us *all* this question.

She pauses here, for effect.

A question, ladies. So how shall we answer? Why are we interested in the typical?

Elizabeth looks down at her own hands, inches apart, flat on the desk as if she were about to rise out of her seat, propel herself out the room. Then she glances lower, at Miss Lockwood's shoes, a kind of slipper, dark blue and still buttoned up inside opaque plastic galoshes. A late snow has left a dirty line around both soles, across the toes. All the streets in Poughkeepsie look this way now, dirty, wet snow pushed up against the curbs, at the rims of sidewalks, underneath the box-wood and privet hedges.

No one speaks.

Miss Lockwood asks the question a second time. She waits. The last of the sun winks at the edge of the window frame and disappears. The classroom falls into shadow. Still Miss Lockwood waits. She does not move to turn on the lights. Elizabeth feels they have fallen out of time in some way, lost their grip on the contemporary. That would be interesting. If you fell out of the order of time, what sort of violent disorder would you fall into?

But this is a kind of power: to make a room go still this way, steal its thunder. That would be a terrific skill to have. That would be beautiful. That is *beauty.* Which somehow depends on the imminence or threat of violence. She will have to think more about this notion. Her breath comes easily now, like moving in an empty house, certain no one will disturb you, but knowing you can disturb if you so choose.

Miss Lockwood is looking at her. Elizabeth can feel her eyes, the blaze of her attention. That gaze is like Robert's: the beam from a powerful flashlight. The unexpected similarity shocks her, physically. She wants to touch Miss Lockwood's cheek, her shoulder under the plum-colored cardigan.

Clearly, Miss Lockwood says, her voice choked with emotion, you all need time to think about this. Good. So then. We will take it up again next week.

She turns her back to the class, gathers her newspapers, her copies of *Life* and *Look* and *Liberty*. The class shuffles notebooks, papers, handbags. Coats sigh as if with pleasure when hands and arms go into them. Miss Lockwood leaves the classroom, and the students follow. Elizabeth does not move. Footsteps recede down the hallway. No conversation. It's a funeral procession for the typical. She hears the groan and slam of the big door. Elizabeth waits awhile longer, until the other girls are far away, back in their dormitories, and Miss Lockwood is making her way through the dirty, slushy streets of town. She imagines Miss Lockwood walking, her body moving fearsomely and beautifully beneath her clothes.

M iss Lockwood told me to find a tutor, Louise Crane says. If I don't, I'll be thrown out of school.

So this is the one, Elizabeth thinks. Louise. Blue eyes as deep as her pockets, that was what people said. Delightful, lovely, unruly girl. Her mother practically invented the Museum of Modern Art.

I'm in college here, she tells Elizabeth, because my grandmother said I had to go somewhere. And it's close to New York City. And respectable. I've already voted myself most likely not to graduate. You're brilliant—

No, I'm not, Elizabeth says. I work like a demon.

Just being in your room makes me feel smarter.

That's because it's Margaret's room, too.

Louise's eyes disappear into a thin glittering when she smiles. Cheshire Cat, only not so sleepy.

But first, let's take a walk, Louise says. I'm afraid the walls have ears.

Being near Louise is like having drunk seven cups of coffee. It's as if she brings New York City with her wherever she goes. Like Margaret, but more emphatic. A glowing aura. Electricity. That's it. Louise's skin is electric. Elizabeth discovers this accidentally, in the library, early one morning, studying Baudelaire.

I can't get it, Louise says. I have to cheat and read the translation. Come help me find it.

Poetry, the 800s, lives at the end of the third row of shelves, the west end of the stacks, the darkest row. The spines of books, gold or silver letters, dust jackets stripped off (where do they put all those dust jackets?). Elizabeth and Louise, half blind, run their fingers along the lettering, guessing the titles. Louise's left arm winds around Elizabeth's waist.

I like you in shadow, she says. I like darker women.

Years later, when she has become an infamous patron of the arts, she will say something very like this to Billie Holiday, the singer, and then to Victoria Kent, the Spanish lawyer.

Elizabeth is silent.

I'm sick of the library, Louise whispers. I think I need to lie down. Come with me.

On the way out, Miss Borden gives them a look. Go have breakfast, girls, she says lightly.

Louise has a single room, for which her mother (really her grandmother) pays extra.

I don't like wasting time, she says. Do you know the girls call me "Auntie" because they think I act like an old maid?

Is that so? Elizabeth says. You could have fooled me.

I tell them to button up their blouses and wear less lipstick, Louise says. I have a large car like a tank, and I drive it very slowly and very well.

Louise is a nervous, clumsy sailor. She brings her tutor to visit Elizabeth in Wellfleet, but there are never any lessons. Together they manage to tip over the sailboat, scattering the centerboard, the oars, cigarettes, sweaters. Elizabeth swims the capsized boat to shore with Louise riding on top, then they lie flat on the dock, let the sun bake them back to a normal temperature.

Sorry about the boat, Louise says.

That's what happens, Elizabeth tells her, when the city comes to the country.

I prefer driving a car. On a proper road. A hard surface you can't sink into. I'm very good at that.

Louise sends the tutor back to New York, saying that she's going to flunk out of Vassar anyway, so what's the use. After that, they sleep and read and smoke and gorge on lobster dinners. At night they take a whiskey bottle and two juice glasses up to their bedroom. Aunt Florence and Aunt Ruby, indulgent and a little foolish, and awed by Louise, turn a blind eye.

Or would it be blind eyes? Louise says. Four blind eyes. Like the mice, plus one.

That would be seven, Elizabeth says.

You know I'm no good at math. I'm good at being the life of the party and exasperating my mother.

After three days, Louise begins to sigh and mope. When she runs out of Chesterfields and has to smoke the aunts' Camels, she declares she must return to Manhattan.

Just wait a day. Please? Elizabeth says. Margaret will come up and bring us the news of the world.

And the Chesterfields?

Yes. And then you can go if you want to. Even though I will be lonely.

Never lonely with Florence and Ruby, Louise says. Are they sisters?

In law.

That's a funny term, don't you think?

It reminds me of partners in crime, Elizabeth says. Do you think I would make a good lawyer?

About the worst I can imagine.

Why? I'm an excellent observer.

Which would make you a very good criminal.

Florence and Ruby wouldn't like *that* in the house.

Louise laughs. You mean a criminal? she says. They may not have any say in the matter. It may have already happened. So much can be accomplished under the covers of darkness.

I think the phrase is *cover* of darkness, Elizabeth says. Singular.

How lonely, Louise says.

Isn't it. Which is exactly what I'm going to be when you don't come back to school next year.

I'll still visit from New York. And you can come down and stay with Mother and me anytime you want.

What will you do if you don't have school to keep you occupied? I can't even imagine.

I'll socialize. I'll *see* people.

Well, don't see too many people, please.

I'll make friends for you, so you don't have to work so hard at it. Mother is training me to be what she is, a patron of the arts, and have salons and run the museum when she's done inventing it. I'll make absolutely the *right* friends. Think of it. All of us together: Mother and me, Margaret and her mother, Miss Marianne Moore and her mother. You can stay with a different pair of us every night.

Elizabeth and Robert drive out to western Massachusetts, a place called Sunk Pond, to sail.

Robert is fascinated and horrified by the four towns nearby, Prescott, Enfield, Dana, and Greenwich, which may be flooded to make a reservoir, as if this would be some kind of live burial. He talks about cellar holes and what might be found in them, what clues about people's lives, what mysteries that could now be solved if you knew where to look. He has very specific ideas: jam jars, pet interments, sodden manuscripts, the water causing them to dance to and fro, caressing these things in its cold embrace. His hand on the tiller seems to turn pale—paler—as he speaks.

Elizabeth doesn't even know she's seeing this transformation until later, until Normandy, another man's hand on a tiller, and her strange errand there. And much later, Lota's hands will remind her of Robert's.

They climb to the top of a small mountain and stare out over the site of the future reservoir. Robert makes the grueling hike without complaint. Now he finds it difficult to stand. Elizabeth sees this and feels distressed and angry. Why does he do this to himself? she wonders. Why does he do it for her?

These towns, Robert begins. But it is hard for him to speak. Elizabeth helps him to sit down beside the path. He shakes his head, disgusted by his own frailty and the future he sees.

What about the towns? Elizabeth says.

People will have to leave, he says finally. Move everything. Even graveyards. Four towns' worth of bodies.

That's progress, Elizabeth says.

Is it? I don't know if I want that kind of progress.

Isn't it inevitable? Elizabeth says. That things fall apart? That Boston would need more water?

I hope not, Robert says.

He's quiet for a moment.

I find myself interested, he says, in what will be left behind. What will never be retrieved. What secrets people have buried below their houses that they will forget to rescue or what they won't want to save.

Elizabeth stares at the top of Robert's head. This would be my life, she thinks. Looking down would be my life. It seems an awful way to begin, a terrible promise. She can imagine it, this whole valley filled with water. She can imagine the loss, but also the beauty of it, a sheet of gleaming water stretched between the hills. And the art. All the broken bits of lives buried under some civil engineer's creation.

But Robert can't. For him, it's all ugliness and disaster.

I'm losing you, Elizabeth, he says. I can tell. I won't be able to bear it.

The green on the scalloped hill is acrocarpous moss, Elizabeth says. It can absorb twenty times its own weight. So maybe the reservoir will take a long time to fill.

But even so, everything will be drowned. The church steeple. Underwater, its bells will become a message to ships. Weightless cars and buses will drift from the road. Just above the surface of the reservoir, weathervanes can still track the wind, but there won't be anyone left to care.

M iss Moore and Elizabeth ride the train to the Ringling Bros. Circus in Queens. They have come to see the elephants, to feed them. Miss Moore hopes there is a snake charmer.

All reptiles fascinate me, Miss Moore says, but snakes especially. The fanged variety. I find I appreciate the sort of thing that makes one shudder. Tattoos, another instance. Though I can see no reason to have my own person permanently marked.

If you are lost at sea? Elizabeth says.

I don't think a tattoo would be much help at that point.

That's true. It wouldn't save your life.

I am curious about tattooed ladies, Miss Moore says. There's a famous photograph from 1907. A circus woman, of course. Against all ideas of female beauty. The very question of what is beautiful.

Miss Moore chuckles, a low rolling sound, like the laughing falcon she has described to Elizabeth. She digs into the satchel for more bread crusts.

The elephants crowd at the fence, ignoring everyone else, the other dozen women and children marveling at the great height, the wholly unexpected beauty. Elizabeth finds this somewhat embarrassing, that they are adults, hauling the two satchels stuffed full of bread. The elephants are massive, great walls of gray flesh, their eyes unblinking, wet, and full of want. The trunks and ears seem to belong on another

kind of creature, they are so graceful and responsive, the trunks especially, the pink nostrils sweeping the bread away, prehensile fingers
folding the soft slices into their mouths. This spectacle of slow feeding
is better than men on trapezes, men subduing lions, tattooed men
lifting thousand-pound weights.

Could we teach ourselves to think of beauty another way? Miss
Moore says. Anyhow, tattooing interests me as much as handwriting
does. It is, if you think about it, another kind of handwriting.

Elizabeth can barely breathe. Miss Moore, her conversation, the
elephants, the other pairs of women who seem to be mothers and
daughters. Finally, they run out of bread. The elephants are sorry
to see them go. Ears droop. Trunks explore the empty air, same as a
human hand grasping.

Miss Moore understands the animals. Elizabeth has seen this kind
of understanding in some men who farm and fish, her uncle and
grandfather, but never in a woman. Miss Moore looks not at the girl
in the pink tutu standing on the back of the horse, but at the horse.

The horse is smarter, Miss Moore says, the horse is keeping the girl
aloft.

Elizabeth can see that now. The girl has only to hold still while the
horse balances her. The girl's eyes are half closed, but the horse's eyes
are wide open, wild, searching ahead.

Because balance is all about knowing what is going to happen,
Miss Moore says. Or trying to find out. Balance is about knowing the
unknowable. Simple as that.

The horse slows, and the girl leaps off, into the center of the ring,
raises her arms, and bows low. The horse, unburdened, slows to a
trot, then a walk, turns, moves back toward the girl. From out of her
pink skirt, the girl draws an apple, which she polishes with elaborate
anticipation. She holds the apple before her, pretending to appreciate
its perfection. Her gestures are large enough to be understood from

where Elizabeth and Miss Moore sit, very high up under the circus tent. The girl opens her mouth and brings the apple closer. Now the horse is directly behind her, and in one swift movement, he reaches over her shoulder and takes the apple, delicately, as the elephants took the bread. The girl mimes surprise, then a flash of anger. The horse chews calmly, carelessly, dropping bits of fruit at the girl's feet. The audience laughs and applauds.

Interesting, Miss Moore says. An apple, a woman, an animal. A new version of the old story.

The unfall. What if it had happened this way, that the serpent wanted the apple more than the temptation?

You'll be traveling next year, Miss Moore says. Mother and I envy your leisurely habits.

Would you and Mrs. Moore think of traveling as far as Coney Island? Elizabeth asks. My friend Louise has a large, safe car, and she's an awfully good driver.

Vassar in the spring is Sleeping Beauty just before the prince arrives to kiss the maiden awake. Childish and false. Everyone is fooled, though, and overjoyed by the stone chapel that green willows weep over and the crenellated gates twined nearly shut with roses. Honeysuckle grows up over the chapel windows, and the gardeners look the other way. The sleeping beauties shrug off their camel-hair coats, rub their eyes, lift their chins, and purse their lips, waiting.

Miss Peebles wants to give us what my father calls an exit interview, Hallie says. You know: What we've learned. What we'll do next.

I haven't a clue, Elizabeth says. If it's an interview, I won't get the job.

Yes, you will, Hallie says. Everybody gets this job.

I keep thinking about mercury, Elizabeth says to her literature professor, Miss Rose Peebles. The way a drop of it will join smaller drops to it. The drop grows larger, but it keeps its original form and quality. Like the past. I don't think you can understand the past in the order things happened. That's the mistake most people make. It's not what happened in the past that matters, it's the present circumstance in which one's consciousness admits that event. You have to have a great deal of patience. You have to trust in the chaos of things. You have to let your senses be reordered. Causality doesn't matter. The plodding ahead of time is the least useful way of understanding what's happened to you. As if the past lives right here inside the present, not behind it. As if the present makes the past real.

I don't know, Hallie says. I think the past politely stays out of sight. The present is noisy but a bit dim.

Slow, you mean, Elizabeth says.

That's what you learned from Proust? Miss Peebles asks.

I think so, Elizabeth says.

And how do you suppose this will inform your future, Miss Bishop?

I think I will have to keep my eyes open. I think of the human eye. And the pupil is the past. It sees what it sees, knows what it knows.

You've lost me now.

Sorry, Miss Peebles. I'm just coming to these ideas myself.

But I think I understand just enough, Miss Peebles says, to know that the eye needs new things to look at. I hope you will be able to travel after college, to find these circumstances, to reorder, as you say. To be in familiar places will clog the works, as you've just explained it.

Yes, travel.

You realize, though, the dangers. Where will you go?

Europe, I expect.

I should be very careful there. The news out of Germany is distressing. I have a friend, a medical doctor, now in Manhattan, who left Berlin all of a sudden after reading Hitler's autobiography. She says this is not uncommon, to be frightened this way by what's going on there, especially for Jewish people. What else could go on, too. I want you to pay attention.

I will, Miss Peebles.

I like this one part of your essay in particular, Miss Bishop.

Miss Peebles turns over the pages of Elizabeth's essay on Hopkins, then reads aloud.

We live in great whispering galleries, constantly vibrating and humming, or we walk through salons lined with mirrors where the reflections

between the narrow walls are limitless, and each present moment reaches
immediately and directly the past moments, changing them both.

That's very complex.

Thank you, Miss Peebles.

And now tell me, what have you learned from Ibsen?

Nothing I didn't already know.

What do you mean?

I know what I learned, Hallie says. A beautiful woman is always
doomed.

Well, that's a relief, Elizabeth says.

And you, Miss Bishop?

I'm not sure.

But she is sure. *Peer Gynt: To write is to sit in judgement on oneself.*
And the future, that it's like a stone in water, sinking and alone.

She gazes around Miss Peebles's office, done up like a sitting room,
with chintz sofa and curtains, silver tea service on a table between the
windows, framed photographs of the Acropolis, the Eiffel Tower, the
Houses of Parliament, bridges over the Danube. She's a very tough
taskmistress, Miss Peebles is, and often young women are invited into
this room to hear terrible news about their futures. Even the desk is a
wide inlaid dining table that appears to have been stolen out of a Sara-
toga mansion. It's easy to let down one's guard and then be savaged.

Did you ever ride the Cyclone? Miss Moore asks.

I don't like roller coasters, Elizabeth says. But I have a friend who does.

Louise drives to Brooklyn, first to collect Miss Moore at her mother's apartment on Cumberland Street. They are surprised to be invited upstairs by Mrs. Moore, who is seventy-three and gray eyed and very serious. The sitting room seems to be occupied more by animals—shells and feathers and painted eggs—than humans, even with the four of them crowded in. Mrs. Moore follows them into the hallway, takes Louise's hand.

Since you are the driver, she says, and thoroughly unknown to me.

She closes her eyes and whispers a short prayer.

Thank you, Louise says.

You will want to stop your car exactly at the intersection of Surf Avenue and West Tenth Street, she says. Any farther and you will be too far for Marianne to walk comfortably.

Louise starts to say they cannot park on the boardwalk, but Elizabeth interrupts.

We will, she says. She has heard that some people who contradict Mrs. Moore are never invited back.

I understand that if a person stands or even sits up very smartly on this ride, his head will be cleanly severed from his body.

Mother, Miss Moore says. I will keep an eye on them.

I'm not worried about them, Marianne. You, however, can be a bit . . . flighty. She turns to Louise. Miss Crane, she says. I have no doubt you will take these two poets firmly in hand.

I will indeed, Louise says. You can count on me.

The Cyclone, Miss Moore tells them, is 2,640 feet long, with six fan turns and twelve drops. The first drop is at a 58.1 degree angle. Each of the three cars on the train can carry eight persons.

Why don't you like roller coasters, Miss Bishop? Really, you must give it a go.

Trial by fire! Louise says.

Miss Moore proposes they sit in the front car. Elizabeth wants to refuse and make a gentle suggestion: the last car, perhaps? She tells herself she could just close her eyes.

You won't be sick, will you? Miss Moore says.

Elizabeth shakes her head, very glad they have not yet eaten lunch.

As he slams and locks the gate of their car, the attendant looks concerned, leans in close to Elizabeth.

Be careful with your mother, there, he says. Some people have a weak ticker and don't know it.

Yes, of course, Elizabeth says. Always. Thank you.

We have a medic and an ambulance right here, though. Just in case.

I don't think that will be necessary, Elizabeth says.

We may need the medic for *you*, Miss Moore whispers.

Louise steps into the last car. She is alone for a moment but soon joined by three other riders, all men.

They look to be reasonable, calm fellows, Miss Moore says. See, that one has brought along his lunch! He won't let Louise lose her head.

I hope not, Elizabeth says.

The ascent is agonizingly slow, the cars ratcheting higher with a sound like wood snapping: branches in an ice storm, kindling in a fire.

Look down! Miss Moore says. It's like we're climbing matchsticks!

The worst thing is that Elizabeth can't see Louise and can't know what reckless thing she might do. She can't see what she imagines to be happening: the man offers Louise half his sandwich, Louise refuses at first, then changes her mind. The park, Surf Avenue, all of Brooklyn falls slowly away behind them.

Oh dear, she says, I've just remembered that I don't care for heights.

Miss Moore smiles appreciatively, as if she thinks Elizabeth has just made a very good joke.

Then this will be your cure, Miss Bishop, she says.

They have almost reached the summit. Elizabeth tries to turn in her seat to catch a glimpse of Louise.

No, no, Miss Moore says. You must look straight at it or you'll miss the experience. When we round the first bend, you'll be able to see Miss Crane. We'll be almost right beside her.

Bent in half, Elizabeth thinks. All kinds of rules get broken on this machine. The notion of time travel flashes into her mind, then out again.

They sit balanced at the top of the Cyclone for so long that Elizabeth believes the entire ride must have broken down. She wonders how they will be rescued. Helicopter? That would be worse than the usual descent.

The car begins to tip, as if in slow motion, as if taunting, and then suddenly it's hurtling toward the ground. Elizabeth wants to close her eyes, but she can't—the wind holds her eyelids open, or is it some kind of paralysis? The earth rushes at them, people below grow larger, sound changes from a low whistle to a fierce whine. Someone two cars back is screaming. It's a girl, a child. Not Louise.

At the last second, they do not, in fact, crash through the timbered gully of the Cyclone but dive upward again and round the curve and yes, there is Louise, waving half a sandwich.

On the next descent, something whips across Elizabeth's eyes (a snake? How could that be, this high up?). She turns to look at Miss Moore and sees the reddish-gray braid has unwound and the pins that held it are blowing into the car behind them, where two men in military dress catch them as if they've practiced this maneuver every day for years. Miss Moore looks strange and beautiful—*unlikely* is the word. A word in spite of itself.

Three more whipsaw turns, and it's over.

The first and last roller coaster ride of my life, Elizabeth says.

At least in the conventional sense, Miss Moore tells her. Really, it's not very dangerous.

I've come to realize I don't love danger, Elizabeth tells her. Of any sort.

It's a good thing to know about oneself, I should think, Miss Moore says. And it will keep you safe or bored or both for your entire life.

But alive, Elizabeth says. There is that.

Louise strides toward them, grinning broadly, her mop of hair blown sideways, gleaming copper in the sun.

Oh, she says. Miss Moore! Now *that* was poetry!

Of a sort, Miss Moore says. Though not completely elegiac, as Miss Bishop would have it.

Elizabeth notices the soft magnetism that seems to swirl between Miss Moore and Louise. In the right light, they might be mistaken for mother and daughter, not so much their looks, but the way they relax into proximity but don't quite touch. It's as if they have known and will know each other all their lives.

All I want to do is kill you. After she whispers these words, late one night, Elizabeth's mother disappears for eighteen years, and when she returns, she's dead. That's how she comes back, as a message from Uncle Jack three days before graduation: Your mother has died in the state hospital.

All I want to do is kill you. It is impossible to talk about such a sentiment expressed by one's mother, and so Elizabeth doesn't. She breathes it, though, in and out, every minute. There's always been the fear, too, that what her mother said is a deed undone and looming ahead in some possible future. Or done continuously, as if neglect were a weapon, a blade driven in slowly, through the breastbone—or no, slanted a little left of center, ever closer to the heart.

And now she is dead. The threat shrivels to a little ache. Although sometimes her heart feels like a sponge held too long underwater. A sponge in the Hudson, a sponge in the ocean.

For some reason, Elizabeth tells Margaret, I really thought, I thought she might, you know, just turn up. Maybe for commencement. She would come to her senses and do the necessary calculations, and she would know what year it is, and where I was. She would have to ask my uncle—and then . . .

I feel so sorry for you, Margaret says. It's such terrible timing.

They are lying on Margaret's bed, Elizabeth on her side and Margaret behind her, half sitting, so that she can stroke Elizabeth's hair. The room has a curved wall of windows—they are in the tower suite, seven floors up, so that the evening sun illuminates them like a stage light, but in a theater without an audience. Everyone else is so far away, groundlings who never even think to look up. Elizabeth has loved these rooms all year: so much exquisite privacy. Margaret's undivided, careful, cool attention. Their conversation about art and poetry and beauty. The first thing in the morning and the last thing at night, followed by the click of Margaret's bedroom door closing, tiny rebuke, with Elizabeth on the outside.

I'm crying all over your duvet, Elizabeth says.

I can wash it. Anyway, it's only tears.

I guess I pretended in my head that I had some family, and I believed it.

And now it's real that you don't.

It's real. I'm sorry to be so pathetic.

Elizabeth lifts Margaret's hand from her hair and tries to pull her into a hug. Margaret resists, moves off the bed and toward the windows.

Do you want something to drink, Elizabeth? she says.

I want everything to drink.

Sorry, but I only have *something*. It's just sherry.

Margaret opens her armoire, reaches down behind the shoes. Elizabeth hears a clanking of glass that suggests more than one bottle. The sound makes her cry again, the camaraderie of it, the promise of an evening talking to Margaret.

I'll take sherry, Elizabeth says.

We'll be your family tomorrow, Margaret says. Remember all the trouble we got into our first year? And my mother still likes you. She'd be glad to have you at our table for the president's luncheon.

Elizabeth rolls over onto her back. The light on Margaret's hair turns some strands a glittery red, as if they were heated filaments.

It feels like I'm losing everything. All at once.

No, you're not. You'll come to New York and we'll all be together, and then Europe.

But not you. Like this.

Elizabeth holds out her arms to Margaret.

Not me, Elizabeth. I'm sorry.

My mother has a friend in Paris, Louise says.

A mother with friends, Elizabeth says. Isn't that something? My mother's friends were probably all lunatics. If she had any.

I'm telling you this for a reason, Louise says. And by the way, you don't need any more of that.

She screws the cap back on the gin bottle, stashes it on top of the bookcase.

Sorry.

It's all right.

I can still reach it there.

I'll see that you don't. You're going to stay here tonight.

I'd love to.

Anyway, my mother's friend, Clara Longworth de Chambrun. The comtesse de Chambrun. And the sister-in-law of Alice Roosevelt. And rich. And eccentric. She has odd theories about Shakespeare, mainly that he was a Catholic.

And so we should meet her?

Eventually. She has an apartment beside the Luxembourg Gardens. My mother will rent it for us.

Your mother is too good.

We both think you should go to Paris.

And get in some trouble.

No, that's my department. You're to be my chaperone. Hallie's going over first. You should go with her. Margaret and I have to placate our mothers for a little while, so they'll let us go off on our own. But they will. They think you're a good influence.

I'm glad Margaret's going, too.

Elizabeth, Louise says. That's never going to change. You need to . . . think about it differently.

I don't know if I can, Elizabeth says.

You will. One day you'll wake up and everything will be . . . The whole idea will just be gone. And you'll be good friends and you'll barely remember this.

I don't think I'm capable of that, Louise.

We don't know what we're capable of, Elizabeth.

Until someone tells us.

GEOGRAPHY II

1936

n their cabin aboard the S.S. *Königstein,* lying still in her narrow bunk, eyes open, Elizabeth imagines burial. For a while, Hallie, in the top bunk, snores gently. Then she hops down, brushes her teeth, and slurps from the tap in the tiny WC.

What are you doing? Hallie wants to know. You're not sleeping. Let's go meet some of the other passengers. I hear they're mostly Germans.

Elizabeth closes her eyes. It's late, she says.

I've met one called Albert Nock. He writes for *The Atlantic.* He's actually American. Elizabeth, you'd like him.

I don't know about that.

He says our itinerary is all wrong. Instead of Paris, we should go to the Breton coast.

We'd be traveling backward.

We've got time. You can't have the Chambrun apartment for another month. Louise won't even be there until then. And it's a good thing. She'd hate this. How did you get us on a Nazi boat anyway?

I looked for the cheapest, Elizabeth says. What does it mean, a Nazi boat?

German. Dangerous. I don't really know actually.

Dangerous. That's funny. I keep dreaming I'm being chased. But by a feeling. Not a creature.

What feeling?

I don't know, Elizabeth says.

But she does know. It's homesickness, but a strange sort. The *stranger's* version: she hasn't had a home for ages, not since her mother went into the hospital and never came out.

Maybe it's the Nazis chasing you.

Do you think this trip was a mistake?

I think it would have been a mistake to stay home, Hallie says. I'm glad you could come with us.

I have a little money now.

Inheritance. Call a thing by its name.

I don't deserve it.

No one ever does, Hallie says. She touches Elizabeth's cheek. No one but you. I for one will be glad to get to Paris and have a social life!

Some passengers, mostly German soldiers, are drinking in the ship's canteen. Hallie and Elizabeth watch a slight young man move from table to table, pressing up against the backs of the soldiers.

What is he doing? Hallie says.

You won't believe it, Elizabeth says. Listen when he comes closer.

The young man bends, whispers to each soldier, *Oh, you are a prince!*

Oh no! Hallie says. I hope he stays away.

He's not interested in us.

The soldiers behave as if they've experienced these attentions before. A few roll their eyes. Elizabeth imagines they've endured much worse.

Or will.

The civilians on the ship are a force of nature, like some previously uncharted and violent weather. They fill up the narrow passageways, pushing past Elizabeth and Hallie without greeting or apology, dark coats whipping open against Elizabeth's legs. The women's heels pound like gunfire, the men's boots like explosions. At six o'clock on the first night, pairs of Germans rush arm in arm from the cabins, steely eyed, forcing Elizabeth to flatten herself against the walls.

I feel like a small bug, Elizabeth says.

It will be better at the table, Hallie says. They'll have a drink and relax. They're just, you know, *reserved.*

The purser leads them to a table in the center of the dining room, already occupied by a man and a woman and two girls, maybe eight and ten, who must be their daughters. Hallie begins a conversation in her phrasebook German—where are you from, where are you going, do you speak English. The man answers stiffly—*München, Antwerpen, nein.* The dining room is crowded and too hot. Conversation roars around them. Elizabeth feels exposed, as if a spotlight is being trained upon their table. She thought there might be windows, even a line of portholes along one wall, but the room is sealed, as if they were traveling in a submarine. The din of talk fades as plates are delivered to the tables. Elizabeth remembers grammar school and the times girls misbehaved and were punished with silent lunch—the cruelty of that. She notices that sounds are being replaced by smells, of cabbage and another sour, yeasty aroma, like spilled beer. When their plates finally arrive, loaded with watery vegetables, a slice of roast, and a hunk of dark bread, the man and woman look accusingly at Hallie and Elizabeth, as if they have prepared this grim dinner.

Hallie takes up her knife, points it at the roast. *Was ist das?* she asks.

The man stares openmouthed as if she has said something obscene. The little girls look at each other and giggle, and the woman slaps the arm of the girl closest to her, the sound of the hand on soft flesh echoing through the dining room like a high-pitched gunshot. The child puts down her fork and weeps quietly for the rest of the meal. Hallie asks again if the couple speak English, and the man says no in a way that suggests he might but would prefer not to.

Elizabeth eats quickly, cleaning her plate in order not to be hungry later. Dessert arrives: a small dish of ochre-colored pudding, which Elizabeth tastes cautiously and discovers is butterscotch. She sees that these little orange pots dotting the tables are the brightest things in the dining room, like votives. The man and the woman take the girls' portions away and hand them back to the waiter as he passes. Elizabeth wishes she might somehow meet these girls later, in secret, slip them pieces of chocolate. The man rises and, without a word, leaves the table, and his family follows.

I don't think I can face another meal with them, Elizabeth says.

It wasn't so bad. Maybe they'll get used to us.

I doubt it.

Those poor little girls. Next time, I'm going to give them my pudding. Or at least try to. The parents can't like us any less.

I think I'm homesick, Elizabeth whispers, later, after they have turned out the light and climbed into their berths, after Hallie has begun to snore. I remember feeling like this when I was nine and missed one of my aunts.

She's not sure why she wants to say the words out loud or who she thinks might be listening. Not Hallie. Not Louise or even Margaret.

Where do the dead go? she asks the air, the ship's iron hull, the ocean below.

The fishnets are closely woven and dyed blue, the same shade as the North Atlantic beyond Douarnenez. Sardines can't see them in the blue sea—that must be the idea. The catch is tremendous, at least twenty boats at the dock below the fish houses, so loaded with sardines and oysters that their hulls ride just at the waterline. A medium-sized wave could swamp them, but no such wave arrives. That's what waves do. They arrive, same as dreams do, same as travelers do, their bags full of flotsam and jetsam, the orderly folding inside always undone by the rough treatment of porters and dockhands.

Elizabeth predicts Hallie will last only a few days in this little town before she escapes to Paris. A few turns out to be too hopeful. In forty-eight hours, Hallie has helped set her up in the Hôtel de l'Europe, a block from the port, and then she's packing her bags again.

It's all right, Elizabeth says. I like it here. It feels familiar.

And think of it this way, Hallie says. I can start making introductions for us. Invitations, escorts, that kind of thing.

Not too many invitations. Please.

It's Paris, Elizabeth. The point is to *go out.*

I'll rest up for it then.

Promise me you'll make a friend here. The cook seems nice.

I'm sure the cook doesn't have time for me.

It turns out, though, the cook has quite a bit of time. Every morning, after Elizabeth has unpacked her books and writing paper at the little table on the hotel terrace, the cook brings strong coffee and warm rolls, and then four hours later, a massive lunch of oyster pie and courgettes, a plate of cheeses and slices of butter cake, explaining that this is the custom, to eat well at midday. She is unfailingly cheerful and quick with a conspiratorial wink. The hotel staff call her Madame. She says approvingly that Elizabeth must have many, many friends at home because she is certainly writing quite a lot of letters.

Madame is, it appears, also the laundress. The fourth morning of her stay, when Elizabeth walks out of the hotel lobby and onto the terrace, Madame is pegging sheets on a wash line. She has hung the line on three sides around the table Elizabeth has chosen the three previous mornings, and then, after she serves the coffee and rolls, she quickly pegs the final sheet, forming a sort of tent, open to the sky and to the view of the sea.

Privée, she whispers, and gestures toward the table piled with books and writing paper. Then she lifts a corner of the tent and disappears.

The bedsheets have been bleached to a brilliant sheen, and they sparkle in the sunshine like light on water. Elizabeth's view is endless water and fishing boats and docks and men. The sky is the color of cornflowers or forget-me-nots. The sheets around her twitch like sails, and then, as they dry and grow less heavy, they ripple in the steady breeze. Elizabeth has a sense of the sea running beneath her, under the terrace, that she is sailing downward toward the port and the bay but never arriving. Muffled voices from behind the wash lines could be human or animal or the wind or something else entirely.

Two hours later, when some invisible presence unpegs the sheets, Elizabeth discovers there is a woman seated at the next table. This woman opens her eyes wide in theatrical surprise and smiles warmly.

I thought someone was over there, she says, but you were so quiet.

Elizabeth guesses the woman is German, and maybe about forty. She wears riding clothes: red silk shirt open at the neck and jodhpurs. Her hair is coal black and close-cropped, styled like a man's with a side part and a slick of pomade.

Madame appears, as if out of the air.

Voilà! she says to Elizabeth, gesturing toward the woman. *Mademoiselle Bishop. Le cirque d'Autriche arrive!*

Well, the woman says, her accent clearly German, I am hardly the entire Austrian circus by myself!

Elizabeth cannot take her eyes off the woman's blouse. The color glistens like rubies or wet nail polish. She imagines when the woman rises from her chair, the seat back will be streaked red.

How rude of me, the woman says. I'm Greta Angel.

She extends her hand across the space between their tables, and Elizabeth does the same. The ends of their fingers just touch. Greta Angel tips her chair sideways to grasp Elizabeth's hand in hers, and both her feet come completely off the ground. The maneuver is amazing—Elizabeth can't really believe what she's seeing—the magical balance of it.

I love the circus, Elizabeth says. I saw the P. T. Barnum last year in New York.

You'll like ours then, Greta Angel says, though it's smaller, of course. I'll get you a ticket. Or two?

Thank you, Elizabeth says. But just one. My friend isn't arriving for another ten days.

Ah, Greta Angel says. She turns her chair so that she is facing Elizabeth. Her gaze is open and unguarded. Patient.

I understand from Madame that you are a prodigious writer of letters. Madame said perhaps you are a diplomat.

Hardly, Elizabeth says. I like to receive letters. And I've found this is the only way.

There is something fine about a foreign letter posted to a foreign address, Greta Angel says. *Poste Restante, Paris.* That's all. And these letters hardly ever go astray. It's a miracle.

The sorting is the magic, I think, Elizabeth says. Behind the scenes.

Yes, I agree. It's the same in the circus. We keep the illusion going.

I understand.

Greta Angel stares intently, as if she is calculating exactly how much Elizabeth understands.

Well, I'm off to work, she says. See you again tomorrow. I'll leave the ticket with Madame if you're not here.

Thank you, Elizabeth says. I'm here every day.

The next morning, Greta Angel does not appear, but her blouse does, pegged into a corner of the wash line enclosing Elizabeth's table. Madame obviously has decided Elizabeth enjoys this sort of Bedouin breakfast. The sky is a bit overcast, and so in this light the sheets have a soft, pearly glow. Amidst them, the ruby blouse is like a slap, a quick bit of violence. Elizabeth stares at the blouse for a long time, then sits down at the table, facing away toward the sea. She stirs her coffee, picks at the breakfast roll, reducing it slowly to a plate full of crumbs. She takes a pen and stationery from her bag, begins a letter to Louise: *Who are you seeing in New York these days? I look forward to your arrival. You'll love it here. I've met a woman who's with the circus. I'm told she trains the ponies.*

The wind rises, and from behind her comes a low tapping. She turns to see the ruby blouse has blown open and up into the air, so that the buttons strike against one of the wooden pegs. Almost before she knows what she's doing, Elizabeth stands and moves into the corner of the washing. She reaches up to untangle the blouse, close the buttons. It's hung at the level of the sheets, so she has to lift her arms high, as a small child would toward a grown-up, toward her mother wearing this blouse, the child asking to be held. She knows how this gesture must look on the other side of the sheet: a shadow play. From the kitchen, from the dining room windows, everyone can see what is happening. She catches the hem of the blouse, smooths the fabric, which has the scratch of raw silk, but softened, buffed away by the body inside. She begins to fasten the buttons, but a gust of wind lifts the blouse away, off the wash line, and into Elizabeth's arms. It would be difficult to say exactly how this happened.

Elizabeth turns quickly and drops the blouse into her bag. She sits down and fixes her gaze on the port of Douarnenez. There is some tumult on the dock below. A boat captain shouts to a group of men standing nearby, *Non, non, non,* and then he begins to pitch sardines at their heads. They duck but do not leave, and then suddenly they storm his boat. He disappears below, and the others scoop up his catch and throw it all overboard. Elizabeth tries to resume her letter to Louise, but the ruby blouse, just visible under books and maps, is a distraction. *Why do you think,* she finally writes, *Rimbaud said about Brittany that the sea air would burn his lungs and the bad atmosphere would hurt him?*

Upstairs in her room, Elizabeth lifts Greta Angel's blouse from her bag and hangs it in the tiny wardrobe. She has already invented a tale that she tells herself is very much the truth: the blouse blew down from the line, and rather than leave it or bother Madame, Elizabeth took it inside and will return it as quickly as she can.

Her intention now is to walk down to the docks to see what happened to the besieged boat. There is probably a very good story, and everyone in the shops will be talking about it. She wants to pick out gifts for Frani and Miss Moore, one of the beautiful baskets or a small blue net for catching crabs. A bottle of cider for later, no, two bottles. She combs her hair, applies a little lipstick. Too much, she thinks, for what I have on. Reflected in the mirror, the half-opened wardrobe, the blouse is a slash of red as if someone has started to paint the wall inside.

With her back to the mirror, Elizabeth unbuttons her shirt, slips it off, and drops it on the bed. She opens the wardrobe and slides the ruby blouse closer. She wonders again at the feel of it, rough and soft at the same time—wouldn't you feel alive and witty and *ennobled* wearing such a thing right up against your plain old human skin? Wouldn't you? She reaches back to unhook her brassiere, drops it to the floor, reaches for Greta Angel's blouse.

The blouse is miles too big, like the men's pajama tops some girls at Vassar used to wear. She always wished she had that sort of bravery, that nerve. And now it's as if the fabric sends a drug through her skin to her bloodstream. She turns to look in the mirror and sees the effect: the red lipstick is a shade lighter than the blouse, but that seems artistic rather than wrong, a subtlety Margaret would approve of. Last year, Robert Seaver took her Christmas shopping and said to pick out anything, and Elizabeth chose a scarf that was a sort of Tiffany window design, with small rectangles of blue and green and yellow, but mostly this same shade of ruby red. He said he was glad she'd chosen something red, and she was both touched and puzzled by his modest happiness.

She unbuttons the blouse, takes it off, returns it to the hanger. She dashes off a few lines of explanation to Greta Angel, seals the page in an envelope, and leaves it at the hotel's front desk on her way out, hoping she has avoided writing something that sounds like a ransom note.

The sailboats for hire are named for nearby towns and local legends: Quimper, Tristan, Isolde, Carnac. They ride gently in their berths, the bright hulls—pink, blue, green, orange—and dazzling white sails inviting, eager. Maybe after Louise arrives . . . ? Elizabeth thinks, but then she recalls Louise flying overboard in Wellfleet, all whirling, splashing arms and legs. A charter, perhaps, then maybe a bit of fishing. The vista from the terrace of the Hôtel de l'Europe reminds her almost painfully of Cape Breton, the sea lying steely blue as mackerel. These French are different from the Canadian Bretons, well-off by comparison, a bit obsequious in the shops, rather than moody and silent, catering to the tourist trade instead of desperate to get away to today's dinner. Elizabeth ducks into a little shack full of baskets and espadrilles. She admires the shoes, same colors as the boats' hulls, with their soft, woven soles. So comfortable for walking. She wonders if they will be fashionable enough for Paris and begins in her head to form the question in French.

Bien sûr, the shopkeeper says. She is a small, compact woman, about sixty, dressed in the native costume: starched black dress with a broad lace collar and the traditional lace *coiffe* that looks like a cross between a maid's cap and a nun's winged cornette. She asks the usual questions: where Elizabeth is from, how long she will be staying, what she plans to do. When Elizabeth mentions renting a boat, perhaps fishing, the shopkeeper scowls. They are not to be used as fishing boats, the shopkeeper tells her, but sometimes that rule is broken, and so there is trouble, the sort that Elizabeth observed this morning. *Vol! Stealing!* The shopkeeper, whose husband is a sardine fisherman, is so incensed that she translates, as if the English could serve as an expletive. *Les étrangers,* she says, and then apologizes.

She doesn't mean us, a familiar voice says.

Elizabeth turns to see Greta Angel.

She means gypsies and that sort, Greta says. I got your note just after you left. Thank you for saving my blouse.

Not at all. I didn't know quite what to do.

What you did was perfectly appropriate, I think.

Greta Angel takes a step closer. Her eyes are large lidded, giving her a sleepy, languorous look, but still full of the candor Elizabeth noticed before, a habit of interested appraisal. She gives off the scents of hay and peppermint.

I should have left the blouse with Madame, I now realize. Do you need it for today?

I would like to have it for this afternoon, yes. Perhaps when you finish your shopping. I can wait a minute or two.

She looks down at the pairs of espadrilles in Elizabeth's hands. Such lovely colors, she says. Very nice for country walking. I could show you a few paths along the coast if you have time.

Elizabeth feels a gathering vertigo, as if she had already been led to the sea's edge on one of the coastal footpaths. But instead of seascape or horizon, she sees only blackness, the emptiness of cold, blue-black space, suffocation. Suddenly, a bell chimes. She turns her head toward a rush of fresh air: a breeze has blown the shop door open, a fine rain has begun to fall, tourists enter the shop to escape, the women's hair is shot with raindrops like gossamer, like silk.

Look at that, Elizabeth says. I think I'll have to stay here for a bit.

But I'm sure Madame would be willing to let you into my room, or go in herself to get your blouse. You can tell her I said it was all right.

Are you sure? Greta Angel says. I don't think this rain will last for very long. It never does.

I want to look at the baskets, Elizabeth says. For a friend who is a poet. She's very particular.

I understand perfectly. You're right. Madame will see to it. I think she rather likes poking into the bedrooms.

I suspect she does, Elizabeth says.

I'll leave the ticket for you. I hope you'll come to the circus tonight.

Thank you, Elizabeth says. I had planned to.

I'll be looking for you then.

Greta Angel reaches to shake Elizabeth's hand, then turns away, disappearing into the misty rain.

That night, at the Cirque Royal, Elizabeth is astonished to crowd into the small tent with what seems to be the entire population of Douarnenez, dressed up in Breton costume. The thirty or so tourists look like bright blooms against a sea of black taffeta and white lace. It will be easy for Greta Angel to see if Elizabeth has come as promised, even if she sits very high up and behind the aerialists' perch. Already, Madame has found her in the crowd and is making her way slowly up the wooden benches, stopping to greet a few of the women and kiss the cheeks of fat babies. Each time she stops, she points to Elizabeth and explains something, smiling broadly. Elizabeth wonders what fame she's acquired: *Voilà,* the American! The marvelous letter writer! *Tiens!* The queen of privacy! *Alors!* The thief of *chemisiers*! But she doesn't mind. To be able to come to the circus alone, she first fortified herself with three tall glasses of cider, one after the other, standing beside the open door of her wardrobe and gazing at the gap occupied this morning by the ruby blouse.

Mon dieu! Madame wheezes when she reaches Elizabeth, pressing her right hand to her bosom. *Bonsoir, mademoiselle!*

Bonsoir, madame, Elizabeth says. She moves farther into the row and pats the bench beside her, watching herself from a tipsy distance and wondering at the same time if the gesture is too informal.

Madame seems not to think so. She half collapses onto the bench, takes up Elizabeth's hand, and gives it a squeeze. Though her white lace *coiffe* is firmly in place, a few gray tendrils escape around her forehead and at the back of her neck. Her skin is lined but supple, creamy white, unblemished, not a single freckle. Elizabeth has the urge to rest her head on Madame's shoulder, and she feels the impulse becoming a kind of magnetism, a force. The cider, she thinks, wishing she had more, a bottle of it cold in her hand.

The circus master announces something through a megaphone, and the tent lights go down for a moment, then blaze up. The crowd is on its feet around her, seeing that the aerialists have climbed in the dark to their perches at either end of the tent, and the spotlights are on them, two men and a woman who swing past one another, then let go and somersault and join in a last-minute clutch. What Elizabeth is struck by is the lack of frenzy, the almost dreamlike precision. And the silence—even the crowd seems scarcely to breathe—broken only by a faint creak from the trapeze and the exhalation of these three bodies moving through the air, apart and together. What must be tiny sequins on their costumes glitter like stars or icicles in the trees at dusk. If there's a net below them, Elizabeth can't see it—another one of the invisible nets of Douarnenez.

Finally, all three aerialists arrive on the same perch, wave to the crowd, and are lost in darkness as the spotlight shifts to the circus master. Elizabeth is still trying to follow the descending aerialists—a spray of tiny lights moves through the darkness toward the floor—when Madame touches her hand again and whispers, *Voilà, votre amie.*

Greta Angel stands in the center of the floor in the ruby blouse, jodhpurs, and black boots, carrying a riding crop painted or dyed the same shade of red. Why? Elizabeth wonders. What is that meant to signify? Or is it meant to terrify?

Greta Angel shouts the one word—*Pferde!*—and the ponies gallop into the ring, six of them, nose to tail, moving as if connected by a wire, or as if frozen in motion and it's the floor that's revolving. Occasionally, Greta Angel makes a slight correction with the tip of the riding crop, to a misstep only she can see. After a minute, six shirtless boys in red trousers run into the ring and leap onto the horses, stand, and balance. Six girls follow, in red skirts and shimmering ruby bodices, and the boys pull them onto the horses' backs and quickly onto their own shoulders. The horses move in formation, around and around the ring, while the humans seem to remain perfectly still. Greta Angel lowers the riding crop to her side. She bows her head and stands still, too, and she becomes the cog in the whole production, the spindle. Elizabeth wonders if everyone around her sees what she does—a blur of red. She feels slightly seasick. She wishes it were another color.

Greta Angel lifts her head and shouts *Genug!* and then *Assez!* It *is* indeed enough. The boys lift the girls off their shoulders and set them on the ground, then leap from the ponies' backs. Greta Angel touches the ponies one by one, and they slow to a canter and leave the floor. The humans take a bow.

Elizabeth leans close to Madame and tries to think how to say, *But the ponies have done all the work,* but in the end, she changes her mind and tells Madame that this is the best circus she has ever seen. The people of Douarnenez are on their feet again, stomping and applauding and calling the troupe back for an encore. The floor remains dark for some minutes, until a single spotlight opens on Greta Angel, who carries a large hoop, which she sets in a stand about three feet off the ground. One of the boys appears carrying a lighted torch and touches it to the hoop, which takes fire. Greta Angel gives a long, shrieking whistle, and a white pony canters into the ring, clearly younger and smaller than the others, looking like a ghost or a leggy cloud. With the red crop, she directs the pony around the ring, faster and faster, and then, with a tap to the pony's withers, she sends it through the hoop of fire, but only once. The pony seems to change course on the other side of the hoop, runs closer to the stands and more slowly. Madame shakes her head and makes a clucking sound, and in a moment, Elizabeth catches the scent of burnt flesh. The horse stops abruptly, its cries like a child's. A boy runs in, and the tent goes dark. The crowd is silent. Madame grips Elizabeth's hand. She whispers in English that Elizabeth should not put this in her letters because it is too terrible.

ouise arrives at the hotel, exhausted from her trip across the Atlantic and oddly pale. She gives Elizabeth a kiss and sniffs a bit at her hair.

Hmmm, she says. The sea air. Let me go wash up. Then we'll talk.

But she turns at the foot of the stairs, exhales loudly, rummaging in the pocket of her coat. She produces a telegram.

It's for you.

Elizabeth can scarcely make sense of the words. They seem lost in a haze, as if the writing itself were an apparition. The message says that Robert Seaver has died from a gunshot wound. Accidental, his mother has written or dictated. Crutches, hunting rifle. He had too much to carry.

Oh God, Elizabeth says. She drops the telegram, reaches for the banister to steady herself, but it is too far away. Her open palm pushes down, down, as if trying to keep the empty air from swallowing her whole.

Barbara told me it wasn't an accident, Louise says.

Because I turned him down.

Madame stands behind them in the hallway, wringing her hands over this most irregular arrival, a guest who will not go to her room when the baggage is already there, waiting. Another guest who is distraught.

Maybe not just you, Louise says.

Did someone else turn him down?

No. I mean all of it, all his life wanting to run and dance and always being such a very good sport about everything he couldn't do. As if conversation and wit were a substitute.

Which they're not.

Madame can contain herself no longer. She grasps Elizabeth's arm. *Qu'est-ce qui se passe?* she says.

That's a good question, Elizabeth says quietly. What *is* happening?

You should write to his mother.

I know. I will. Madame thinks I am the most amazing correspondent on earth.

She covers Madame's hand with her own. *Un copain,* she says, *est mort.*

Oh! Madame says. *Désolée. Mes condoléances.*

She asks a quick flight of odd, embarrassed questions, half-stifled chirps. Do they need a doctor? Will they need a telephone? To send a telegram? Will they return to America?

No, no, Elizabeth says. None of that.

Now I will go up and unpack, Louise says.

I'll be in the bar, Elizabeth tells her.

The circus has gone, as Greta Angel said it would, inland, through the forest to Rennes. Elizabeth can chart their path on the great map behind the bar, the vast forêt de Quénécan, its emptiness illustrated by a horse, a deer, and a wild boar, all three the same shade of rust brown and quite still, facing east as if waiting for some important piece of news. The bartender brings a glass of water, and the two of them stare at it. Then he says, No? He turns to take hold of a bottle from the shelf in front of the map. The empty space reveals the brightness of the boar's jagged silvery tusk—or is it a tooth, or a fang?—and this revelation causes Elizabeth to notice the wild eye of the horse and the way the deer's antlers resemble branches of coral. She imagines the circus ponies breaking out of the caravan in a great hullabaloo, their wild stampede away from Greta and her red crop, and into the trees, their great, whinnying relief.

The new liquid in her glass is the color of root beer. It's sweet and perfumey, like gin. Rum, the bartender says, but she's not sure that's right. It carves a path down through her chest, a sluice of heat and a contrapuntal rise of sadness, then vague goodwill. If only Robert had known this sensation. Her head feels lifted off her shoulders, flying on its own in a cloud of fiery pale chemicals, high above that mapped forest. She will get to Rennes ahead of the circus, before any of the animals.

Louise slides into the seat beside her. She signals to the bartender and points to Elizabeth's glass.

You won't like it, Elizabeth says,

I might.

Should I go home?

His mother didn't ask you to.

She still could.

That's true. So you should be prepared for it.

But I don't want to leave. We just got here. Hallie is waiting for us in Paris. God, I sound so selfish.

You do. Like a spoiled child. Have you been writing to him?

No. Though he's been writing to me. I thought it best to let go myself.

You're right. Now, take one last gulp of that awful stuff and show me the village.

Elizabeth shakes her head. I can't.

You have to. You promised this was a gorgeous place. You said it was just like home, right down to the smells.

E lizabeth wants ice cream, and then she wants to sit in the sun and drink a bottle of cider. After that, whiskey. Louise, of course, says no, takes Elizabeth's arm, and steers her toward the water. There is a marina at the south end of Douarnenez harbor and above it, the yacht club.

Let's rent a boat, Louise says.

Robert loved to sail, Elizabeth says.

So do you.

It's too still.

At the marina, there is a clutch of people and commotion and what appear to be twenty or so small craft moving back to the docks. Elizabeth comes to understand that this is the return of boats from a canceled race. The sailors call up to those watching: No wind! Some of the boats have to be towed, and these sailors seem the most cheerful. All are men, except for one crew of three women. Louise and Elizabeth watch this boat, the *Isolde,* ease into the dock. The women throw out fenders, secure the lines, and climb ashore. They stand for a moment, scanning the crowd.

I wonder if they're allowed inside, Louise says.

As if answering her question, one of the women looks directly at Louise and Elizabeth and smiles. They disappear into the yacht club, emerging in a few minutes on the upstairs terrace. They stand along the railing, gazing down at the other boats docking, furling sails, stowing gear. They don't talk much among themselves. Elizabeth thinks their silence seems comfortable, their lean bodies loose, waiting calmly for whatever will happen next. She longs to be with them. The desire takes her quite by surprise. She touches Louise's elbow, nods her head in their direction.

Who do you think they are? Louise says.

Maybe they would take us out in their boat.

We don't even know them.

You could go ask, Elizabeth says. They might say yes to you. Everyone does.

And I suppose you'll just wait here, and then I'll wave you over?

Something like that.

Why I do these things for you, I have no idea.

Because your mother told you to try to make me happy.

Elizabeth watches Louise with a mixture of awe and envy: her particular confident walk, part swagger, part glide, as if she is always moving in the direction of what she wants. At the end of the jetty, Louise comes to a gate, waist high, latched from inside, clearly meant to keep tourists and strays off the yacht club terrace. She turns her head to look at Elizabeth, but she's too far away to read the expression. Then she simply reaches over the gate, opens it from inside, steps through, and drops the latch as if she's been entering parties this way all her life. Which, of course, she has.

She walks straight to the crew of the *Isolde,* and though Elizabeth cannot hear the words, she knows that Louise is complimenting the boat, asking if the race will continue, what plans they have for the afternoon. In the pantomime, Elizabeth can see that Louise is offered a drink but declines. The conversation seems to be proceeding quite slowly, but with much smiling. At times Louise lifts both hands into the air, as if conducting an orchestra.

The sky brightens. A puff of breeze cools Elizabeth's neck. She deliberately turns her head away from Louise and the sailing women, toward the sea, flat gray glass, a barely perceptible undulation, a sound sleeper breathing beneath a blanket.

The last time she was in a boat on water like this was with Robert, off Nantucket. She wonders whether she wants to revive that memory fully, or erase it: the moment she knew she should have turned the boat back toward land but didn't because the wind was rushing them along so swiftly. And then it was too late. Robert said they made a good pair, and then he completely lost his head and proposed marriage. She hears herself refusing, the sound of her voice echoing over the water, percussive. And then Robert shot himself. She closes her eyes.

So when Elizabeth hears her name carried on the wind, she isn't sure if the sound is fact or dream, Robert or Louise, and then she's not sure which she prefers, Robert alive again or the prospect of sailing with these women. She can never make this choice, so does this mean she's glad Robert is dead? What kind of monster would she be then? Maybe suicide doesn't really exist. Maybe it's just a different kind of murder. Elizabeth wonders if she will never not be lonely. What was it Miss Moore wrote about that? The cure for loneliness is solitude.

Then it's clearly Louise's voice, calling her to come. Elizabeth rises from the bench, turns toward the yacht club. It feels like leaving Robert behind.

The women are German, from Berlin, taller and older up close—probably in their thirties—than they appeared from a distance. Louise introduces Elizabeth in a jumble of languages: *amie, Begleiter, classmate.* The women are Marie, Ann, and Sigrid. Again, they offer drinks, and before Louise can speak, Elizabeth accepts. The sun shines silvery through the clouds and the wind pipes up, but the race has been postponed indefinitely.

Sigrid, who is a bit younger and speaks more English, offers to go to the bar. Ann and Marie watch her leave as if she might not come back. Elizabeth senses a pause, a sort of deflation, as if now, without Sigrid, they will not know how to make themselves understood. Louise steers them toward a table set for a meal. The breeze frets the edges of the blue paper place mats. In a mix of French and English, Ann explains that they have come to Douarnenez from Paris, where they live in Saint-Denis. They left Berlin in January, she adds, but does not explain. Louise gives the comtesse de Chambrun's address and the date of their arrival. Sigrid returns, balancing a tray of pints. The beer is the color of honey. Sunlight travels through the glasses and across the table, over the pairs of hands.

What about your parents? Louise says.

Ann, Sigrid, and Marie look at one another, but their expressions betray nothing.

We miss them, Sigrid says. My mother can visit. Not my father. Yours?

Never, Elizabeth says.

Morts, Louise says. *Tot.*

In Saint-Denis, Ann and Marie teach at the university. Sigrid works at the German embassy in Paris. The way she says this, her voice halting machinelike, her gaze unmoving, makes Elizabeth pay attention. Sigrid's eyes are the same shade of blue as a Siamese cat's. Miss Moore would have noticed this immediately, Elizabeth chides herself. This blue is a bottomless shade: a person could see for miles through these eyes, far into Sigrid's mind, out through the back of her skull, into the past, the history of Germany, the origins of the universe. She has the look of someone imprisoned. Elizabeth begins to notice that Ann and Marie treat Sigrid as if she is a kind of talisman, a touchstone, a divine creature moving among mortals.

The men at the next table have sent them a round of beers. They are English. They give out their names, calling across the space between tables: Colin, Andrew, Michael, Ian, Robert. *Robert.*

We would be a matched set, Louise murmurs.

Englishmen always shout, Sigrid says.

They look into their glasses and nod, except Sigrid. She stares directly at the men, as if appraising pieces of furniture or birds in cages. Elizabeth is relieved to discover this English Robert looks nothing like the dead American Robert. The name could somehow be renewed. *Robert* might exist without grief being attached to it.

I'm Elizabeth, she shouts back.

Louise, Ann, and Marie try to quiet her, all three at once. Sigrid throws back her head and laughs.

Elizabeth looks down and sees Sigrid has fashioned an origami sailboat from the place mat.

When the beers are finished, Sigrid says, *Ist ja gut!* and leads them out of the terrace and down the steps to the docks. The *Isolde* is a Colin Archer 25, brass and teak, clean and trim. Louise and Elizabeth wait while the others step into the cockpit, move lines, gather cushions from the lazarettes. Then Sigrid helps them aboard. Her hand is warm, the palm soft. Ann and Marie speak German to each other, instructions about the sails, the dock lines, the fenders. Sigrid takes the tiller.

Five may be too many for this boat, Louise says.

Sigrid shrugs. A crowd is always safer, she says.

Louise begins to explain but seems to think better of it.

Sigrid steers a tight turn away from the dock and into the wind. Marie hoists the sail, jibes the boom, and the *Isolde* moves lazily toward the mouth of the harbor and then out into the sea.

The famous herons, Sigrid says, pointing south. They have their own island. Also an orchard and a tropical garden.

The wind remains brisk and steady on the prow, their travel both breathless and slow. This must be how the dead go. Elizabeth imagines her mother's body and Robert's are the cargo, ballast for *Isolde.* The île Tristan is heaven, Ann and Marie the Valkyries, and Sigrid is Charon. Elizabeth glances at Louise. Who is she then? The coast to starboard is emerald green and almost too bright. The gray-blue sea heaves, massively going somewhere. If this trip could take forever . . . She refuses to complete the sentence.

These cushions will probably float, Louise whispers, though the boat barely heels.

Sigrid tacks away from the coast. *Isolde* searches for wind like an animal trailing a scent (a boat has a nose, after all). Those were the best days at the sailing camp in Wellfleet, when the boat was flesh and blood. The wind was blowing at six knots, and the hand on the tiller and the rudder in the water and the sail filling were all the same thing. One could almost disappear, like the following wake, a mild disturbance and then water folding back in on itself.

The herons stand in a line with their backs to the mainland, the cormorants and guillemots below them, as if waiting for admission to the old sardine factory, to gobble up all the scraps. The moons of magnolia flowers glow, surreal, too many for one sky. Elizabeth can recognize myrtle and quince, the spiny pink skirts of mimosa flowers, a giant stand of bamboo. It's hard to know exactly where in the world one has suddenly landed. Such a tiny island, but crowded with its own lighthouse, fort, chapel, beach, cliffs as blank and imperious as Dover's. A pirate's den, the guidebook says, also once a refuge for an earthy poet who had an affair with Sarah Bernhardt.

To the north, there is open ocean. Sigrid tacks and turns the *Isolde* back toward Douarnenez harbor. The wind fails to nothing, and the boat drifts whimsically. Ann disappears into the hold, and then they hear the pop of a cork. Ann hands up a bottle of wine and a sleeve of paper cups. Louise pours, and they raise the cups in the direction of the lighthouse. Ann joins them to sit beside Marie, touching her arm and the inside of her wrist casually, without self-consciousness. Louise looks away, but for a long moment, Elizabeth stares. The wine is white and crisp and very cold. *Sancerre*, the label reads. Five minutes more in the *Isolde*'s icebox and it would have frozen. Again, Elizabeth imagines Robert's body, borne along, now borne back to Douarnenez. Unburied. She wants to leave him here.

We will meet in Paris, Sigrid says to Elizabeth as they motor into the boat slip. I'll make sure of it. In the meantime, take care of this.

She hands Elizabeth the blue origami sailboat.

Clara, comtesse de Chambrun, director of the American Library in Paris, has agreed to rent her apartment beside the Luxembourg Gardens to Elizabeth, Louise, and Hallie. The countess and Mrs. Crane are connected by an intricate web of commerce and politics. They are each, Louise says, admirers of the other's husband's name, and so they play a certain game. When Louise offered a sum of money for the rent, Clara wrote back that it was too much, and Louise returned a letter naming another price, and Clara rejected that, too. In the end, they paid no rent and had the services of a cook and housekeeper.

When Elizabeth and Louise meet Clara at 58 rue de Vaugirard to claim the key, she wants to know which one of them is the writer.

Your mother told me, Clara says to Louise. She thought that would make me believe you were all calm, neat girls.

We are, Louise says. Elizabeth is the calmest and neatest of us all.

Clara looks dubious, but then she fixes her gaze on Elizabeth. Her expression softens and her eyes widen, as if she's had an idea.

Very good, Miss Bishop, she says. And you're still young, too. Those qualities could be useful later in life.

Clara smiles, with some hesitation, as if she's afraid the necessary parts of her face might not work correctly. She is tall, with a long nose and jaw, like a horse. She should smile more, Elizabeth thinks, to lessen the effect.

Clara does not invite them to sit. There is a suitcase packed by the door.

Thank you for all this, Louise says. We would be glad to pay you something.

My husband believes in generosity, Clara says, that it is a more reliable kind of intimacy. But now, in this era, in Europe, I am not so sure. Perhaps you can take me dinner, or to tea. Like friends.

Of course, Elizabeth says, without knowing why she's spoken up so quickly.

Though you know I am older than your mothers, Clara says. My daughter, Suzanne, would be your age.

Elizabeth hears the *would be*. I'm sorry, she says.

Oh, Clara says. Her heart. It was . . . But where is your friend?

Hallie decided to stay in a pension in the sixteenth, with her mother, Louise says.

Clara sighs, clearly relieved. The third bedroom, she says, Suzanne's bedroom, is very small. You would be crowded, I think. No one sleeps in there anymore.

Later, after Clara has called the driver to fetch her suitcase and left with him, Elizabeth finds the photographs, arranged on the dresser in the small bedroom:

Suzanne at nine months, in that bedroom, sitting in the caramel-colored leather chair, holding a world atlas as if she's reading from it, as if she were announcing the names of countries, lamplight beaming down over her face and hands. Her fingers tracing the edges of the continents.

Suzanne held by Clara in front of the Christmas tree: a slyly humorous shot, in which a teddy bear ornament hangs directly above Suzanne's head as if it's her idea, as if she is thinking the little bear into existence.

Suzanne at five (someone has written the ages), leaning against a tree in the Luxembourg Gardens, a pose meant to be casual but looks as if it must be excruciating, as if the cleft of the tree had suddenly of its own accord yanked Suzanne's arm up at a forty-five-degree angle, and Suzanne is trying to pretend that such a horrifying thing has not happened.

The next year, Suzanne wearing a sweater the exact color of Japanese iris, arms crossed, a blond braid falling over her left shoulder. Some question in her eyes, some worry or fear, above that gap-toothed smile.

At fifteen, embracing Clara on the Pont des Arts.

"Seventeen, after the diagnosis." Suzanne's fierce smile, the smile of heedless youth, the smile that says, Fine for you to admit there might be an end to your days on this earth, but I'm going to live forever.

The largest photo, nine-year-old Suzanne wrapped in a white blanket, looking at a picture book with a man, perhaps her father. The book is *The Nutcracker*, so it must be Christmas 1911. No sign of damage to Suzanne's perfect little heart. No inkling. No war yet. That's three years hence.

Just like now.

The champagne like stars on their tongues, as the monk once said, and the wild strawberries in summer warmed by the sun and shockingly sweet. Louise's hand on Elizabeth's hesitant, her skin like a child's: soft and untroubled. The light over the Seine this same softness, but really the opposite—old light, well broken in. Like leather, chafed from years of use, a saddle, a jacket, and Elizabeth believes if she could touch this light, that's how it would feel. Children's voices in the alley sounding at first like church bells, but then as they walked closer, like cats. The jangle and shriek of perfume on Saint-Germain. The racket at night outside the apartment. Chocolate so bitter it's almost like tasting chalk. *Chalk-lit,* like the white cliffs. The large beer called a *formidable.* Actual church bells. The feel of Clara's oldest books and the smell of them giving Elizabeth an ache below her eyes, in her nose and ears. The clocks in the apartment going off nearly constantly. The crazy quilt of languages around Notre-Dame. The quiet in certain parks. How the early evening light on the île Saint-Louis feels exclusive, carefully set down at dusk, so perfectly does it fill the streets. Even the ice cream tastes better there. Steak in the tourist cafés, though, tough as an old boot.

Elizabeth would like to become more French, but she knows she never will. For one thing, the French are small and thin, and while she is certainly small, thin seems to be forever out of reach. Louise, though, is often mistaken for a wealthy Parisian, and Elizabeth wonders what must be said about them as a pair. *Louise has brought her friend from the country! Louise's friend the Swede! What does it mean, Canadian? Aren't Canadians simply French who are confused, who missed the boat? Or took the boat, rather!* Louise receives an invitation from an ambassador's wife to visit their house in Neuilly, another to attend a salon in the Latin Quarter. Bring your somber little friend, the wife says. She and Louise laugh about that, but still it makes Elizabeth sad.

Clara tells them the maid, Christine, and Simone, the cook, are worried because Elizabeth and Louise appear to have no suitors. Louise proposes they send themselves flowers, great, towering bouquets, a new one every day, until the maid grows tired of sloshing water and dropping petals.

In odd moments, Elizabeth misses New York City. Paris, though a delight to the senses, sometimes seems a little dull. She reads days-old American newspapers and keeps a running tally of all they've missed in New York, talks and concerts and theater openings. But also world news: it's strange, Elizabeth feels, to be in the middle of so much and learn nothing until they read it.

Louise, she cries, throwing down the newspaper, listen to this: American citizens traveling on ships of warring nations do so at their own risk.

No more Nazi boats, Elizabeth, Louise says.

I only booked one way. And what will Margaret do?

I'm sure her mother will only put her on an American ship. If she lets her travel at all.

We'll have fun when she gets here.

Aren't we having fun now? Louise says.

Of course we are.

But the Louvre with Margaret. She's been imagining the two of them roaming the place on rainy afternoons, and Margaret's running commentary. She knows everything Margaret will want to see. *The Wedding Feast at Cana. Woman with a Mirror.* The Géricault portrait called *The Woman with Gambling Mania*—Elizabeth has already found it on the second floor of the Sully Wing. The woman in the painting is wearing a white kerchief and holding a crutch. Her face, the expression. She looks like a simpleton, but she's an individual, Margaret says. You think you might understand her and feel for her. He paints her with such sympathy.

And then Margaret says this, which causes Elizabeth to love her all the more: I think a madwoman and an artist are alike in a way. They're intense and single-minded. They cannot be distracted from their passions. They're not like normal people. Isn't that right, Elizabeth?

The apartment *de la comtesse* appears to have been furnished by a madwoman, with too many writing desks, love seats, family portraits, clocks, and Moroccan knickknacks, mostly an enormous collection of small incense burners strung on ropes and chains. These, Christine explains in French and in hysterical pantomime, are apparently used to fumigate Clara's many visitors by shaking the vessel around their heads and shoulders. Every drawer in every writing desk is locked, Elizabeth discovers when she searches for pens. Christine claims the keys were lost *il y a mille ans,* a thousand years ago.

The multitude of clocks don't keep the same time. Elizabeth and Louise argue about this.

We could adjust them, Louise says.

All of them? Elizabeth says. That would take hours. And maybe the countess likes it this way, all the staggered ringing. Maybe she needs it to stay awake.

It keeps me awake, Louise says.

It doesn't seem to.

All right, so I do sleep pretty well, but not so well that I don't see you reading Robert's letters. Put them away, why don't you? Or, better yet, throw them away.

Yes, Elizabeth says. That's just what I'll do.

I shouldn't have said that.

You're right.

Elizabeth asks herself why on earth she rereads these letters, and she never has a very good answer. The memory of Robert Seaver burns in her mind. His hands, calloused on the inside from gripping crutches his whole life, but soft to touch, to hold. His hands felt like the writing paper he used, and so it comforts her some to touch the letters.

Elizabeth knows Louise also wants her to stop writing to Robert's mother, but she can't. She feels she has to explain herself. Maybe it is out of guilt, but more likely that Elizabeth isn't convinced of anything—she wonders if she could have loved Robert and been his wife, that she might have liked the way she could have been with him, that she still longs for something he could have given her that Louise can't. Which is a life like other people's. She can see all those lives, the way she can see the outline of a tree in the fog: really, it's just that you know the tree is there. You can't actually see it. It's faith, a kind of frantic belief that the world doesn't change very much or very quickly. But, Elizabeth wonders, what if she really wants change, really wants a steady life that resembles other steady lives? But why on earth would she go home, stay in one place? She and Louise could travel for years on the Crane family money.

And Louise is generous. Elizabeth knows Louise would take her to the ends of the earth. She says so, and then, she says, when we come to the end, we'll start over. But won't we have seen it all by then? Elizabeth wonders. Will we want to see it again? Does she love Louise? Can she love anyone? What is love anyway? When has she felt it, ever? Drinking. That's when. No, not just drinking. That summer two years ago, when she was falling in love with Robert. And then with Louise (and with Margaret, if she's honest). It felt like that, falling, as if she were plummeting, tumbling, sinking backward onto a soft bed, helpless. That's why they call it falling in love, the drop of it, an excess of gravity. Warmth, wonder, a calm surprise. *Oh. Look. Here you go.*

You're facing forward, but the world rises behind you, disappears past your shoulders, over your head. What other sensation is like that? Elizabeth wonders. A vacuum? A vortex? Neither sounds pleasant.

There is a photograph on the bedside table, the childhood portrait of Suzanne and her brother, René, in which they appear to be blond angels, dressed in white linen, and backlit. After Elizabeth buys the pair of doves at the market on rue de Lutèce, and after she paints the small wooden cage, she keeps the doves next to the photograph, thinking children and singing birds should, whenever possible, be in close proximity. But they shuffle and coo at all hours, so she moves both the birds and the photograph to Clara's bedroom, which they reserve for guests. In Clara's handkerchief drawer, she finds the other picture, the one in which Suzanne has been crying. She looks as if she is about to be struck.

Clara phones to ask Louise and Elizabeth if she might come back to the apartment someday soon. To collect a few things, she says. This visit is arranged for lunch, but Clara arrives hours late, in the middle of the afternoon when Elizabeth is alone. Clara stands for a few minutes in the front hallway, staring into space, as if she's forgotten why she wanted to come. Then she crosses the hall and disappears into her bedroom. Silence, a breath of it, until a clock chimes the quarter hour. Elizabeth calls out, asking whether she would like some refreshment, and Clara says yes, if it's not any trouble.

Use the Limoges, Clara says. In the china cabinet.

Elizabeth finds the Limoges cups, white with skeins of pink roses. Her hands shake a little as she carries them from the kitchen, pours the tea. They settle on the sofa.

I hope I'm not interrupting your writing, Clara says.

Heavens, no, Elizabeth tells her. I'm afraid I'm having a sort of dry spell.

That must be terrible. I myself have never had a dry spell that way. I'm writing a memoir now, you know.

I didn't know. How lucky to be so prolific.

It's not luck. You sit down and you do it.

I've heard that.

If you were writing, Miss Bishop, what would it be about?

About? Elizabeth replies.

I think that's the polite question, Clara says.

Poems about clocks, Elizabeth says and laughs.

At first, Clara is angry. You mock me, she says.

Mocked by clocks. How extraordinary. Isn't that what we all are?

She wishes she had something stronger to pour into this pretty little teacup. Clara stands abruptly.

I dislike tea, she says. Really. We ought to have an honest-to-goodness drink.

Clara looks as if she might be about to cry. She leaves the room and returns with a glass decanter half full of glittering amber.

Scotch, Clara says.

I like scotch, Elizabeth says. I like it very much. Too much, probably.

Clara pours out two generous tumblers, and they drink. Do you want something to eat? she asks.

No, thank you, Elizabeth says. I want the full effect. I want to get very drunk.

Good, Clara says. So do I.

They drink for a moment in silence. Light streams through the tall windows, falling hard on Clara's face.

The thing is, Clara says, I find myself wishing for you to be my daughter. I know that's odd. That was the reason I rented you the apartment. Not because of Louise and her family, but because of your ages. Suzanne would be a bit older, but not much. And I would have loved for her to turn out like you. An independent person who knows what she thinks.

But I *don't* know, Elizabeth says. I don't have any idea. I just go along. Drinking and getting up in the morning. Because the clocks wake me. Otherwise I might not get up. So I suppose I should thank you for the clocks after all. She studies Clara's large hands. Nobody really ever wanted me for her daughter.

Well, I do, Clara says. I want it immensely.

Why? Elizabeth asks.

I can introduce you to some of my friends, Clara continues. I do know some very influential people. Readers who might appreciate your work. You do seem a bit lost in the shadows.

In that moment, Elizabeth remembers her father lying in the snow. He is blue, like snow shadows, like the evening into which he has fallen. His jacket and trousers are blue, too. His hands beside him seem to have more to do with his clothing than with his body. Elizabeth stares from the porch of their house. She is three. She stares and stares. She cannot help herself. The world is nowhere, lost to her. Inside the house, her mother rests in the darkened bedroom, taking apart the blanket, stitch by stitch, each bit of thread a loss, a disappointment. Soon her mother will be sent to the institution.

She knows her father is dead, though she doesn't know the words for it. She knows he now has nothing in common with the world. Before, he was like the fox, like the birds, like the sky, above her, the blue of his eyes a kind of smaller version of sky, the flecks of brown in the irises like the birds that drift there. But now he is more like a machine in the barn, still until someone makes it go, or the broom in the kitchen closet, a tall wooden thing whose purpose might be decided by her mother but mostly left in darkness.

Before her, the figure in the snow, a vision, a ghost.

Also invention. Her father died when she was eight months old, so she could not have seen this. And yet. And yet, who knows what sights and sounds and visions an infant's memory can hold.

That's very nice of you, Elizabeth says. But you hardly know me.

True, Clara says. I'd like to get to know you better. And you must call me Clara. How are you liking the apartment, apart from the clocks? And the *quartier*?

It's a lovely apartment, though I do think I'm somewhat allergic to your antique books and incense burner and your rugs, and perhaps the draperies. I've had this problem since I was little. Maybe Christine could dust more?

I will certainly speak to her, Clara says. She stands and walks to the window. She lifts a panel of drapery, sniffs, makes a face.

Anyway, we'll be traveling in the next month or so, to Rome and perhaps Madrid.

Clara stands very still. Elizabeth wonders if she's heard someone at the door or the telephone.

How long will you be gone, Miss Bishop? she asks.

Two weeks, maybe three. Please call me Elizabeth.

That's quite a long time. I think I shall miss you girls. You must . . .

Clara turns away suddenly, crosses the room to the large writing desk, produces a ring of keys from the pocket of her skirt. She unlocks the middle drawer and removes a red leather book, the size of a small Bible.

I have contacts, she says. Friends you might call on. Just in case.

That's very kind, Elizabeth says.

Such interesting cities, Elizabeth. Though quite tumultuous now, I understand. The rest of Europe seems to be in a stew of revolt. Please be careful. I wouldn't want anything to happen to you.

Clara unlocks another drawer and lifts out a box. Calling cards. Of course she would have those, Elizabeth thinks. Clara selects three cards, begins to write on the backs of them. She looks up once, at Elizabeth, her gaze uncertain (as if Elizabeth might have quietly left the room), then tender, her smile gentle. Motherly, Elizabeth thinks.

You should have these, too, Clara says, holding up a card. As you move about the world, you sometimes want to leave a bit of yourself behind.

I do, Elizabeth says. Though I had not thought of it quite like that.

While Elizabeth is being treated for an infection of the middle ear, Louise brings her the English newspapers and chocolates. Mrs. Crane insists she have a nurse, and Louise hires a Russian woman called Nina, who bakes bread, makes endless cups of tea, and knits, small pink-and-white mittens for an army of little girls. The pairs are attached by a long braid of yarn that will travel inside the child's coat, up her sleeves and across her shoulders, invisibly from hand to hand. The sight of these attached pairs illuminates a dim memory: a large black glove on the ground, Elizabeth reaching to pick it up, her mother saying no, no, her voice a screech from far away. Elizabeth is afraid to turn and look, afraid she won't recognize the woman making that terrible sound.

My muse now seems to have folded its wings, Elizabeth writes to her friend Muriel in New York, *and stuck her head under one of them.*

But she hasn't flown the coop, Muriel writes back. *That's promising. Close the window, so she can't escape.*

She doesn't want to escape. What would she do in the world anyway, besides feel silly and exposed, out there with Gide and all the other exhibitionist writers in Paris? And everywhere else.

What am I doing here? Elizabeth says to Nina, who will not understand her, not really.

Nina cups her hand around her own ear, smiles as if she knows a secret, and bows her head over her knitting.

What makes me think I can write anything, ever, at all?

Nina rises and comes to stand by the bed. She places a cool hand on Elizabeth's forehead, frowns, holds up the bottle of sleeping pills.

A good idea, Elizabeth says.

Nina leaves the bedroom. Elizabeth hears her in the kitchen running water into the kettle, arranging tea things on a tray. If only such questions could be answered by the taking of tea, the wisdom of Earl Grey and Lapsang Souchong, whoever he was. She closes her eyes.

And then, what seems like a moment later, Clara brings in the tea tray. This may be a dream, Elizabeth tells herself. I should just keep still until it's over.

I know I'm a bit of a surprise, Clara says. My husband thinks so, too.

Oh! Elizabeth says. I wasn't . . . Nina didn't say you were . . .

This room is so dreary, Clara says. No wonder you're ill.

It's allergies really. And bright light seems to give me a headache.

But Clara has already opened the drapes. Sunlight pours over the carpet and across the bedclothes. Elizabeth waits for the pain that will certainly bloom along her jaw and up into her cheekbone. Clara busies herself arranging cups and saucers. She assumes or remembers that Elizabeth takes milk and sugar.

I haven't any idea why dry leaves and hot water are medicinal, Clara says, pouring out a splash of tea. Not yet. You want it stronger.

Thank you for coming, Elizabeth says. But I'm really doing so much better.

I wanted to make sure. You know sometimes you let an infection like this go, and it just gets worse. And the next thing you know, you're just . . . beyond.

Elizabeth watches Clara arrange and rearrange the cookies on the tray into neat rows, then a circle, and finally into a star. Her concentration is brittle, liable to shatter at any moment into something that might be embarrassing.

I'm catching up on my reading, though, Elizabeth says. I'll need more books from your library maybe this week.

They'll be waiting, Clara says. That's the beauty of a library. American books waiting for all you flummoxed American readers.

Flummoxed! Elizabeth says. Well, I suppose that's true. My French is still so hopeless. I wonder if that makes the surrealists easier or more difficult to understand.

Probably easier, Clara says. You know, I've found myself rereading Edmund Burke. I'm not sure why. Ignorance makes things appear beautiful. Of all the funny ideas. Though I think I may be misquoting.

She hovers over Elizabeth awkwardly, bending to adjust the pillows. Elizabeth resists the urge to close her eyes.

Thank you, Clara, she says.

Well, you don't want to harm your back. If a girl your age spends a long time lying prone this way . . . Anyway, my husband has got me doing all this reading. He thinks I'm a bit at loose ends. He says it would be good for me to contemplate beauty. I have no idea why. Who has time to consider beauty anymore?

What do you mean?

I mean I would think twice about going to Rome right now. Or anywhere in Spain. People I know would try to dissuade you.

I know. But we're here. In Europe, I mean.

You picked a difficult time.

It picked us. College graduation. I mean, what else do girls do? And I have some money. Inheritance from an uncle.

Not from your mother? Mrs. Crane said she heard—

Not from my mother. I think that tea is probably strong enough now.

Yes, of course it is.

Clara pours their tea, then settles herself in the armchair beside the bed.

You're smart. You and Miss Crane and Miss Miller. You're smart not to tie yourselves down with husbands just yet. They tend to not want one to do anything useful. Just to be available at a moment's notice. Pack up, Clara darling, we're going to Morocco tomorrow! Dinner tonight at the embassy, darling! Sometimes I don't even know which embassy until the car pulls up in front. And then I have to think quickly—do I shake hands with this one, or not? Do I bow or curtsey? Do I use a knife and fork or, God forbid, my fingers? Does this one know English or French or German? Am I even allowed to speak?

Clara sits back, out of breath, and gulps at her tea.

So, she says finally. You're smart. Even if it hurts a little.

The last postcard from Robert Seaver, forwarded with the mail from New York, reads, *Elizabeth, go to hell.*

Where is that? Elizabeth says, where's the hell he requests I go to? No, not requests. Directs me to go. Banishes me. Where he is? Maybe he told me to go to hell to meet him there?

I need to take you for a walk, Louise says. We need to get out of this apartment. Get some air.

No, Elizabeth says. Or yes. You're right. Let's go into the Luxembourg Gardens, down to that statue. The angel. Some angel. Oh damn it. Any angel.

I don't think the angel statue is in the Luxembourg.

No? All right. The statue of George Sand then. I want to go stand there. George Sand looking over her shoulder.

Yes, Louise says. Let's go now. Just get your jacket.

They leave the apartment, make their way out into the street. Parisians drift past them, glassy-eyed, frightened.

Is he really dead then? she asks. How could he be dead and send a postcard?

He sent it before, Louise says. He must have.

But what if it's a hoax?

There's little margin for error here, Elizabeth.

But there's no proof either.

It's not a hoax, Louise says. You know it's not.

They are standing in front of the statue. George Sand. Womanly and thoughtful, her stone dress rendered impossibly light, filmy about the shoulders and throat, gray at the hem as if she's ghosted through the streets of Paris for sixty years.

She's not looking over her shoulder, Elizabeth says. She's been disturbed from her reading. Look. Her face is completely blank. No emotion.

She's marble.

I wish I was.

I don't like this kind of mess for you.

What do you mean by *mess*?

You know what I mean. Entanglements.

You can't stop that, Elizabeth says.

But I can try. It's not good for your writing.

Well, the mess comes for you no matter what, doesn't it? Even if you go thousands of miles away and across an ocean. I probably killed him.

You didn't. If anything he killed himself. But it was probably an accident, like his mother said.

He said he couldn't bear losing me. And I said—what did I say? I don't think I said anything. I think maybe I said I would be traveling for a while after graduation. And he asked why would I do that, and I think I said something about the weather. How it was so unpredictable. Something like that. Something neutral. Impersonal. I shouldn't have done that. I shouldn't have encouraged him. I was just trying to . . . I don't know what.

I know what, Louise says. Look at the statue again. She's been shocked by something. She's holding on to the low wall or bench or whatever it is because otherwise she'll fall down. If Margaret were here, she'd be able to tell us what it is, what news George Sand has just heard. She'd be able to tell us why this (Louise takes a small guidebook from her pocket and reads) François Sicard sculpted her in a dress and not trousers. She'd tell us it's 1847 and George Sand has just heard that Chopin died.

Oh, Louise.

Or it's 1849 and Marie Dorval has died. Marie Dorval, to whom she wrote, *I want you either in your dressing room or in your bed.*

That's not in the book, Louise, Elizabeth says.

No, it's not. It's in my head.

If Margaret were here, she would never tell us any of that.

That's right, Louise says. Exactly.

Clara appears nearly every day, without warning, seeming sad and unlike herself, a little lost. She walks past Elizabeth or Louise in the foyer and wanders through the apartment as if she can't quite remember how she used to navigate through the rooms, even though no one has moved a single piece of furniture. This little journey changes her mood, restores equilibrium. She returns, takes stock, and announces with her usual certainty that Elizabeth can't possibly be well yet because she still looks exhausted.

The morning after Robert Seaver's postcard, Elizabeth is still half drunk. She wakes with a pounding headache. Her room, the bathroom, the kitchen appear fuzzy and tilted. And there is Clara, standing inside the front door, waiting for someone, for her. Clara looks desperate. Clara wants to please someone. The expression is familiar, and at first she can't place it. Then she can. She says the words before she can stop herself.

You look like your daughter.

Clara shakes her head, turns away to set her handbag carefully beside the little basket that holds the day's mail, the house keys, coins for the delivery boys, a black-and-gold fountain pen.

I suppose I do, Clara says. Only, as you know, she can't be looked at any longer, so what does that really mean? She leads Elizabeth into the sitting room.

I want to tell you something, she begins. I used to believe that money and position could protect me. But then my daughter died, and my work on Shakespeare was made a laughingstock. So I have new work to do. I loan library books to Americans, and I travel. I worry and want to do some good in the world. And now I find myself drawn to you—as if something in you calls out.

I can't imagine, Elizabeth says, what such a call would sound like. A screech?

Sometime in the next month, Clara says, I believe I will be making a trip to Normandy. I have some business there. It's a place you ought to visit.

I'd like to get back to the sea.

Yes. I recall that you are fond of sailing. Perhaps you could help me.

How would Clara know that, about sailing? Elizabeth wondered. Maybe from Mrs. Crane. There's no telling what Louise's mother might have said.

I doubt I could be much help, Elizabeth says.

You would be perfect, Clara says. She stares into her glass. I would have asked Suzanne. We used to travel together quite often. She especially loved New York, as I believe you do. I took her there years ago, to begin college.

That must have been very exciting.

And then she begged me not to leave. And I said she needed to grow up.

Oh! Elizabeth says. How awful.

For whom? Clara asks.

The question rings through the empty apartment. Clara must have spoken louder than she meant to. She makes an odd gesture: she puts her fingers to her lips, shushing herself.

Elizabeth feels her face redden. For both of you, she says.

It was. How could I have done such a thing, Elizabeth? How could

I have refused my own daughter? She came back by herself. And then the midnight call from the doctor, the mad drive to the hospital, the arrival too late.

Elizabeth takes it all in, silently. The clocks chime all over the apartment.

There's so much time in here, Elizabeth says.

Yes, Clara says. It's all in here. All that time. So much of it. But out there—

Here she rises from the sofa, crosses the long sitting room to the windows.

The world looks so perfectly green, Clara says. If I let my gaze drift just out of focus, I can see Suzanne at play beside the Medici Fountain, gathering the little white clover flowers, a pink dress billowing around her.

She closes her eyes.

I'm sorry, Elizabeth says.

There she is again, Clara says. Five years old. She's writing with a black-and-gold fountain pen. The café near the École Militaire. What was the place called? La Terrasse?

I sometimes tell myself Suzanne isn't gone forever, Clara says. Even though I remember holding her cold body in the hospital. No, she's just away. That's easy enough to imagine. I'm so often in Paris now that I can tell myself Suzanne is alive in New York—and soon she will come for a visit. I imagine she will look older, thinner, more oddly dressed than the last time.

I do the same about people I miss, Elizabeth says.

I wasn't a good mother, Clara says. Why did I spend so much time going on about Suzanne's clothes? All those wasted minutes. I could have been talking to her, finding out who she was. Once I took a photograph. From behind the camera I said, I'll show you how ghastly you look in that outfit.

That photograph, Elizabeth thinks.

Clara lifts her head, Elizabeth sees, to take in the sky, the enormous pillowy clouds drifting by.

There's time everywhere, Elizabeth says.

She doesn't know what she means. She might go to the window and embrace Clara, and she waits for the desire to pass. Louise will be home soon. Louise would not understand. Or maybe she wouldn't care. Maybe it was Elizabeth who did not want to be caught in such an odd and pathetic tableau with a woman she hardly knows. That was an odd way to put it: *tableau.*

There was a man named Robert Seaver, Elizabeth says, who proposed marriage, and I refused him. He shot himself. Now I've received a postcard from him.

What did it say?

Go to hell.

Clara turns from the window. Her eyes are dry.

I know it's early, but is there any more scotch? she asks, then laughs, a sound like choking.

I think so, Elizabeth says. I think I left some.

Of course there's more! Clara cries. I bought it, didn't I? And I bought extra. I stocked the bar before you arrived! I polished the glasses!

I'm grateful, Elizabeth says. I promise I'll replace what I drink.

I wish Suzanne had sent me a postcard, Clara says. Just one. Though I would have preferred thousands. A postcard every day.

But not telling you to go to hell, Elizabeth says.

No, not that. Though I would have deserved it.

I don't know if I deserved it. I don't know.

My daughter died, Clara says. When a person dies, you can't argue with her anymore. I'd like to take you to see the *Mona Lisa,* which Suzanne detested. She said it was possibly the world's most stupid famous painting. We had a disagreement about it, and now I would like to end it by telling Suzanne she was right. It is indeed a stupid painting. I would absolutely capitulate if I could have my daughter back. Yes, I would say, you are absolutely correct. The *Mona Lisa* is too small to capture all this attention. And yes, the smile is—what outrageous thing did Suzanne say that time?—the smile is not mysterious, it's *foolish,* like an inebriated girl who wants a man to know she's had this bit to drink and is open to suggestion.

It is foolish, Elizabeth says. I don't like it either.

You remind me of her, Clara says. I've told you that before. And you—I see myself, too. You think privacy will protect you. But it won't. You need to come back into the world. That was what I said to Suzanne. You're so dreamy, so impractical. You can't live outside the world.

Well, now she does, Elizabeth says.

Clara moves to stand behind the sofa. She places her hands on Elizabeth's shoulders. Elizabeth leans her head back to look up into Clara's face. The expression is both tender and wolfish, full of need.

You'll come to Normandy with me, yes? Clara says. As Suzanne would have?

Elizabeth doesn't answer. She hears Suzanne's dead voice: *I hate the* Mona Lisa *even more now because I'll never have a chance to see that smile on myself. Because now I won't ever again be in the ladies' lounge in a bar, looking at myself in the brightly lit mirror, practicing that smile of invitation, that clairvoyant gaze, so when I go back out into the murk and smoke and the crowded tables, I can get what I want.*

Since the postcard, Robert Seaver's mother has begun to call from New York. Every day at five. Like clockwork. Like everything else in this apartment.

Did he say anything to you? Mrs. Seaver wants to know. Did he ever write about his difficulties?

No. Never. Elizabeth says this emphatically, every day.

But Mrs. Seaver persists. Then she is silent for five days, but on the sixth morning, there she is, looking as if she has walked the entire distance, even over the ocean, ringing the bell of 58 rue de Vaugirard.

For a moment, Elizabeth experiences an electric confusion. It is Robert, but dressed incoherently, in a woman's hat and coat, come back from the dead, or not dead at all. Adrenaline fizzes her skin, darkens her vision at the corners.

Then Mrs. Seaver collapses in Elizabeth's arms. The taxi driver helps Elizabeth get her to a chair, suggests a drink of water. He leaves, then returns with Mrs. Seaver's coat and baggage, which she has left in his taxi. She has apparently traveled with only one small suitcase.

I had to see you, Elizabeth, Mrs. Seaver says. Even though everyone said not to. It's too dangerous. *You won't be able to get home.* That's what they said. *There are soldiers everywhere. So many Germans. A woman traveling alone isn't safe from them.*

It's all right, Elizabeth says. You're here now.

Mrs. Seaver seems unable to breathe.

I had to talk to you, she says. You have to tell me why he did this. You're the only one who might know.

Elizabeth pays the driver, helps Mrs. Seaver upstairs and into the guest bed. She sends the cook and the maid home early. The only way to comfort Robert's mother might be to lie to her or tell her about the postcard. Or both.

As the sun sets, the bedroom door opens slowly, and Elizabeth has the sensation that Robert will be the one to appear, that she deserves such a haunting. The being that will emerge from the guest bedroom will be hideous, a sort of gargoyle come down off the sheer façade of Notre-Dame. She waits, heart hammering. Mrs. Seaver clutches the door frame and the wainscoting as she makes her way down the hall.

Oh, Elizabeth, she says. I don't think I can go on without him. How can you?

I don't know, Elizabeth says. I have to, I guess. We both do.

The doves woke me, Mrs. Seaver says.

Not the clocks?

The clocks are just music. Who are the children in the photograph?

Elizabeth tells her.

The poor mother, Mrs. Seaver says. She must have had a terribly hard time.

Elizabeth suddenly remembers years ago her mother telling her to say goodbye to her dead cousin, Arthur, and lifting her up so she could see inside the coffin. She remembers how small Arthur was, like a doll. How the roads were so completely obscured by snow, and the snow still fell, blinding them. They had a hard time getting to the graveyard. And then, of course, they had an even harder time leaving Arthur there alone.

Elizabeth nods, afraid to speak. She doesn't want to say that even now, more than ten years later, Clara is nearly paralyzed by the death of her child. Sadness never ends, and regret is impossible to escape.

The question is whether to introduce Clara and Mrs. Seaver, bring grief to grief, mothers who do not know how to go on. Louise says no, absolutely not, a meeting will terrify them. But Elizabeth looks at it differently, selfishly. She imagines sitting with them, between the two mothers, listening to the clocks tick and chime.

Come up sometime, Elizabeth tells Clara. When you're out walking in the morning. If you feel like it. I have become a hopeless insomniac, and at dawn, Louise has just come in and gone to bed. She sleeps like a rock. She doesn't say she has a visitor or that Mrs. Seaver likes early mornings best, sitting quietly with her American coffee and staring down into the courtyard where nothing grows and into which no one ever enters.

And so one morning, very early, Clara arrives with a paper parcel of warm brioches. Introductions are made. Clara sits in the large blue armchair. Mrs. Seaver and Elizabeth arrange themselves on the sofa. And then only the clocks speak. Elizabeth remembers sitting in the pitch black of her grandmother's house when she was ten. Her aunt and grandmother occupied the darkness, and no one said a word. Still, the room was raucous with feeling: anger, regret, longing. Her grandmother's knitting needles tsk-tsked. Occasionally her aunt sighed, a sound like ripples on water.

It's as if we were all strangers, Elizabeth thinks, my aunt and my grandmother. Myself, too.

Now, in Paris, so many years later, it's the same. Why is that? The clocks jabber, jitter, their cries unsteady, overlapping. Listening to them, one has the sense that they are trying to come into union, order, agreement. They are very near to reconciliation, the chimes and bells moving closer together the way it happens on a bright day outside that a person's shadow aligns and unifies with her body as the sun climbs higher in the sky.

Finally Mrs. Seaver stands and raises her coffee cup toward Clara and Elizabeth, then walks into the kitchen, pours more from the pot on the stove. She does not return to the sofa or to her preferred seat overlooking the courtyard. Instead she crosses behind to stand at the large casement windows that give on to the Medici Fountain. Elizabeth glances at Clara, who does not seem to see her or anything else.

I don't know what to do, Mrs. Seaver says. I think I might as well let myself go mad. Just give in to it.

You can do that for a while, Clara says.

That's not what she means, Elizabeth says. She means forever.

If that were the case, Clara replies, she would already have done it. She would not be here. Suddenly, she lunges out of the blue chair and hurries across the room to stand beside Mrs. Seaver. You would not have been able to cross the ocean!

The last word is nearly a shout.

You can't dishonor him that way, Clara says.

Mrs. Seaver says nothing. She might step away from the window, go into the guest room, and close the door, but she doesn't move.

I travel, Clara says. My husband and I keep moving. We don't dwell on it.

That's not true, Elizabeth says.

Clara turns. What are you talking about? she says.

Elizabeth shakes her head. Every single minute we've spent together you've been doing just that. Dwelling.

Clara glares at her. That's private, she says, biting off the last consonant.

All at once, Elizabeth sees the mother Clara must have been to Suzanne. She wants to refuse this vision. She wants all mothers to be perfect, devoted, sane. She wants to believe her own mother had been the one exception to a great rule of the universe.

Mrs. Seaver nods, as if to resolve some inner quarrel. It was the polio, she says. That, and losing you, Elizabeth. She turns away from the window.

I'm sorry, Elizabeth says.

He loved your voice. He told me that. Many times. *Her voice has so much life and color in it,* he said. *It's so rare.* I don't think he could bear the thought of never hearing your voice again.

What did he mean by rare? Elizabeth says.

I'm not sure.

This, Clara says. Look.

Elizabeth rises from the sofa and stands between Clara and Mrs. Seaver, and they watch the bands of rose and violet and gold arc and blaze over the Luxembourg Gardens. They stare hard, as if they must get the full meaning. They stare until the color fades into nothing, into plain daylight. The clocks sing like a drunken girl, first a little growling, then a bit of tune, high notes and low.

Louise lets herself in the front door, and still Elizabeth and the grieving mothers do not turn, even after she disappears into her bedroom, even after they hear a splash of singing, a long, contented sigh, and the ringing of her shoes, dropped, one and then the other, to the floor.

The drinking helps until it doesn't. But then it helps again the next day. At first, Elizabeth feels camaraderie with the entire world, every man, woman, and child, animal, vegetable, and mineral. After that, there is anger and irritation. Then sadness. Then (sometimes) sleep. In the morning, the sensation of walking along the edge of a very high precipice, below which lie sharp gray rocks, glinting shards of glass, raised tips of bayonets, explosive devices with wires trailing from them like a woman's long hair. Elizabeth understands that she is not allowed to stop or step back—in fact, stepping back would mean falling off the other side, where the rocks below lie hidden in shadow. The person who best understands her does not write or call. The person whose touch means everything, the brush of lips, the touch on her back from this person, nothing.

Silence. Robert, Mother. A whisper of Suzanne, always, in this apartment.

Margaret, in a different way.

The drinking causes the pain, the loss, to feel farther away. The pain starts to *get lost!* First, the pain drifts into the next room, then out the front door. In a half hour, the pain stands outside the apartment building in the middle of rue de Vaugirard calling halfheartedly. Then it wanders over to the Medici Fountain and tries to wash its face. In an hour, it's lighting a candle in Notre-Dame. Later it's in

Gare Saint-Lazare, stepping onto a northbound train. Then it is in Douarnenez, gazing out to sea. Douarnenez, in a rented sailboat.

The poems take too long to write—the lines, each word, each letter comes with excruciating slowness. All day long she sits at the window and watches the courtship of doves. Their breasts are pink and orange and brown. Not gray as is commonly believed. Spots on their backs like inkblots, like all those missteps in every poem. They dig into their own feathers with their beaks, a repeated, quick puncturing. It looks quite painful. They do this for hours, perched side by side, and what comes of it? Finally, they begin to groom each other, kiss with their beaks, which looks like fighting. Sometimes the wing feathers lift to reveal the sleek blue-gray bodies, as if they were the secret. Suddenly, the male hops on the back of the female, both staring off in the same direction. It's very quick, this part. Then they fly off separately, east and west.

Sigrid. Where is Sigrid?

Just across the river. Of course.

I could fly over there, Elizabeth thinks. Over the Seine joining itself again off the prow of the île Saint-Louis and bearing countless schools of little fish running in verses. Above all the grim Haussmann buildings standing lined up like colonels looking for work, high above Margaret, her face turned away from me, Mother and Robert and Suzanne lying down in the dark. I could do it. I could fly. If only she would send me an invitation.

Remember the Germans who took us sailing? Elizabeth asks Louise.

They were fun, weren't they? Louise says. I'll call Ann.

Sigrid invites Elizabeth to meet her at 78 rue de Lille, the German embassy, and from there walk to a café for lunch. She waits for Elizabeth in the embassy's front garden, then guides her inside to tour the building. The large reception rooms are lavishly decorated with bouquets of flowers the size of small children and hung with portraits of dour German statesmen and tapestries depicting scenes from the *Nibelungenlied*. There is a melancholy dilapidation about the sofas and chairs, covered in gray velvet, as if no one has time to sit anymore. Elizabeth is introduced to the deputy ambassador, Ernst vom Rath, whose attention becomes suddenly more focused when Sigrid tells him Elizabeth is an American, though perhaps Sigrid has also said something more. Then Elizabeth hears *Dichter,* and vom Rath seems suddenly lit from inside. He insists on showing them some of the private quarters, including a state apartment on the second floor. This, he says, is where the führer will stay when he comes to visit. *Bien sûr,* Sigrid says, her voice sounding oddly mechanical. Elizabeth notices that more bouquets of fresh flowers stand in the small entry hall, on the dining room table, and on a low dresser in the bedroom. She wonders if the visit is today or tomorrow. She realizes vom Rath thinks she writes for an American newspaper.

Vom Rath asks where they will have lunch, and when Sigrid tells him, he is very pleased. A writer should be there, he tells Elizabeth in

English. But the most important writers dine at Le Boeuf sur le Toit, he says. André Gide, for example.

I was supposed to go to a party for him, Elizabeth says quickly. But I was too shy about my bad French.

Sigrid and vom Rath nod politely. They smile. Expressions of general solicitude flash, then diminish. Still vom Rath does not let them go, even though there is nothing left to see besides the room full of telephones and small desks where Sigrid works. It is as if they are silently conferring about something. They direct Elizabeth ahead, and she feels quite sure if she glanced over her shoulder, she would see them pointing at her back and exchanging looks.

The door to the German ambassador's office is closed, though voices can be heard from inside. Sigrid and vom Rath stand for a moment, listening unabashedly. They step closer to the door. Elizabeth is stunned to see this. It's a melodrama. She wishes Louise or Margaret were here to witness the comedy of it, the pure theater. She expects vom Rath will turn to her, put his finger to his lips, and wink. She wants badly to take her camera from her pocketbook and snap a picture of vom Rath. His large blue eyes give him a look of perpetual surprise, and his mouth twitches as if he's holding back laughter or having a great deal of trouble keeping a secret.

Finally, there really is nothing left to show or tell, so vom Rath allows them to leave for lunch. He seems deflated, saddened, as he waves from the front steps of the embassy, as if left behind on dry land, while they are a ship setting sail.

He seems to think you're never coming back, Elizabeth says.

He's . . . How do you say it? Sigrid asks. She rubs her eyes with her fists to pantomime weeping.

Emotional?

Yes. At Le Boeuf, they call him Notre-Dame de Paris.

Elizabeth wants to laugh, but she understands the significance of what Sigrid has just told her. They walk one block and go into the café. They sit and order omelets and a *pichet* of wine, but then Sigrid suggests they move to a table outside so that the sun will warm them.

What do you write about? Sigrid asks when they are settled again.

Not very much, Elizabeth tells her. This and that, small things.

Small things can become larger.

That is my hope.

Sigrid reaches quickly across the table to touch Elizabeth's hand, a gesture at once meaningful and abstract, automatic.

Marie and Ann, she says, they are my mothers.

Elizabeth waits for the sentence that will explain this turn in the conversation. The omelets arrive with a salad of lettuce and tomato. The colors on the plates seem electric and weighty, larger than the words for them: yellow, green, red. Even the steam rising off the omelets has a kind of heft. They wait for the wine, which the waiter brings in a green pitcher, a shade darker than the salad, with two small glasses.

At home, Elizabeth says, we would use these for juice.

Such as orange juice? But in France, you don't have a wineglass until evening.

That's good. So the luxury is later.

Exactly. May I read your writing one day?

One day, Elizabeth says. I haven't anything with me now.

This is very nice, Sigrid says, pointing her knife at the plates. She reverts to French, but slowly, so that Elizabeth can catch the words for *eggs* and for *this afternoon*. She taps the little wineglass with her knife. Elizabeth lifts the glass and drinks quickly, as if she has been instructed, and Sigrid laughs.

Speak to me in French, Elizabeth. Practice so you can meet Gide one day.

Elizabeth can make a sentence one word at a time: *Vous me dites qu'est-ce que je dois faire.* Tell me what I must do. It is flirtation, but also a very interesting and productive method of conversing: one can only express what is elementary and true, what can be done. It is impossible to say too much or tell a lie. One can talk about what's on the table: *les oeufs, la fourchette, du vin. La serviette*—no, under the table, clutched in the fist, that one. *La bouteille d'eau* like a window between them, Sigrid's fingerprints around the middle of the bottle where she has lifted it to pour. Everything else floats in gulfs of silence. Elizabeth wills herself to eat more slowly, take smaller sips of wine. Sigrid seems to be doing the same, dividing her tomato slice into eight (Elizabeth counts to herself in French), pouring the wine a finger at a time.

They comment on the passersby in a kind of shorthand or beginner's language lesson. *L'homme qui porte le chapeau brun. L'enfant pleure. La dame a perdu quelque chose,* accurate observations but without context, whole empty worlds around them. It would be utterly frightening to know the story of the brown hat or the child's tears or the woman's loss. It would be *overstatement.* Too much.

Even when Sigrid asks a difficult question, the spell is not broken. Why do you travel? In English, please. She seems to know the answer might be complicated, or private.

To see the world, Elizabeth says, thinking of Clara. She's not sure why, but she holds up her little wineglass, thinking it might be a symbol.

To drink the world? Sigrid says.

To see beauty and live near it. It's what I'm supposed to do after college. To be free. To visit the old masters and the places they mastered.

You should be careful, Sigrid says. There is not really any such thing as free.

She leans closer, lowers her voice.

To master a place is . . . It does not always end in beauty. This is why we left Berlin. Women like us cannot have the life we want there.

I understand.

Even in Paris, a woman my age, unmarried. A German woman. My position here is not secure.

You should be married, Elizabeth says. Is that right?

Tomorrow, Sigrid says. I would like to see you again.

Yes.

We will have something even more French than this. A German woman is going to make you more French. That is unusual.

The next day, a drink in the late afternoon at Le Tournon. When Elizabeth arrives, there is already a whiskey waiting for her. Sigrid says very little, but she looks at Elizabeth as if she's expecting an answer to something that is part question, part challenge. Sigrid has ordered *huîtres gratinées.* She speaks to the waiter in German, and he replies. He brings the oysters, and their conversation continues, as if Elizabeth were not present, even as he comes and goes and attends to others in the bar. There is a certain pretense of deferential service, but they are talking about something else, not *huîtres* or whiskey or even the weather. She hears vom Rath's name repeated four times. Then the waiter hurries to the bar and returns with two glasses of champagne. After that, he disappears into the kitchen and does not come back.

Lovely, Elizabeth says. You seem to know the waiter.

He is also from Berlin. It is good to have people who will feed you.

Louise and I have been talking about that. We'd like to invite you and Ann and Marie. When Margaret is here.

You haven't spoken of this Margaret before, Sigrid says.

She is a dear friend. She's a wonderful painter. And a scholar. We lived together in college. Once we ran away together, but the police found us. She's a very good cook.

I see. In that case, I will take you somewhere.

Up rue du Bac, and there is the river, stretching before them like a lazy afternoon. They stop on the Pont des Arts, gaze into the water ruffling like upturned petticoats, like the edges of the oysters.

Champagne makes Paris more like itself, Elizabeth says.

Sigrid says nothing, watching the river, watching Elizabeth. They continue past the east side of the Louvre, toward the stock exchange. On the street behind is Dehillerin, a shop for cooks. Louise has mentioned it.

It's like a church, Sigrid says. She opens the door for Elizabeth.

Inside is quiet as a church or a library and full of men, studying cutlery, copper pans, gleaming silver molds, marble rolling pins, small tools used for intricate and arcane tasks like curling butter. Sigrid leads Elizabeth through the narrow aisles. Hundreds, maybe thousands of knives, pans for all sizes and shapes of tarts: spades, clubs, diamonds, hearts, animals, stars. Eiffel Towers, small, medium, and large.

A wooden staircase descends to a catacombs full of pots. The walls are cool stone. We might be under a castle or a church, Elizabeth whispers.

One might buy a saucepan two inches high, a metal pot shaped to hold a fifty-pound fish, or a kettle one could bathe in. Sigrid lifts a ladle large enough to scoop up a baby. All of these vessels sit waiting to be filled and emptied, again and again. What Elizabeth loves, though, is the lack of the clever, eye-catching display one sees in American department stores, as if these objects know they are singular and essential. When they are needed, they will be sent for or sought out. This is the luxury of assurance.

The men stay upstairs. Sometimes Sigrid and Elizabeth hear a murmured greeting when the front door opens, but mostly there is only the shuffle of feet, the distant clang or thud of utensils returned to their bins, not chosen. Sigrid stands very close. Elizabeth feels not so much the heat of Sigrid's body or her breath, or even her own body, but rather the space between them, which seems to diminish incre-

mentally. This sensation is at once painful and hilarious, the uncer-
tainty, the men upstairs, here below the absolute dead silence of metal
and crockery, the deep absence inside stockpots, the smooth grooves
of ladles, the waiting sluice of sieves. All of which Elizabeth has been
imagining as animated, and that is some of the hilarity, too.

They stand this way for forty seconds, maybe sixty. A minute is a
long time in the world of cooking things (Elizabeth will say this later,
thinking of Dehillerin's cellar rooms). The feeling is pleasant: stillness,
silence, rapt attention. Pleasant but not enough.

It is not clear who has stepped closer, but the back of Elizabeth's
right hand brushes Sigrid's left wrist, the knob of bone. Neither steps
away. Elizabeth becomes aware that she is holding her breath, and she
tries to exhale without moving. Sigrid's right hand, she observes, is on
the rim of a yellow ceramic dish, for *gratinées,* oval, but really shaped
like a large eye, the interior white, as if the pupil and iris had been
removed, a blind eye. Sigrid's hand is open, flat on the rim, as if she
is keeping the dish from rising off the shelf, as if she were trying to
prevent its inevitable levitation.

They hear a footfall above, breath and presence at the top of the
stairs. Vom Rath, Sigrid says slowly. I have more work at the embassy
this evening.

Aren't you afraid to go there?

The safest place to hide from an angry person is just under his nose.

All right, Elizabeth says. She places her hand over Sigrid's, then
beside it, lifts the gratin dish.

Yes, Sigrid says. This is what you need. Maybe you will write something about it.

Upstairs, at the counter, the clerk speaks to Elizabeth in English,
asking where she lives in the United States.

How did you know I was American?

The clerk glances at Sigrid but then gives a tiny shrug.

Is there an address to ship? he says

Elizabeth tells him no, she intends to make a gratin here in Paris, very soon.

Use only the best cheese, he says, and he gives her the address of a shop nearby. Tell them I sent you. Show the dish.

He signs a card: *Émile.*

Elizabeth thanks him in French, but Émile is resolute, replying in slow, measured English, as if she might not even speak her own language.

Outside, Sigrid waves for a taxi, then grasps Elizabeth's shoulders and turns her toward rue Montorgueil, the cheese shop.

Don't forget. Émile said *the best.*

She steps into the taxi, directs the driver. The taxi waits for an opening in traffic. Sigrid stares straight ahead. At the very last moment, she turns, smiles up at Elizabeth, presses her fingertips to the window glass.

All right, all right for now. Rue Montorgueil shines with the commerce of nourishment. The round cheeses in the shop window glow buttery yellow and orange, suns and planets caught just this minute in the act of revolving away.

Elizabeth can't help thinking of the two of them together, in Sigrid's apartment in Saint-Denis. Not at Clara's. She tries to concentrate on the light in Sigrid's bedroom, only that, but then the light fades, as it does every day out in the world, and she's left with the bodies, the whole scene in her mind becomes flesh and shadow, except for Sigrid's blue eyes and red mouth, moving from Elizabeth's throat to her collarbone to her breasts, lower. After that, it's not that Elizabeth's imagination fails, it's that her vision goes dark, as if in a swoon, and she's left with sensation, heat, gentle pressure, fingertips, pulsing from the inside out, voices murmuring beneath the shadows, commanding, pleading. *Ich würde sie gern ficken. Worte machen viel aus.* The words are important. The words make all the difference.

ANAPHORA

 1937

On rue de l'Odéon, there is the famous bookshop, its front window crowded and crowing with the works of Irish writers. Elizabeth has been avoiding the place. It seems so awful to waltz in and present oneself out of the blue, but just as bad to be discovered having not done so.

All right, Elizabeth, Hallie says. I'll take care of it.

Of course I know you, Sylvia Beach says. I have an advance copy of your poem in *Life and Letters*. It's very good. "He cannot tell the rate at which he travels backwards." I admire that. Such a beautiful scan. And "He thinks the moon is a small hole at the top of the sky." Actually, I've thought that for years but never put it into words.

Sylvia invites Elizabeth to see Giraudoux's play about the Trojan War, which, she explains, some people think is really about Mussolini.

Men love war, Sylvia says. They think it solves everything. And Frenchmen cannot forget how Germany has dishonored them throughout history.

Frenchmen have a particularly aggressive temper, I've noticed. We've learned to steer clear of them in the street.

How can you tell which ones are the Frenchmen?

Gauloises, Elizabeth says. They're either smoking them or they smell like them. Like someone's eccentric great-uncle.

Sylvia appears surprised, stopped in her tracks. Elizabeth has noticed this happens when someone is talking seriously and she makes a joke. Or a funny observation. She is trying not to do this so much, at least not with strangers. Talk about the play, she tells herself. You can do that. Pretend you're in school talking to Miss Peebles.

I love Helen, Elizabeth says. I love how she visualizes in color what will happen and what she sees in black and white will not happen.

I do, too, Sylvia says. Helen has no intentions. Only images.

I understand that, Elizabeth says.

But it means that beauty can be used to mask the ugliness of war.

Not beauty, Elizabeth says. I think beauty is too pure to mask anything.

I don't know, Sylvia says. Beauty and purity seem like antique terms nowadays. Ideas for children. The world is getting so ugly.

Elizabeth feels a kind of hollowness in her chest. What if I am still a child? she wonders. What if I'm stuck there, always admiring childish things, beset by childish ideas?

I like children, Elizabeth says, somewhat defensively (she hates that tone). They're so helpless and good.

If we keep acting like children, Sylvia says, and then she pauses. This war is coming. Only children can't see it. Mussolini's in Ethiopia. What do you think *Axis* means? Do you think Germany and Italy will sit still there in the middle of Europe and be content to deal with their Jews and enlarge their borders a few miles here and there? They won't. These Nazis have already committed terrible crimes. They love power and order. They're cruel. They're just getting started. And they hate children.

And so Elizabeth begins to hear it, too, below everything. The gathering war. It is so often the shallow breathing of metal: the steep sides of warships, the chambers of rifles, empty shell of helmet, packed shell of bullet. The swastika, a headless spider, legs whirling and buzzing so fast they appear to be still. If there were ever a quiet moment in Paris, you could hear all this noise. You say *Versailles*, and most of the people in the room think you mean the treaty violation to the east and not the house of excess to the west. Conversation takes the shape of denial. The list of what one must deny grows longer every day.

A man at a party in the Latin Quarter says drunkenly that the poets should be very nervous.

Why is that? Elizabeth asks. I know a few poets in America.

Well, they had better stay there, the man says.

A tall woman with the face of a sweet horse takes his arm. Elizabeth realizes this is Ann, Sigrid's guardian. I understand the führer reads Goethe, she says. And Ibsen.

I dream almost every night about tanks, Elizabeth hears herself say.

She takes another sip from her glass, as does the drunken man. She imagines that their two heads dipping into their wide martini glasses must look like the courting doves outside her window.

How frightening, the man says.

Sometimes, Elizabeth continues, in my dreams, I'm standing next to a plaster wall full of bullet holes. Do you ever think that gunfire in the movies is a sort of amplified and stretched-out version of doves cooing?

Ann and the drunken man seem to hold their glasses more tightly. They stare. Someone new comes into the room, a beautiful woman, a film star, and there is sudden applause for her.

Doves? Ann says at last, choking on the word so that it sounds like *ducks.*

And Wagner libretti, another woman says. Hitler also reads those. They are his favorite.

Elizabeth realizes this woman is German also. She may, by who knows what circumstances, be quite familiar with the führer's reading list.

Louise steps in at this moment. Please save me, Elizabeth begs with her eyes.

Elizabeth, Louise says. I see you've found Ann. From the sailboat in Douarnenez

Certainly, Ann says. She was just making a stupendous metaphor about doves.

Now, Elizabeth, Louise says. Not here. This is a party.

I don't know about that, the drunken man says. It's more like a train platform packed with nervous, foolish people who can't see what's coming.

In three days, Louise says, Elizabeth will have her poems published in *America.* Isn't that right, Elizabeth?

Groups of people have paused in their conversations at exactly the same moment, and the words fill in a coincidental silence, and so news of Elizabeth's publication rings like an announcement made to the entire party. Guests seem to stand at attention, regimental. Elizabeth notices that most of the women have chosen to wear olive green skirts and jackets, or gray or blue. She finds this terrifying. The intelligentsia of Paris stand at the ready, an army. The men, of course, wear their usual dark suits. The men are always ready for battle, spoiling for a fight. This battalion of guests turns toward Elizabeth and smiles, delighted to celebrate.

Like an engine that sputters and catches, conversation starts again.

Borders are always the problem, a man standing behind Elizabeth says. He is some kind of British, but not, she doesn't think, posh London.

For you, of course, a woman says, the silvery notes of her laughter ascending, a pianist paying scales. *Glissando,* that's the word.

You live on an island, Ann says to him, speaking over Elizabeth's head.

And we like it that way these days, the man says.

If I were you, Ann says, I wouldn't be so *selbstgefällig.* She pauses, and her smile fades.

The word is chilling, even though almost no one who hears it knows exactly what it means. The way Ann says it is both a warning and a plea. *Get your silly heads out of the sand.* All the drab-colored women look as if they might never be happy again.

Louise, Elizabeth discovers, has an abiding interest in brothels. She calls it *my curious philanthropy:* she wants to befriend the women—girls, really. No one except Elizabeth seems to think this is strange. Louise says it's a bit like social work, the rather unconventional sort her mother raised her to do.

She arranges an introduction to Mademoiselle Indira, the dusky-skinned proprietress of a house near the Opéra. She invites Louise and Elizabeth for tea. When they step out of the apartment building, Clara is standing on the edge of the sidewalk, as if she has been waiting for them.

Oh, she says. I was just coming in, but it's not important.

You can go up anyway, Louise says. Christine is there.

Nothing urgent, Clara says.

The pause there on rue de Vaugirard is awkward. Louise pushes up the sleeve of her jacket and checks her watch. Clara stares at Elizabeth as if she wants her to receive a telepathic message.

I don't want to make you late, Clara says finally. I'll just walk along with you for a bit if that's all right. Are you comfortable in the apartment? Are you finding your way around Paris, Miss Bishop?

I am, thank you, Elizabeth says.

Elizabeth sees clearly, as if the word is inked across Clara's forehead. Clara is lonely.

Louise seems to understand this, too—this is the best of Louise, her empathy—and she links her arm through Clara's.

Maybe you'd like to join us, Madame Countess. We're on an unusual mission.

Louise explains. As Clara listens, her expression moves through abrupt changes: disbelief and distaste soften to sympathy and interest.

Mademoiselle Indira speaks eleven languages, Louise says. She can say *hello, bonjour, guten Morgen, ciao, hej, hola, olà, goedendag.* She is the mother to her young ladies.

Indeed, Clara says. She won't mind that I've tagged along?

On the contrary, Louise says.

Elizabeth wonders what *contrary* Louise will provide.

Perhaps she'll take me for an advocate, Clara says.

A protector, Louse offers.

I would be that, of course, Clara says. A protector of girls. I would like to take on that role.

If Mademoiselle Indira is surprised to see Clara with Louise and Elizabeth, she doesn't let on. She takes their coats and leads them into the parlor, where nine girls, almost all of them appearing younger than twenty, sit, dressed as if they are about to leave for church, in a palette of pastels, white gloves, hats with veils, identical pearl necklaces. The girls say hello, one at a time. Mademoiselle (*not Madame,* she tells them pointedly) Indira pours tea into painted china cups, each a different floral design, so that it seems each girl is clutching a small bouquet. For a few minutes, everyone is quiet inside a steamy cloud of bergamot and mint.

I believe I know your son, Comtesse, Mademoiselle Indira says. She smiles as if she's given Clara an expensive gift.

Elizabeth nearly spits out her mouthful of tea. She cannot look at Louise. Clara remains perfectly composed.

René, Mademoiselle Indira says, as if Clara needs prompting.

Do you? Clara says.

Or I know *of* him, I should say. He's just married the premier's daughter.

She's quite delightful, Clara says. And the apple of her father's eye.

Comtesse, Mademoiselle Indira begins. You have an international perspective. Do you think there will be a war?

The question makes a small explosion. Teacups chatter in their saucers, though the girls have hardly moved. They seem to know they are not being looked at in the usual way. Still, it must be familiar to them, the way Mademoiselle Indira attracts the attention to herself and to any man in the room, as if they have been hit by a spotlight. One girl, possibly the youngest, rolls her eyes. Elizabeth tries not to smile, and the girl sees this. Elizabeth wishes they could go somewhere else to talk.

I'm concerned, Clara replies. Though the French and English don't seem to have an appetite for war. Still, there are countless small acts of subversion everywhere, carried out by private citizens.

I'm afraid we are completely unprepared anyway, Mademoiselle Indira says. No ammunition. We might as well be children having a snowball fight.

Germany will not be reasoned with, Clara says.

But you can hear it coming, Mademoiselle Indira says. A kind of rustling in the leaves.

How poetic, Louise says.

You Americans have your heads in the clouds, Mademoiselle Indira says. Only you'll find soon enough that the clouds are really a ceiling, and you can't sleep up there forever. You can't protect yourselves.

Dreaming Americans. In their armored cars of dreams.

I don't think we're that bad, Clara says.

Look around you! Mademoiselle Indira is nearly shouting. Look at my girls! They are the ones who will be crushed by your dreaming!

Louise glances at Elizabeth. Her expression seems to be asking, *Is this really happening?* But also, *You'll be a dear while I fall in love with Indira, won't you?*

Mademoiselle Indira's girls know how to diffuse tension. It's their second calling. The youngest, the eye roller, turns to Clara.

Madame? she says in heavily accented English. Would you like to see my room?

We all would, Louise says, rising quickly from her chair.

Simone is the girl's name. She is small, maybe a whisper taller than Elizabeth. Her hair is black and thick, cut to hang just below her shoulders, and there's a wave to it, a kink. Elizabeth wonders if she is Jewish—the question sits in her brain like a stone—the prominent nose, the dark eyes. The muscles of Simone's calves flex and relax rhythmically as she climbs the stairs, like a heartbeat. There is something about her men would find attractive: a forthright gaze, willingness, curiosity, intelligence. These are terrible abstractions. So: those shapely calves, the curve of her backside, the arch of her eyebrow. Also an oceanic calm. Vast. A calm that seems to extend outward, infinitely.

Simone's bedroom is at the top of the stairs, the first on this hallway. Elizabeth wonders what this must signify. Popularity? Discretion? Simone turns the handle, opens the door, and inside they see what might be a girl's bedroom in a country home. A rough-cast iron bedstead, a pieced quilt in blues, yellows, and browns, lace-edged pillow shams, an armchair covered in chintz, a needlepoint rug that covers the entire floor.

That must have taken centuries to make, Louise whispers.

The large dresser seems to stagger under the weight of a gigantic mirror framed by winged cherubs the size of grapefruits and the lesser weights of a vase of dark purple gladiolas and three photographs—an older couple, then a young boy, then four teenaged girls, one of whom might be Simone herself. Reflected in the mirror, Elizabeth sees the detail she missed (how could she?): resting on the pillows is a row of dolls wearing dresses clearly sewn by hand.

Oh! Elizabeth believes her heart will break. The whole room swirls as if she's stood up too fast, then stills itself, resolves back to someone else's childhood, this one in which they stand now. She wonders: When there is a guest in this room, does Simone gather the dolls tenderly and set them in the chair? Or do they tumble in sideways and upside down, faces pressed into the chintz, grateful and fortunate in their empty porcelain heads?

I am worried for Simone, Mademoiselle Indira whispers to Elizabeth and Louise on the way downstairs. Her parents sent her from Warsaw. It's a miracle she got to me. At the moment, her accent is attractive, but I worry that will not last very long.

As they are preparing to leave, Clara takes Mademoiselle Indira's hands in hers. You are doing necessary work, she says. I should like to put you in touch with someone I know. Natalie Barney. She's an American, too, but you mustn't berate her as you have me. Her views are extraordinarily . . . open. If she believes a cause is just, she doesn't care who it offends.

Clara turns to Elizabeth and continues. Miss Barney holds a salon on Fridays at her pavilion on rue Jacob. She appears to be quite fond of writers, especially women. I could send a letter of introduction if you'd like.

Thank you, Elizabeth says. But I don't know if I'm enough of a writer yet.

Well, Clara says briskly. Natalie Barney will be able to tell you.

Louise, too, has heard about Le Boeuf sur le Toit.

Boeuf meaning *ox* in this case, she says. Ox on the roof. It's named for a ballet, a plotless thing, really an homage to Brazilian music, from ten years ago.

The place is supposed to be jam-packed with writers, Louise says. Painters, too. Musicians.

It sounds like it may be too much, Elizabeth says. I'd rather stay home.

But just think of all those sorts of people in one place, Louise says.

Exactly, Elizabeth says. Doesn't that scare you to death?

Let's just see if we can find it. In daylight. Think of it as a dress rehearsal.

The next morning, they cross the river at the Pont d'Iéna and walk north past the Palais de Chaillot, crowded with carpenters and stonemasons hammering though last-minute work on the exposition pavilions. Despite the commotion, Elizabeth notices, there is no excitement, only grim purpose, a great deal of shouting by a few men whose hands, she sees, are almost always empty. No one looks at them, not even at Louise, who is observed and admired everywhere in Paris. Here instead, she's greeted with disdain and vaguely threatening glances.

I'm not sure we're welcome here, Louise says. They must wonder why we aren't at work.

I hope that's all they wonder, Elizabeth says. I'm going to dash across to that shop for writing paper. I'll catch up.

Elizabeth starts to turn away, and then she sees what will happen a moment before it does. Two men carrying a load of lumber appear around the corner of rue Benjamin Franklin. The man in front watches his shoes as he steps off the curb, then glances up suddenly at Louise, who is walking a bit ahead on the narrow stretch of pavement. She turns and gives him an apologetic smile and a wave. She glances across the street at Elizabeth, and the man follows her gaze. His brow creases and his eyes narrow. They are exactly like boats on a collision course, and so, Elizabeth believes, the man will certainly realize this, and bear a little to the right. But he doesn't, and then a horrible rage comes over his face. Louise is not watching, half turned back toward Elizabeth, calling out that they must walk a bit farther north. So she does not see that the front left corner of the boards is aimed right at her head. The man spits tobacco on the ground and quickens his pace, causing his partner to stumble, lose his balance and his grip on the lumber. The man in front realizes their load is falling and that he must get out from under it. He glares at Louise and shifts the boards off his shoulder, slinging them to his left, so that they will certainly strike Louise square in the chest. Elizabeth rushes back and grabs a fistful of Louise's coat, pulls her out of the way. The boards fall at her feet, tumble onto her shoes.

The man begins to scream in German. Elizabeth pulls on Louise's coat. Let's go this way, she says.

Louise seems frozen in place. The fallen boards block both the sidewalk and the street. The screaming man seems as though he doesn't need to breathe. Louise begins to apologize, and the man steps forward, over the boards. His boots are enormous. His gloved hands are black mallets at the ends of his arms. His voice sounds like the popping of a toy gun, low-pitched, staccato.

Dogs, he is saying. Both of you.

Another man breaks from the crowd, calling in French. Though slightly built, he is a foot taller than the screaming German, and Elizabeth relaxes her grip on Louise's coat. When he is close enough, the German steps forward and lands a blow to the taller man's throat, knocking him off his feet. Louise turns, finally, and they run back the way they've come, toward the Place d'Iéna. At the river's edge, they stop. No one has followed them.

What did I do? Louise asks, over and over. What was he yelling? What did he want?

Elizabeth says nothing. She wonders instead what he saw, and she tries to banish the thought. Two women. That's all.

I keep seeing those boards on the sidewalk, Louise says. That would have killed me. I keep seeing those boards.

I do, too, Elizabeth says.

They were floorboards, she is beginning to realize, honey-colored grain. Tourists will walk over these boards, back and forth, scuffing but also polishing them with the sandy dirt off their shoes. But now the boards are lying in the street, like they would have been fifty years before, boards across the muddy streets of the city, a civility so women wouldn't ruin their skirts in one day, a courtesy.

An hour later, they are standing outside Le Boeuf sur le Toit.

Why did we come here today? Elizabeth asks.

I thought it would make you less afraid to come at night, Louise says.

I'm almost ready to believe at night might be safer, Elizabeth says.

They circle back to the Luxembourg Gardens. Elizabeth watches a child play with a mechanical toy, a horse with a dancer on his back. The child is trying to make the toy go, but he cannot. She watches as the child's interest turns to frustration and then to rage. His mother (or is she a nursemaid?) occupies a nearby bench, oblivious or unmoved, turning the pages of a book too quickly to be reading the words. She seems troubled, too, undone by something beyond her reading. So she does not notice when the child flings the toy into the grass. He sits quite still then, apparently subdued by his own gesture. The little horse and rider land close to the path, so Elizabeth can see the detail, the flowers on the dancer's costume, the large key in the horse's belly, the pole that pierces both horse and dancer. It must be painful, to be run through that way, even so neatly. Though after a while you might get used to it. The toy seems violent and dangerous, lying there sideways in the grass. A child should never be allowed to see such a thing, let alone touch it.

At Le Boeuf, Elizabeth and Louise stand just inside the doorway and peer through the cigarette smoke, looking for Sigrid. She seems to take shape out of the haze and noise and leads them to vom Rath's table. Vom Rath stands, kisses them on both cheeks, calls for more champagne. Sigrid introduces them to three men who work at the embassy. Elizabeth knows she will never be able to remember their names. When they are seated, Sigrid whispers about the young man beside vom Rath. His shirt is white linen, almost blinding. Expensive.

A gypsy or Polish boy, Sigrid tells them. A Jew.

He's quite attractive, Louise says. And that shirt.

He is sometimes mistaken for one of the waiters, Sigrid says. I've heard his shirts are stolen from a mortuary, off corpses.

Elizabeth observes a languorous, brooding, sleepy-eyed way about this boy, as if he's just come from bed. The impression of rumpled sheets, the smell of sweat and wine. He drinks champagne and does not say a word, except to whisper across the table to Elizabeth that his name is Hermann. She finds him interesting to look at, something incendiary about him. He watches vom Rath with violent attention. When vom Rath leaves the table, Hermann does, too, like a shadow, only darker. When they return, fifteen minutes later, vom Rath motions to the empty chair beside Elizabeth, and Hermann sits obediently.

Hermann knows Yiddish poetry, vom Rath says. He would be pleased to recite for you.

Undzer shtetl brent, Hermann begins.

Sigrid translates: *Our town is burning . . .*

Hermann has a low, clear voice. Elizabeth leans closer, but really she has no trouble hearing him below the din of Le Boeuf. Though she can't know what the rest of the words mean, she hears music and feeling, imagines the words making a slow sad march from right to left, the Hebrew letters running below the lines like tears down the white face of the page.

Vom Rath eases himself gracefully out of another conversation, a hand on the man's sleeve as he looks away, and leans in to listen to Hermann, his expression at once ravenous and pitying and terrifying: *I will eat you alive but only after I say a little prayer over your pretty white body.* When the recitation is done, vom Rath applauds. Then he blinks quickly, as if awaking from a nap. *J'aime le cinéma,* he says, *et la flânerie,* then he closes his eyes again. For half a minute, he appears asleep or dead upright, or listening to music no one else can hear.

Vom Rath's eyes open, and his gaze slides sideways—Elizabeth watches this happen—as if he's counting or waiting. He has, in fact, Sigrid says, waited a week for Hitler to occupy the upstairs rooms at the embassy, but now it appears this honor will not be bestowed. He looks like a jilted suitor, and Elizabeth almost wants to take hold of his beautiful pale manicured hands, give them a squeeze. She realizes then that he is looking at the young men passing by their table.

Hermann finds this prolonged silence intolerable. The champagne glass in his right hand begins to tremble. Elizabeth glances away at Sigrid, then at Louise, to see if either has noticed, and in that instant, Hermann drops or throws the glass against the table, and it shatters into a thousand tiny pieces that land and shine like sequins on their clothes.

Le Boeuf falls silent around them, though patrons seated at tables at the edge of the room continue to talk. It's like being underwater, Elizabeth thinks, the light dim and wavering. A moment later, a woman nearby screams and then stands abruptly, knocking over the drinks on her table. Other voices, male and female, shout in languages Elizabeth does not recognize. The sound of glass breaking seems to move through the room like a giant wave. Vom Rath grasps Hermann's arms, lifting him out of his chair. They move quickly past the bar and disappear.

Fifteen months later, on Kristallnacht, the memory of this evening will again frighten Elizabeth deeply.

Sigrid puts them into a taxi on avenue Pierre Ier de Serbie. I'm sorry the evening was spoiled, she says. My colleague is going to get us all in trouble.

Come with us, Elizabeth says to Sigrid. I don't like the thought of you out alone tonight.

Or any night, Louise says.

I'll be all right, Sigrid says. Ann and Marie will be expecting me. And your friend arrives tomorrow.

That's true, Elizabeth says. But you will want to meet her.

I don't think so, Sigrid says.

She closes the taxi door, speaks to the driver, pushes a handful of franc notes into his hand.

I think we will have a different kind of fun once Margaret gets here, Louise says. At least I hope so.

Elizabeth does not realize this is the last view of Sigrid she will have for some time, though she does take note of the sad smile, the long arm raised to wave goodbye, Sigrid's red hair glowing like flames around her face, the beam of lamplight out of which she disappears.

Elizabeth is thinking of Margaret, their reunion tomorrow, Margaret's laugh, the comfort of her presence. Then Louise will hire the car and they will all three drive south, through Sens and Tonnerre to Dijon. I'll ride in the back seat, Elizabeth decides, like the child behind the parents. So I can lean forward between them to talk. So Margaret won't have to miss anything along the way.

We must have more churches, Margaret says, to balance our life of pleasure. In five days, you've made me into a heathen!

Margaret would want churches anyway, for the art and for the open empty spaces above, for relics and chalices and cruets. Altar cloths, tapestries, candles, salvers, all those Catholic trappings, which when separate are just housewares and decoration. Years later, she will organize an exhibition of collages for the Museum of Modern Art in New York, because she loves the modulation and connection of objects that by themselves have less meaning.

For Elizabeth, it's a relief to escape all the talk of war, and the work, work, work of all the writers in Paris, which makes her feel stuck and lazy. All those writers writing—it's as if she can hear them, the purr and tap of their brains and machines. They're sleek and coiffed, sharp as if they have a fine edge. Refined. They seem to drink in moderation. They all know one another. She recalls Clara's comment about Natalie Barney, that Miss Barney would be able to say whether or not Elizabeth was enough of a writer. She pushes the thought from her mind.

In the rented car, they drive southeast from Paris to Sens, where they meet their English-speaking guide at Saint-Étienne. He tells them this is the oldest Gothic cathedral in France.

All Americans, he says, want to see the robes of Thomas Becket. They are shocked when they see no bloodstains.

Only Americans? Louise says.

Yes, the guide tells her. History eludes them.

Becket's robes do in fact appear too clean, floating there behind the glass. They resemble, Elizabeth thinks, a giant purple stingray, hung up by its nose, alive and waiting.

What if, Elizabeth says, things could know what will happen to them? If that robe could know the future when Becket was inside it.

If only they could speak, the guide says.

If only, Louise repeats.

Another Becket play, Margaret says. I hear it. Just what the world needs!

Please, Margaret! Louise says. She's on vacation.

I am, Elizabeth says. Marianne Moore says she's amazed by my life of leisure.

The crypt is partly Carolingian, the guide tells them. There's some music in that. She wishes she could stop counting syllables every time this man speaks and just listen for the information.

The Cistercians had an abbey at Fontenay, which is still mostly intact but hidden deep in the woods, away from the château, though the royals engaged the monks to keep their doves and their hunting dogs. It was a noisy, smelly place, even the scriptorium, where manuscripts were copied. It was overrun with animals, all crowded together close to a stone fireplace where monks could warm their chilled hands. In the Romanesque style, Margaret tells them, so no decoration. Like a pure heart or the souls everyone strives for. Monks slept in rows on straw in a long, unheated room. The ceiling arches above like ribs inside the belly of a whale. Each monk dreams he's Jonah. Forty separate pleas and rescues cloud the air at night.

In Semur, they climb an old road above the town to its Notre-

Dame, to meet first a stony doubting Thomas in a tympanum over the north doorway.

Inside, the eye is drawn first up to the stained-glass windows. Representing the guilds, Margaret reads. Elizabeth stares for a long time at a butcher in a red tunic (so the blood won't show), his gleaming white axe raised behind his head. The animal before him gazes out as if to say, *I know, I know. You do what you have to do, but must it always be this way?*

The cathedral at Vézelay, the guidebook says, is believed to house Mary Magdalene's femur. The English explanation in the crypt reads, *once thought to be.*

Outside the crypt, Louise stops suddenly, grasps Elizabeth's sleeve.

Look at this, she says. It's so . . . female.

Oh my, Elizabeth says. I see.

But, she thinks, this is how a man would be looking. What a man would be thinking. The stone, the marble highly polished, inviting. Perspective leads visitors into the dark, round mystery of the reliquary. You want to rush inside, bury yourself. The very thing you want most, need most, whatever it is, must be hidden there. The thought makes her warm and flushed. The porches, the folds of stone to be passed through first. Smooth and gleaming wetly in this light. And always the question: What will you find there, what transforming ecstasy? Maybe the bones of the Magdalene will magically knit back together.

A priest hurries toward them, his face red with exertion.

Les femmes sont interdites, the priest is saying.

Women are forbidden? Louise says. That's idiotic. *Stupide!*

He grasps Louise roughly by the arm and leads her out of the crypt.

Va te faire foutre, he says in a whisper so violent Elizabeth hears it as a shout.

* * *

In the car, they are too stunned at first to speak. Louise leans forward and rests her head on the steering wheel. After a minute, she says quietly, He told me to go fuck myself.

Sorry, Margaret, she says. The rest of the country hasn't been like this.

We can go back to Paris, I guess, Elizabeth says.

Not yet, Margaret says. He's just one person.

In Dijon, Margaret discovers an English-language bookshop.

That might be sort of a comfort for a while, she says.

Louise says she would rather take a walk.

Margaret and Elizabeth begin with Travel, which is beside the door. Baedekers with their cranky observations, walking guides, some French history mixed in. Belloc's *The Path to Rome,* D. H. Lawrence on Sardinia, Morton on England, Halliburton. Small leather volumes that would fit nicely in their pockets. They move farther into the store, which is surprisingly deep, a series of small windowless rooms lit by soft bulbs in metal cages that sway as a breeze moves through the shop.

Where are the coal miners? Margaret says.

Or is it a subway car? Elizabeth says.

A subway bookstore. What a good idea. Maybe there could be coffee service, a bar car open in the afternoons.

Margaret stands a few feet away, wrestling large art books off and onto the shelves. Just to be near her is soothing, almost as it was in college.

On the shelf marked Poetry, Elizabeth spies Miss Moore's first book and opens it. It's signed *To Harriet from Mummy.* A little darkness falls at the edge of Elizabeth's vision. Mothers give volumes of poetry to their daughters. Life in another universe. The only logical thing to do is buy the book.

She carries the book to the front of the store. The bookseller brushes glittering motes of dust off the cover.

I hope you don't mind it's used, he says.

Not at all, Elizabeth tells him. I like for books to have an afterlife.

So do I, he says. Obviously.

He glances around the shop. There is a kind of emptiness in his face, familiar, paper waiting to be darkened by words.

It was actually my mother's idea, he says. As I wasn't much for business or sports.

Nor am I, Elizabeth says.

She watches as he lifts sheet after sheet of white tissue from beneath the counter, then scissors and tape. His long, pale fingers work slowly with little flourishes, as if he were handling a needle and thread, as if the finished product were to be a wedding dress rather than a wrapped book.

There, he says, offering the parcel with both hands. No charge.

But of course I'll pay.

I insist. He winks. What Mother doesn't know won't hurt her.

I see, Elizabeth says. I am a conspirator.

You are. And I hope you will come back and conspire again.

Outside and across the road, someone has put in a bench in the shade, next to an overgrown garden.

Louise appears, fighting gravity, walking stiff legged, like a cripple, so as not to hurtle downhill. She stops and holds up her hands, palms open, thumbs splayed as if to frame a picture. Elizabeth realizes she and Margaret have placed themselves just so, framed by nasturtiums and roses.

You two make a lovely composition, Louise says. Very calm.

She sits down beside them. You can't quite get to the top, she says. There's a church and a very large house. Of course a priest's.

Her eyes fill with tears.

I hate him, too, Elizabeth says.

Louise nods. Priests ought not to be so damn stupid, she says. Especially not in France.

One more cathedral, Margaret says. Even I have had about enough.

What have you got there? Louise takes the white paper parcel, peers through the sheets of tissue. You visit a shop you have at home and buy a book you already own.

Miss Moore will like knowing she's been abroad, Elizabeth says.

I think this would all be quite too much for Miss Moore, Louise says. I think the circus is about all the abroad she can take.

It's true. Miss Moore would be appalled and frightened. Hitler, all the uncertain certainty of war. Something awful is lying in the shadows, in wait, some bloodied, menacing, monstrous thing that no one can even imagine.

nd so in the center of Dijon, on the façade of yet another Notre-
Dame, they touch the owl, which is supposed to bring good
luck.

But it most certainly does not.

At three o'clock, Louise declares they must return to their wayward
lives in Paris, even without redemption. She decides to follow smaller
roads through the fields as much as they can and then return to the
A6 at Auxerre. The windows are down, but it's quiet in the car. Louise
drives, consulting the map at each crossroads. Beside her, Margaret
leans out the window and lets the wind toss her hair. Elizabeth dozes
and wakes, having dreamed in the geometry of arches and porticoes.
The word *narthex* comes to her as if a species of wingless bird, its sudden appearance a messenger from the spiritual world. The fields they
pass make patterns like tablecloths and counterpanes, and that seems
beautifully logical: corn and wheat from these fields lead to the table.
The work of harvesting leads to sleep. This idea is just spinning out to
resolution when Louise rounds a curve, and a large car swoops past
from behind. The road is too narrow, and Louise veers too far to the
right. The wheels start to slide on the sandy shoulder, and Louise tries
to correct, but the sand gives them no traction. The car turns over,
spills them out, then bumps upright and stops. Quickly and quietly,
a moment of flying (later, they will wonder at the complete silence

of it), and then the world fallen on its side. Elizabeth scrambles to her feet and so does Louise, but Margaret doesn't move. Her eyes are open, blinking against the sunlight. She says the word *what,* but without inflection. Elizabeth sees it before Louise does, Margaret's right arm, severed above the wrist, pulsing blood into the sand.

Louise runs toward the field across the road, yelling help in English and in French. Two men look up, drop the hoe, the rake, and sprint toward them. When they see what's happened, one swears loudly and turns pale, but the other tells him *Non!* and yanks the handkerchief from around his throat, kneels beside Margaret, grasps her bleeding arm, and fashions a tourniquet just above the wound. This all happens so fast it seems magical, time folded in upon itself. The large car has returned. The driver loads Margaret into the back seat, Louise climbs in, and they speed off, back to Auxerre, five miles away, where there is a doctor. Elizabeth stays with their car.

I am thinking about time, she says out loud, to no one.

For a few minutes, the road is perfectly empty, the air still. Elizabeth does not look at anything, can't really see anything. A delivery van approaches, slows. The driver asks a question, *Ça va? Qu'est-ce qui s'est passé?* Elizabeth can barely answer. *Accident.* The word is the same in French, probably in every language. More vehicles arrive and stop. Everyone wants to know, to help, to take her somewhere else, away from the smashed car and the blood pooled in the sand. It's almost the solstice, so the sky will stay light for a long time. This part of the road is on a little rise—she can look over the fields and think the words *tablecloth, counterpane, brickwork, wood grain.* Once, when the road is empty, she calls Margaret's name.

What is wrong with me? she says to no one. Margaret isn't lost! Margaret isn't hiding somewhere nearby!

After some time, maybe an hour, the large car returns. The man tells her they will drive to Auxerre. Elizabeth asks if Margaret is all right, but he either does not hear her or does not understand. His silence is terrifying, nearly unbearable.

The hospital in Auxerre is horrifying, primitive, unclean. Blood streaks the floor of the examination room. Elizabeth recalls the stained-glass butcher and his hatchet. Margaret's severed hand is rolled up in white gauze and left on the lip of a gray stone basin. Elizabeth is afraid someone will throw it away. She stands beside the basin, her own hand cupped around Margaret's. If necessary, she will put the hand into her pocketbook for safekeeping.

A priest hovers outside the treatment room until the doctor invites him in. His cassock sweeps the bloodstained floor. He tells them in broken English that he has heard the news and has come as fast as he could. He asks what has become of the driver. Louise steps forward and begins to explain. The priest puts his hand quickly to his forehead as if he has a sudden pain there. His eyes are a frightening shade of blue, like a cold, northern sea. He surveys the three of them—Louise, Margaret, Elizabeth—and then he says the accident occurred because a woman was driving the car. Louise tries to explain: a larger car forced them off the road. There was nothing they could do. The priest shakes his head, makes the sign of the cross on Margaret's chest, anoints the bandage on her severed right hand, blesses the surgeon who will perform the reattachment.

Mrs. Miller's scream, there on the dock at Le Havre, sounds to Elizabeth like an echo from a long way off, from the other side of the ocean, from another country. Questions of meaning and injury swirl between them: What happened? What is the hurt? Can it be soothed? Whose fault is it? And who is asking these questions? Elizabeth wonders. Is she asking? Or is it Mrs. Miller? Or both of them at once? And then Mrs. Miller faints dead away, into Elizabeth's arms. A dockworker hauling lines nearby helps Elizabeth lower Mrs. Miller onto the ground, where she lies at their feet, thin and pale and silent. The man says he can stay as long as he's needed. His lips move. He produces a pouch of tobacco and rolling papers from his shirt pocket but seems not to know what to do next.

Someone somewhere is mending a ship, an ironworker, a black-smith with salt on his skin, in his hair. They can hear the clang of mallet on metal. The two sounds, Mrs. Miller's scream and the iron-worker's hammering, fuse in the air, hang there.

But minutes after screaming and fainting, Mrs. Miller is suddenly all right. More than all right. She is in charge. She opens her eyes, smiles at the dockworker, thanks him in perfect French. She stands, looks around, alert as a sandpiper, calls for a porter. Mrs. Miller is accustomed to people coming when she calls them, and she is rarely disappointed. This seems to Elizabeth an astonishing quality—in a mother or anyone else. The porter calls a taxi, and Mrs. Miller puts Elizabeth in first, behind the driver, then walks around to the other side. She asks in her perfect French for the train to Paris. In the station, she pays the fare. She wonders why Elizabeth only bought a one-way ticket.

Every time, even years later, when Elizabeth arrives in or departs from Le Havre, she will hear that peculiar bell of hammer and whistle of scream. Even after the British and Americans bomb the city and port into rubble and ashes and blood, after Auguste Perret builds it up again, including the massive church of Saint Joseph, which points its large accusing finger of a steeple straight up at the sky, Elizabeth will hear Mrs. Miller's scream.

During the three-hour ride to Paris, Mrs. Miller asks odd and even ghoulish questions. Did Margaret cry very much? How large was the scar? Was the surgeon good? Experienced? Would Margaret now be a cripple? Elizabeth says she doesn't remember about the crying or the surgeon and doesn't know about the future. As for the scar—it was awful. Mrs. Miller would soon see for herself, and she may faint again.

Finally, near Saint-Denis, Mrs. Miller leans her head back. Tears run out of the corners of her eyes. She pats the seat beside her like a blind person, finds Elizabeth's hand, holds it for a moment.

I'm so glad, she whispers. I'm so glad she's alive. I'm so glad you were with her. You must move with her to my apartment. She will need you to be close by. You're very dear to her, you know. You always have been.

Back in Paris, Elizabeth receives a very odd letter from Clara:

Dear Elizabeth,

I was very sorry to hear about your friend's accident (you know all news of Americans reaches me eventually). I understand you were also involved but suffered no great harm. Physically, I mean. And yet, violent events can also harm us mentally and spiritually. I believe you are back in Paris. I would very much like to see you again for coffee or luncheon or really any such engagement as you might have time for. I trust you are staying until your friend can travel. I have missed your company, and I have very important matters to discuss with you. Remember that I had mentioned a trip to Normandy. I believe that the timing would be helpful for you.

With all good wishes,
C. L. de Chambrun

Elizabeth shows the letter to Louise.

She would make me very nervous, Louise says. She seems quite fond of you.

She's sort of grown on me. She's a mass of contradictions.

It's your great gift, you know. One of them. You give people lots of room to be themselves.

I don't know what that means.

And you are so morally attractive to someone like the comtesse de Chambrun, someone with a name. No tantrums, no indiscretions.

Not at least where anyone can see.

Within a week, Elizabeth realizes that Margaret's mother is a problem.

Two problems, really, Louise says. She pretends not to blame me, but she does. I can tell every time I walk into the room. Pretending not to is worse than just saying it. And she's scaring Margaret with all her worry and attention. Margaret needs to rest.

Elizabeth knows, however, of another problem, the worst one: Margaret will never again be able to use her right hand. It's obvious in the peculiar, loose curl of the fingers, as if they're about to grasp a pencil, frozen in anticipation. No one will talk about this, but Elizabeth understands that Margaret wants to. Margaret wants to know so she can begin to live accordingly. But everyone—doctors, nurses, her mother, Louise—assures her. No, no, dearest. You're going to be fine. You're going to draw and write long letters and all of that. Margaret looked at them first with disgust, but now she simply turns her back to them, faces the sofa cushions or the wall.

One morning, before dawn, Elizabeth sits down on the sofa, lifts Margaret's feet into her lap. Margaret tries to move away, but Elizabeth holds on. She strokes the paint on Margaret's toenails, a bright coral, the same shade Mrs. Miller wears. Margaret relaxes a bit, gazes up at Elizabeth.

Well? she says.

Elizabeth rubs Margaret's feet. I'm going to tell you. You need to know.

I'm going to lose the hand. Is that it?

Elizabeth nods.

Lose it how though? Lose it like—amputate?

No, sweet, no. No, not that. Heavens, no. But function . . .

Elizabeth cups her hands around Margaret's feet, keeping them warm, keeping them whole, attached.

The room goes still around them, as if time has been sucked away because there's no place for it now. What's time good for anyway, why is it worth having if you can't do what you want with it? Elizabeth knows they are both listening for some sound that will contradict the truth of what she's just said: Margaret's mother, the doctor, a car horn.

The sound of the car horn that could take it all back. If the car that forced them off the road had made any sound before it appeared beside Louise's car . . .

They are listening for that.

Margaret has closed her eyes.

I thought so, she whispers. I think I knew all along. But nobody wants to say that. Even I don't want to say it. What will I do?

Your left hand will get the message, Elizabeth says. It will rise to the occasion. Literally. (This makes Margaret smile, just a little.) People will help you.

I don't want any help.

Well, that will have to change.

I think I'd like to sleep now.

Margaret swings her feet off Elizabeth's lap and onto the floor, moves to stand, tries to push away from the sofa with both hands. Sweat beads her forehead. Her face goes gray with pain.

You can't do that, Elizabeth says. I'll help you to your room.

She takes Margaret's left arm, grasping under the elbow. She runs her right arm around Margaret's waist. They pause together, as if waiting for music to begin a dance step.

That's good, Margaret says. Thank you.

Margaret sleeps in the small maid's bedroom. It has the feel of a ship's cabin, though there is a large window with a view of the île de la Cité. The ceiling is quite low. A narrow passage runs from the door straight to the bathroom, between the single bed and the dresser. Margaret chose this room over the two larger bedrooms at the back of the house, even though they are quiet and face the courtyard. I like the confinement, was how she explained her choice. Restrained. I can't roll around and hurt myself.

Elizabeth understands perfectly. The room is a blank canvas, too, since no one bothers to decorate a maid's room. That's left for the maid to do herself if she ever has a spare minute. The walls gleam off-white, bare except for four nail holes and the shadows of the pictures those nails once held. It is interesting to imagine what the maid (whoever she was) would have wanted to look at in the few minutes between climbing into bed and falling into exhausted sleep. Not food. Not Venus borne on the half shell. Certainly not a wealthy Renaissance family with their adult-featured children and small, beribboned dog.

This afternoon, the room looks more like a nun's cubicle. Two nuns in the room now, one of them wounded. She helps Margaret into bed, turns to leave.

Don't go yet, Elizabeth. Not until I've fallen asleep. I've taken the pain pills, so it won't be long.

Of course I'll stay.

Sit here beside me.

Elizabeth sits on the bed and Margaret curls around her, lying on her side, her knees bent and her hands clasped under her chin, as if in prayer, the lost hand covered by the good one. In three minutes, she is snoring gently.

She watches Margaret sleep. Margaret is a beautiful sleeper (she is a beautiful everything), eyelashes spidering on her cheek, lips slightly parted as if anticipating a kiss, her breathing a little, bouncy hum. How strange, to be so good at something and never to know it.

Elizabeth stands up carefully, moves slowly and silently toward the door, even though she can tell the pills have drawn Margaret into a deep slumber and it will be hard to wake her. She lets herself out, closes the door, and walks to the living room, to the large windows. Now the apartment belongs just to her, the early morning light making the same promise: this is yours, do with it all you can. She will walk to rue de Rivoli and find something nice for Margaret, a sweet, *petits fours, profiterole, pain au chocolat, pain perdu.* Lost bread. The shops will just now be unlocking their doors, though in the bakeries, the ovens will have been burning for hours, the bakers already done half a day's work.

She gathers her pocketbook, the shopping bag made of woven string, which appears as if it won't hold anything much but expands to carry a week's worth of meals. She lets herself out of the apartment, soundlessly. A Parisian marvel, this bag, a small delight. Elizabeth wants to make Margaret happy. She always has, and she always will.

Outside, Elizabeth notices the translucent gleam of morning, and she wonders again how it's possible that the first light of day is so pale. How is it that the sky goes from flat dark to this absolute white and then darkens again into blue? She wonders how to get that phenomenon, that question, into a story or at the very least into a letter to Miss Moore. What is the thing that happens at five a.m. when night goes to pearl? It would be lovely to stay in this moment for longer than a few minutes. The street is nearly empty, and so Elizabeth decides to take the roundabout way, through the place de l'Hôtel de Ville, passing the good bakery, the friendly one, where behind the counter there is a young woman with green eyes and hair black as coal.

Just before she's reached the *mairie,* she hears the sound of footsteps—a crowd of people—and quick breathing. There is no one else nearby, and so she feels a vague dread, very small, a point really, at the back of her skull. She stops walking, moves closer to the *mairie* portico. A light shines from inside: someone here could help her if need be. She turns to face the sounds and sees not an attacker but Sigrid, her skin the same pearl as the dawn sky.

I'm sorry to frighten you, Sigrid says. I was waiting . . . I have been waiting . . .

You should have called, Elizabeth says. The words sound harsh, dismissive, and immediately she is sorry.

I was afraid to disturb you. I heard about your friend.

Close behind are four women, walking very fast, three in dark dresses and the fourth a bride. They stop, too, under the portico, very close to Elizabeth and Sigrid, all of them pressed into the shadows. The three attendants (they wear the same style of dress) talk at once, whispering, surrounding the bride, smoothing the folds of her gown, adjusting the veil. The bride is weeping, shaking her head. *Non, non,* she says. One woman runs her index finger slowly over the bride's lips, a gesture that is both tender and electric, nearly unbearable to watch. Elizabeth hears her say the word *pas,* for *no* or *not.* She decides in that moment that the attendants are giving advice. Don't love too much. Never give your whole self away.

The attendants finish their million last touches and step away from the bride. They notice Elizabeth and Sigrid standing just beyond them, and one takes the bride's arm, turns her around, a kind of silent presentation.

Très bien, Elizabeth says. *Bonne chance.*

Où est le bébé? the bride asks.

Elizabeth says she doesn't know.

The bride stumbles a moment, but her face stays completely still, as if she is blind and deaf. A man in a soldier's uniform appears. Green and gold medals shine on his chest. He wears a red *képi* on his head. He says nothing and does not smile. The attendants guide the bride past him, toward the lighted hallway.

Just before they enter the *mairie,* an older woman rushes out of the darkness carrying a bundle. The bride lets out a tiny sob and opens her arms, clutches the baby to her chest. The woman puts her finger to her lips and hurries away.

Elizabeth turns to Sigrid. She wants to ask what they have just witnessed. She wonders if Sigrid feels the same way she does, that some subtle violence is about to take place. The men must already be inside, waiting for the women and this child. They listen, for what Elizabeth is not even sure (a cry? gunfire?), but there is no sound other than the creak and distant rumble of a city coming awake. The fearful event must be unfolding rooms away, in the interior, the heart of the building. Though the moment appears to have resolved itself, her initial fear, a prickle of high-pitched dread, a whine, settles in her head, the back of her neck.

I'm sorry, Elizabeth says. I ought to have called you.

Is it very bad? Sigrid asks. What happened to your friend.

I think it is. But we can't let her know that.

I am terribly sorry. I know you love her very much.

It's difficult to watch her suffer.

In fact, it's intolerable. Elizabeth thinks she will have to get out of Paris. She must go to the sea. And she will have to make the trip alone. Margaret can't go, of course, and probably Louise won't want to. She's having too much fun. Parisians treat Louise like a beloved pet, and she becomes more sleek and assured under their attention. Like a cat, and all of Paris is her sunny window. Elizabeth believes Louise will take her to Florida, but that won't be for weeks.

And Sigrid. Elizabeth looks at her now, as morning blooms around them. Sigrid's creamy skin, her pale eyebrows and eyelashes—she looks completely unguarded, vulnerable, as if everything about her is out in the open, completely exposed.

You can't leave Paris, can you? Elizabeth asks her.

It isn't safe.

I'm sorry.

Are you going away again?

I think so. Something is crushing me.

Sigrid places her hand on Elizabeth's shoulder. The gesture is neutral, utterly mystifying.

It's as if the growing daylight makes Elizabeth's path clear, certain. She will go back to Douarnenez. Or to Saint-Malo. Or maybe to another town, the one Seurat painted, in Normandy, sailboats in the dotted bay. Elizabeth thinks she would like to get out on the water, look back and see all of France before her. The Seine is decent water, but there's no horizon. You can cross a bridge and have half of it behind you, but you can't stand and look at it all day—you'll either block traffic or be taken for an idiot or both.

Tell me before you leave, Sigrid says.

I will.

Sigrid steps away from the *mairie,* turns north again toward the river.

When Elizabeth returns to the apartment, Margaret is still sleeping. Louise also has come back. Her coat reclines along the sofa, glossy with appreciation. If you put your face close to the coat, you would hear it purring. Elizabeth makes herself a cup of coffee, consults the train schedule in the kitchen drawer. Trains run north from Gare du Nord and Gare Saint-Lazare. She could arrive in Caen in two hours. A bus or taxi to the seaside. Someone would know of a nice town with a good hotel. She is not really afraid to travel by herself—in fact, she would welcome that lovely suspension between cities. But arrival and then finding herself alone, that's another thing entirely. She sits down at the kitchen table, feels the apartment breathe. Women sleeping, separate in their beds, the beauty of it, faces slack, their dreams tumbling and curdling in the air above their heads.

Elizabeth knows the real reason she can't go alone. She will not even make it out of the bar at the train station. She will stay and drink until someone has to come and bring her back to this apartment. She will drink to all of it. She will raise glass after glass, beguiled by suitcases tucked under tables, the alert gaiety of travelers, their eyes glazed here in the place between home and destination, eyes on the departures board, eyes on clocks.

The clocks. Then she knows: Clara. Clara will go with her. Some time ago, and now just recently Clara mentioned a trip to Normandy. Clara is always eager to escape.

Elizabeth knows the telephone number by heart.

E lizabeth, Clara says, and her voice softens. How lovely of you to telephone. How is Margaret?

It's a hideous situation, Elizabeth says. She's had some setbacks. She's in a great deal of pain. There was an operation last week to sever nerves.

Clara's sigh could have come from the mourning doves pacing the roof outside.

But, you see, she doesn't need me every minute. Louise is thinking of making a trip to Florida, to buy property. I'd like to get away.

Clara offers her country house, near Versailles, but Elizabeth hears a reluctance in her voice, a little tease. She says no, thank you.

I want to go farther. The coast. North. Normandy. The trip you mentioned.

Clara's voice turns bright. Of course! I know a town, Arromanches, up quite a steep hill, so there's a marvelous view of the sea, and a comfortable hotel.

She wants, Elizabeth believes, to be asked but fears she won't be. They talk about how the weather might turn, the storm season, and Elizabeth wonders if she really and truly wants Clara to go with her. But she does. The idea fills her with such calm: Clara will direct them here and there. The hotel will be fine, the restaurants excellent. Walking beside the sea will be splendid, the hikes not too difficult or tiring. Clara will know how to rent a sailboat, and she will let Elizabeth steer.

Will you come with me? Elizabeth says finally. Or take me along with you?

Clara does not speak. The silence lasts so long Elizabeth wonders if the connection has been broken. She wonders if she's got it wrong, that a journey with Elizabeth is really the last thing Clara wants. Then she hears a tiny gasp, almost a sob.

Of course, Clara says. I'll book the train. When shall we go? And the hotel. I'll phone right away.

I'd like to go right this minute, Elizabeth says.

Clara laughs. I know, but we can't do that, she says. She sounds like a mother talking to a fanciful child, wishing she could make the fancied thing happen.

Elizabeth listens to the voice, the tone and style that have always been Clara's: a grief-stricken person struggling to be sensible. She wants Clara to go on talking, maybe forever. That will be the pleasure and the wonder of this trip. Clara's talking.

Meet me tomorrow, Clara says. Café Varenne. On rue du Bac. To plan our little journey.

E lizabeth arrives twenty minutes early to have a drink by herself, to prepare for the great storm that Clara can sometimes be, the formidable comtesse de Chambrun. She settles at a table by the front window, next to two women. She orders a whiskey and soda, and glances at a newspaper someone has left behind. *La France est le poids decisif pour la paix ou pour la guerre.*

How would you like love to be at the end of your life?

Elizabeth listens as one of the women, an American, asks this of the other. She believes they do not intend to be overheard.

Calm, the other woman says.

Not me, the first woman says. I want a perfect riot.

Well, her companion says, then I imagine you'll be divorcing James.

No, not yet. First I'll try to set him on fire.

The women nod. They clasp hands across the table, furtively, then let go as if they've received an electric shock.

Elizabeth pictures the burning man, burning James. How quiet he is. Just a crackle now and then. The women are still not speaking. They gaze at each other. At any moment, she imagines, they will rise abruptly, scatter a few francs on the table, leave the café. One of them has rooms nearby.

But they don't move. Silently, Elizabeth urges them out the door. Go now. The older woman sighs, drops a cube of sugar into her steaming cup.

Tell me about marriage, the younger woman says.

Well, it gets better, and then it gets different. Actually, I read that somewhere, and it feels true.

That's what I was afraid of.

The women smile. Elizabeth can't stop watching them, even though any second now they will notice her staring. She drinks them in, fills herself with the puzzle, theirs and her own. What is it, she thinks, that we are all working out here?

I sent you telegrams, the younger woman says. Did you get them all right?

I received two, the older woman says.

I sent four. Did the package from Istanbul arrive?

No. So much gets lost in the mail, Elaine.

Elaine stares, disbelieving.

Elizabeth can tell the older woman is lying about the package from Istanbul. Elaine thinks this is the worst moment of her life, but it won't be.

Margaret once told her a story about going to a bridal shop with her cousin and her aunt. Before her cousin's fitting, they watched a mother and daughter. The daughter was quite young, a bit plump, very happy to be engaged to be married. Engagement to a man had made her beautiful. She tried on dress after dress. In each one she looked increasingly lovely. And she knew this, the daughter, knew it deep in her heart. For the first time, happiness had cast its spell, transformed her into the most gorgeous woman in all of New York City.

It sounds like a fairy tale, Elizabeth said.

Just wait, Margaret told her.

The mother, though. The mother's expression never changed. No, she said, just the one word, no, each time, to each dress while her daughter blossomed, shone, diminished the women of Manhattan. Five times for five dresses. Finally, after the sixth no, the daughter's face went blank. Not sad. Just nothing. Margaret had to leave the shop.

To kill your child like that, she said to Elizabeth. I still see that dead face. It is as much a crime as with a knife or with bullets.

Elaine is being killed this way, Elizabeth can see. Murder by repeated small refusals, murder by silence.

You are there, Robert wrote on a postcard (not the last one). *I am here. I remember.*

Elizabeth did not write back.

Clara arrives in a swirl of cape, midnight blue, wearing a hat pierced on one side by a peacock feather. Elizabeth is not at all surprised to find she knows Elaine and her older companion, called Susan, from the American Library. Clara stands beside their table. She acknowledges Elizabeth barely, with the smallest incline of her head, a gesture that seems to say, *Just sit there for a moment and listen.*

We were just talking about the end of our lives, Elaine says.

Really? Clara says. Did you get some notice?

No more than anyone else, Susan says. It's an amusing topic, don't you think?

I find myself thinking a bit more about the end of the world, Clara says.

Of course, Susan says.

You've been away from Paris quite a bit, haven't you? Elaine asks Clara. Dorothy's been running the library all by herself.

And doing a marvelous job, Clara says. She was a find, wasn't she?

Yes, but we miss you. Are you traveling with the count? But no, my brother says he dines at Josephine almost every night.

Elizabeth watches Clara. Her smile does not waver.

I travel when I can, Clara says. It's one of life's last amusements, isn't it?

Where should *I* go then? Susan says.

Clara leans on the back of Susan's chair, staring down into Susan's teacup as if she's reading the leaves at the bottom.

For you, she says, I would suggest a warmer climate. I was quite taken with Tunisia a few years ago.

But travel's quite difficult now, isn't it? Susan says. So many people mobbing about, displaced and all that.

And all that, Clara repeats, her voice flat. Still, you don't want to miss anything at the end, do you?

Absolutely not! Susan says, lifting the check from its little dish.

I've got to run, Elaine says. She opens her wallet, offers a handful of coins.

Nonsense, Susan says.

Elaine clatters the coins into the dish. Her gaze at Susan is raw, imploring. Elizabeth aches for her. They rise from the table and shake hands with Clara, leave the café. Elizabeth observes a quick *bisou* between them and their departure in opposite directions.

It is fashionable these days, Clara says when she's settled in beside Elizabeth, to talk about death and the afterlife.

I think maybe that's always fashionable in Paris, Elizabeth says.

You're right. The French love to dabble in this dire stuff, and appear brave, and then go home alone to their cold, dark rooms and cower like the rest of us. They say there is no heaven, but in the middle of the night, they want it so badly that they cry out until their cats jump off the bed in alarm.

Elizabeth laughs.

It's not funny, Clara says. At my age you have to admit you're going to die.

If I had more whiskey, Elizabeth thinks, I would contradict her.

You don't think about dying yet, Elizabeth, Clara continues. In fact, you may arrive at middle age and still believe you'll live forever. Honestly, I don't know what you'll believe. Writers are different, and I'm sure I don't know what to make of poets. Maybe you'll think you can read every book and see every painting up until the moment you can't. But I know a few things about heaven . . .

How do you know? Elizabeth says.

Because I have a rendezvous there already arranged. Heaven is not about weightlessness. You can't fly or swim.

Oh my.

Clara squints one eye as if she's trying to glimpse something in the distance. It's very dark in heaven, I imagine, she says. Except for the kind of light that's . . . I don't know the word. It's hard to describe. Think of bright sunshine on water.

Glare, Elizabeth says.

Exactly. So two kinds of blindness.

Why would anyone want to go there?

To say good night one more time. Or forever, really. I think that time gets stretched, and you can stay in that last embrace forever.

Now I'll have that whiskey, Clara, Elizabeth says in her mind. How is it that I can want to be with you, and at the same time find it painful as all hell?

Clara gazes out the café window, as if she's looking for Suzanne. Elizabeth suspects that Clara always chooses this kind of table, in cafés, restaurants, even in the winter, all those times a table farther back would be preferable.

Clara opens her hand as if to admire it, then presses her fingers to the window glass.

You realize, Elizabeth, Clara says, that the Germans will be here, too. And soon. They cannot be contained. They can't be satisfied. You'll look out a window like this and see them in the street. The only thing you can do is be ready.

I won't be here, Elizabeth says. I'll go home before that happens.

And you should, Clara says. But first I need you to help me with something.

She glances at her watch. Elizabeth waits for her to explain. A pair of nuns enters the café, sits at the table next to them. They ask the waiter for coffee. Or rather, the elder nun asks. She holds up two fingers, the way some artists painted Christ's gesture, while the other hand holds an orb or points to the fiery sacred heart burning in his chest.

Do you like children, Elizabeth? Clara asks, raising her voice slightly.

I think so, Elizabeth says. I'm afraid I haven't had much experience with them. I mean I was one, once.

Clara smiles, sphinxlike. Do you believe, she says, they are innocent and in need of our care? Do you believe they come into the world knowing nothing and owing nothing?

Well, Elizabeth says. Yes to the second part. But I don't think they know nothing. It's going to sound somewhat mad. She notices the nuns are listening, so she lowers her voice. But I have a feeling that when babies are born, they know everything, and growing up is the process of forgetting.

That's an interesting theory, Clara says. Is it religious?

I can't think of where it came from. Where I grew up, the Baptists and the Methodists mixed freely. The churches were across the road from each other. Sometimes if you were late for one service and all the seats were taken, you could just go across to the other. Especially in winter when you wanted to be out of the cold.

I like the idea of that, Clara says. But I'm not sure it would work in most parts of the world.

No, Elizabeth says. I don't believe it would. Certainly not today.

Are you in some kind of trouble, Elizabeth?

Trouble? If you mean about the accident, that was settled. Louise had to pay a small fine so her insurance would cover the rest.

What about you?

I wasn't involved at all. I didn't have to go to the trial.

So the police have no reason to think about you?

No, none. Why are you asking?

Because of my connections, Clara says. I am always what the authorities call a person of interest. And since we will be traveling together, I thought I ought to see where you fall on that spectrum.

I think I'm quite outside it, Elizabeth says. So you don't need to worry about . . . besmirchment.

Elizabeth, what a word! Clara says. She appears to be both shocked and amused.

I don't know if it is a word. But I like it.

Elizabeth watches Clara glance quickly at the nuns.

They are rather a presence, she whispers.

The older nun reaches inside her habit, extracts a franc note, and places it over the rim of her cup. The nuns stand, then seem to float around the table and out the door. Their feet are not visible.

In all my time here, Elizabeth says, I've never once seen a nun in a café. Really, I've never seen one of them eat or drink. All they seem to do in Paris is pray or herd lines of schoolgirls.

They are quite mysterious, Clara says.

Like this entire conversation, Elizabeth thinks. She feels as if she's being interviewed for some sort of work, but she has no idea what her job might be. Even stranger, Clara seems to be auditioning, dressed in costume: the cape, the feathered hat. She feels she is watching strangers in a play, in this strangest of theaters.

Sigrid is waiting inside Sylvia's bookshop.

I am going to tell you a story, she says. Before you go away. You will think it is about me, but it isn't.

Why will I think that?

You'll see. Listen. A tiny little girl was walking with her sister in Berlin. They were going to school. The little girl was four. She could walk only a few steps and then she would start to complain. Carry me, she would call to her sister. I am so tired. My feet are tired. My legs are tired. My eyes are tired from the sun.

Hurry up, her sister called over her shoulder. I am going to be late. I have to take you to Auntie's first so you can play all day and eat cakes and sleep, and then I have to catch the bus to the university and work all day to make sure the men understand what the English professor is telling them because they are too stupid to study their lessons at home.

Why are they so stupid? the little girl wanted to know.

Because they are lazy. Like you are being right now to walk so slowly.

The little girl stopped walking and stamped her foot.

I am not lazy! You are the lazy one!

The little girl had come blazing into the world, her sister recalled, with this fiery temper, a supernatural intelligence, and a beautiful face.

Perfect Cupid's bow mouth, eyes the color of Dutch iris, a halo of bright red hair.

This is about you, Elizabeth says.

No, Sigrid tells her. Just wait. It's not.

She turns away from Elizabeth to gaze out the shop window and speaks as if she's telling the story to the street below. Elizabeth almost finds it strange that no one stops to pay attention, to stare up at Sigrid, try to decipher the words.

The sister could stand to be called many things but not lazy, not even by a child. She believed she was perhaps the most conscientious woman in Berlin. She was certainly the most generous. For instance, when her mother died last year and her father, sick himself and easily frightened, left them, she decided she would not send her baby sister to the orphanage as her hysterical relatives suggested, but rather take care of her at home, keep the family together. What family? her uncle shouted. You are completely out of your mind!

If you don't hurry up, she said to her little sister, I am going to leave you right here.

Carry me! the little sister demanded. I can't go as fast as you.

I can't carry you. Look at me! I have this bag of books and papers written by stupid men. I am weighed down by the ponderous thinking of these idiots. I would carry you if I could, but right now I just have to get you to Auntie's before I lose my job.

Her little sister began to cry. She sat down in the gutter. She tore the large white bow from her hair and threw it into the street.

Seeing this, her sister's heart heaved as if it could sob on its own and began to break open. Her heart broke in half. But this is a curious, ungainly thing, half a heart. It doesn't function properly. It cools and hardens.

She would teach her little sister a lesson. She would walk ahead for a few minutes and then come back. Her sister would be afraid and be quiet and she would learn not to make such a scene. She walked to the next block, then the next, almost to the edge of Weissensee, and then she couldn't hear her sister's cries any longer. Good, she thought, she must have realized. She must be waiting quietly for me to come back. Maybe someone has returned her bow, too. Then we will be on our way. I don't think I will be very late.

She reached the spot where her sister had been sitting just in time to see two policemen dragging her away by the arms, yanking her arms high over her head as if they would pull them off her body. Her sister was silent, her body limp, her white knee socks fallen down to her ankles.

Wait, she cried and ran after the policemen. Where are you going? That is my sister.

The policemen turned, let go of her sister's arms. She fell in a heap between them. A bloody scrape bloomed along the right side of her face, streaked with mud. Her head rolled oddly on her neck. Her blue eyes stared at nothing.

Dreckige Jüdin, the policemen said. She deserved to be thrown into the street.

Elizabeth watches Sigrid stare out the window into the gutter along rue de l'Odéon.

The children cannot help themselves, Sigrid says.

n two days, Elizabeth and Clara are inside Gare du Nord, at the bar, which Elizabeth knows she will be able to leave in time to catch the 14:14 train to Caen because Clara will tell her to drink up. Then Clara will pay the waiter, stand decisively, collect her suitcase and pocketbook from beneath their little table, and instruct Elizabeth to do likewise. But for now, she is enjoying a glass of wine and Clara's stories about the American Library patrons.

My borrowers are quite clever, Clara says. And naughty. There is a great deal of mischief in the stacks.

Elizabeth is astonished. Some monumental change has come over Clara.

It was quite sedate the time I visited, she says. Very serious patrons at work. Mothers reading to their children.

Really? Clara says. One gentleman scholar recently pointed out that Baden-Powell's *Scouting for Boys* sits right up against the works of W. H. Auden. *Bolt upright* was how he put it.

Oh, Clara, Elizabeth says, laughing. I love Auden. He knows about everything.

Indeed.

And he's very courageous in the poems.

And very good in the stacks.

My goodness!

Do I shock you? I find I can say certain things to you that I wouldn't dare say to anybody else.

The train is called, and Clara stands. She lifts her own wineglass as if she is going to deliver a toast to the bar, pausing for effect. Elizabeth can see that Clara is gazing over the heads of their fellow travelers and out of the bar, into the mêlée of the station. She glances down at Elizabeth, then up at the departures board. She seems suddenly confused, lost. Afraid.

Clara? Elizabeth says. What's the matter?

I thought, Clara begins. Then she shakes her head vigorously, oddly, as if in the grip of some palsy. She looks into her wineglass, then sets it on the table. Elizabeth has to exert enormous self-control. She wants to take up the glass, finish the wine.

Time, Clara says, reaching for her suitcase. I'm not accustomed to this, Elizabeth. I rarely carry my own luggage. It's refreshing, though, isn't it? *Allons-y!* Platform seven!

Clara leads the way, maneuvering efficiently through the crowd. Elizabeth worries that she'll lose sight of Clara, that Clara will somehow escape. *Escape* is the word she hears in her head, and she must remind herself that Clara wants to lead, that leading is Clara's *raison d'être,* the air she breathes.

And then Clara is gone, disappeared, swallowed. So many tall women in black coats, grasping black suitcases. Platform seven. Signs clearly point the way. In French. *Sept.* Elizabeth feels the impulse to stop, stand still in the middle of Gare du Nord, let the crowd swirl around and ahead, leave her alone in its wake, even though she knows this can never happen. More travelers will enter the station and take the places of those who have boarded trains. The surge of people will never stop, not for hours, until the middle of the night. By then, Clara will have come back, taken Elizabeth by the arm, as if she were a child. Clara's child. Suzanne.

Elizabeth wonders if Suzanne has something to do with Clara's odd moment in the bar just now. She moves sideways to slip between a father and his son, then a group of soldiers, next a clutch of nuns. She catches sight of Clara slowing, stopping, turning to look. Clara's expression is alarming, bereft. Her mouth opens to shout, but then she sees Elizabeth and her face changes in a sort of jolt, as if she has received a blow. She waits for Elizabeth to catch up.

Don't get lost, she scolds. We don't have time for that!

Sorry, Elizabeth breathes. This crowd is tremendous.

No daydreaming. Save that for the train. No writing poems in your head in the middle of the station!

Elizabeth feels at once angry, sad, ashamed. Where else to write poems? But she settles her arm closely around the waist of Clara's coat, exhales, allows herself to be led. They board the train, find facing window seats. The man seated on the aisle offers to hoist their luggage into the rack overhead, even before Clara has the chance to charm him. He speaks to them in German, and Clara replies in kind.

He is a businessman, Clara explains to Elizabeth when they have taken their seats and the German has gone back to his newspaper. He is looking at properties in Normandy.

You discovered all that while he was lifting our suitcases?

Clara nods, does not smile. It is best to take a person's measure as soon as possible, she says.

I wonder what measure he took of us? Elizabeth says.

The man looks at them over the top of his newspaper. He speaks again to Clara in German, and something tightens in her face, though her smile is radiant. *Ja,* she says. *Danke.* She reaches across the aisle to touch Elizabeth's cheek. She turns again toward the German, explaining something. Her eyes dart between the German's face and Elizabeth's. The German's eyes open wide. He stares at Elizabeth, smiles broadly, nods his head. He seems to approve of whatever it is that

Clara has told him. He reaches inside his suitcoat and produces a small pad of paper and a tiny silver pencil, shows them to Elizabeth as if they were the most marvelous *objets,* tucks them away again. He mimes applause.

Elizabeth wishes Sigrid were with them. She would be able to get to the bottom of this strange melodrama. And Sigrid would like Clara, because Clara would treat her exactly as Ann and Marie do, like their mischievous, magical child. Sigrid would have four mothers. Wouldn't that be a wonderful extravagance!

The German settles back in his seat, returns to his newspaper. Clara opens her large black pocketbook and draws out an orange, which she begins to peel. The train shudders, moves forward. Elizabeth is relieved to discover she has the seat that faces the direction they are traveling. She wants to see the north suburbs of Paris as they pass through, parts of the city she has not thought to visit. Clara starts to offer a section of the orange, then changes her mind. Paris slips past, clattering, bridges of ochre-colored stone, buildings staring with dead eyes, ends of roads, a man smoking above the tracks. Good, let it go by, put it all behind. Clara moves to sit beside Elizabeth, then splits the peeled orange in two, hands half to Elizabeth, along with a handkerchief. The orange reminds her of Key West, Louise, all of Florida. The state with the prettiest name. And so much ocean!

She can hardly wait to get to the sea.

Is it lack of imagination that makes us come to imagined places, not just stay at home?

QUESTIONS OF TRAVEL

 1937

Twenty miles south of Caen, the train brakes, not dangerously, but quickly, so that there is a certain discomfort for the passengers, the sensation of one's heart nudging against the rib cage, the brain sloshing ahead of itself. No crashing of baggage, though, no cries of pain. The closest town is called Domfront, the German businessman tells Clara, who translates for Elizabeth. Maybe there is an emergency.

After a few minutes, Elizabeth feels a kind of solemn hush come into their car. Passengers on the left side of the train who have been leaning to peer out the windows sit back in their seats and stare straight ahead. This happens all at once, as if choreographed. It's like the first notes of the organ, and suddenly you remember you're in church and not gossiping at the market.

Then, on her side of the train, she sees what the others have: a funeral procession. The small white coffin (Heavens! A child, Clara says) carried on the shoulders of four men in black suits passes at the front of the train. The mourners who follow appear slowly, one by one, sometimes in pairs, having walked, one heavy foot at a time, over the tracks in an awkward kind of gait: climb, step, stop, step, climb. Following the coffin is the priest, or maybe a monsignor, in brilliant purple robes and a golden stole, looking too festive, outrageous. He carries a small crucifix, which catches the sun and turns into a blade in his hand.

Maybe it's meant to be thrown in on top of the coffin, Elizabeth thinks suddenly, the violence of the gesture surprising her.

A man and a woman follow the priest. He helps her over the railroad ties, and it's slow going. Once beyond the tracks, the woman stops, shakes herself free of the man's hand, turns, and begins to run back the way they've come. The man lunges to catch her but misses, holds out his arms, shouts something that must be her name. Now passengers across the aisle turn to look out the windows, and Elizabeth sees it, too, the woman hurrying past the line of mourners. Some try to stop her. Others shake their heads and let her go.

On Elizabeth's side, the pallbearers, coffin, and priest move on, passing beyond a line of plane trees. They become opaque then, as if viewed through the screen on a confessional, people and objects turned into geometry: a white rectangle, aloft, behind which is another rectangle, perpendicular, violet and gold, moving parallel now to the stalled train, in the woods. This is not a graveyard (no church), not a cemetery. Why bury a child here, that place where frightened children are led or left or lured, both in and out of dreams? Maybe it was the father's idea—or the priest's—and the mother can't bear it, won't watch. She doesn't want to see it happen anywhere, her child dropped into the ground and left alone. The shiny cross won't be any use under all that dirt, those shards of leaves, no matter how soft the moss might be.

The left-side passengers are holding their breath now—something new is happening. *Oh! Tiens!* they whisper. The train's engineer has come down out of his cab. He's walking down the line of mourners and into the trees to the west. Elizabeth wishes she could see his face—how grim or sad. He's going to get the mother and bring her back—Elizabeth knows this as if she were the man himself. Without the mother, his train can't go anywhere. He disappears into those opposite trees, his pale blue jacket and red neckerchief an inverse of the priest's garb. Everyone waits, inside this train and outside in the glare of the sun. Somewhere in the next car, an infant wails and is hushed (how was this accomplished so quickly?). In a few minutes, the driver of the train reappears, carrying the mother in his arms. She does not struggle. She has not fainted. He is a large man, and she is small and frail, her arms twined around his neck and her legs like birch sticks, spilling from the black satchel of her dress. His mouth is very close to her ear—he must be whispering to her. They pass through the line of mourners, over the tracks, past her husband, who bows his head and follows. Behind the scrim of trees, Elizabeth sees the little splash of red neckerchief stop between the coffin and the priest.

Soon the mourners have cleared the tracks. The driver returns, then disappears from Elizabeth's view. The train shudders, begins to move forward. The forest has become impenetrable, as if the trees closed ranks against the world of the living. Nothing more to see here. Move along.

Clara stares, then cranes backward for the last slice of view. When she turns forward again, Elizabeth sees that her face is chalk white, her eyes enormous.

What did he say to her, do you think, to bring her back? Elizabeth asks.

I would give my life to know, Clara says.

So would I, Elizabeth thinks, and she cannot let go of the possibilities, even though she cannot put them into actual words an actual person might say.

t is evening when the taxi from Caen arrives at the Hôtel d'Arromanches. Clara has booked two rooms with baths and sea views. She asks the management to send up sandwiches and cider and bids Elizabeth good night. She is obviously very tired, and Elizabeth is glad for the privacy. She is pleased to discover the rooms do not adjoin. She unpacks her suitcase, and after a tall, sandy-haired boy brings the supper, she settles herself by the open window and listens to the sea. Voices chime up from the bar, though not the words themselves, just the cadences of speech. It's very soothing. The sandwich is good: butter, cheese, ham, a huge slab of bread, the cider a happy, heady fizz, but gone much too quickly.

It's after ten. Elizabeth is not accustomed to late nights in Paris, but today's travel has jazzed and jangled her in some way, caused her to wonder about this eagerness to flee with Clara and to the place of Clara's choosing. Flee to this: to the sound of the sea, the view of breaking waves where the light from below casts itself over the seawall. She should take up her travel diary, continue studying the French surrealists, but really she understands them perfectly, that the amalgamations of dreams are beautiful and true and not so far beyond us as we think they are.

Women's laughter drifts up from the bar. The old thirst. The usual thirst. She wants another drink. Maybe the hotel will sell her a bottle to keep in her room. She must go ask now before it gets any later.

In the hallway, she turns left, away from Clara's door, and takes the stairs two flights down to reception. The boy who delivered her supper sits on a stool behind the front desk reading a newspaper. He appears shocked to see her and asks in English if the countess is unwell. Elizabeth tells him that the countess would like a bottle of spirits, gin or scotch. She is appalled by her own lie and the involuntary manner of its telling.

A short, slight man, middle-aged, with a prominent nose and watery blue eyes appears beside her.

Jenever, he says. *Oude.*

Pardon? Elizabeth says.

He's telling you what to buy for the countess.

Jenever? Is it good?

Bien sûr, the man says. He kisses the tips of his fingers.

All right, then, Elizabeth says. How much? She shows him a twenty-franc note.

No money, the boy says. On the bill.

He and the man go across the reception area and into the bar.

She should just hurry away, back upstairs, and try to forget her thirst. Clara will certainly look at the bill and feel—what? Elizabeth isn't sure. But the old need keeps her rooted there, her mind ticking over itself as if she were trying to understand or remember. And then it's too late. The boy is back, holding out a bottle wrapped in brown paper.

The countess will like it very much, he says.

Elizabeth searches the boy's face, listens for any trace of irony, but there is none. The man behind him is nodding.

The bottle is made of burnt-sienna-colored clay and comes with amusing instructions printed on the label: *Selon la tradition, la première*

*gorgée doit être prise sans tenir le verre, mais en pliant le dos pour appli-
quer sa bouche au verre.*

Why not?

Elizabeth places a water glass on the windowsill, pours to the brim,
then, without touching the glass, bends to take the first sip.

The sea shouts approval.

After breakfast the next morning, Elizabeth and Clara arrange their chairs at the Café de la Plage to face the small, calm harbor of Port-en-Bessin, and beyond it, the sea, which seems today a lolling, lazy being, undulating and degenerate. Odalisque, Elizabeth thinks. Unaccountably, this makes her want to send a postcard to Miss Moore and her mother. Not of boats, but a drawing of seabirds maybe. Or the seashore. And on the back she would write, *There's not much between here and Coney Island. Isn't that odd to think about?* She would add something more, light and breezy, since her last letter, about Margaret and the accident, must have been terribly distressing.

I will be sixty-four in October, Clara says. That's a long time to live. I've published a memoir, you know, last year.

Elizabeth nods.

It's made a bit of a splash in literary circles, Clara says. I quite like writing.

You do? Elizabeth says. Can you teach me to like it?

Clara looks puzzled, then deflated. Elizabeth understands Clara was expecting to have a tête-à-tête with someone more enthusiastic about the whole enterprise.

I was joking, she says quickly. I'm just such an awfully slow writer.

You're young, Clara says. You'll get faster. You will because you'll see that time speeds up. At my age, time is just a blur. So you've got to work like a whirlwind to get it all down.

Elizabeth nods, though she suspects otherwise. She wants to make Clara happy. She imagines a snowstorm of paper. That's what a whirlwind would look like. It would be unreadable.

So will you do another volume? she asks.

Oh my, yes, Clara tells her. She lowers her voice to a whisper. I shall have to in order to tell all the secrets.

Are there many?

One or two. But I think there will be more.

Elizabeth wants to say, Tell me one of the secrets, but she's afraid Clara might expect she would respond in kind.

Also, Clara is saying, something will have to be written about the Paris exposition, and the strikes and the Popular Front lowering the standards of art and literature. You know what I mean, Elizabeth, don't you?

I think so, Elizabeth says.

But enough of that. You wanted to escape Paris. And I have a few people to see here.

I can certainly amuse myself for an afternoon.

They will want to meet you, though.

Clara seems suddenly flustered. Elizabeth notices she has twisted her paper napkin into a ragged coil.

All right.

That can wait until tomorrow. Why don't we see about renting a sailboat? I only hope you're as good a sailor as you told me. The English Channel can be unpredictable. Maybe we should charter a boat instead.

Elizabeth starts to say she's sailed in the Atlantic before, since she was a child, but it occurs to her that a charter might be more restful. And then she might fish, close to the harbor. Clara doesn't seem like a fishing sort of person, though. She doesn't seems like an anything sort of person. Away from Paris, she seems sort of empty, like grand experiences slide through her, like a coin in a broken slot machine. The coin comes right back out again at the bottom of the chute, your very same coin.

A charter would be nice, Elizabeth says.

Yes, Clara says. I thought you'd see it that way. I've already arranged a boat for tomorrow.

Elizabeth wonders when Clara might have done this. In her head, a tiny bell rings, but she doesn't want to upset Clara.

A young mother strolls past, pushing a little girl in a blue pram. The child is singing and the mother laughs at her song. The child is about five, obviously too old for such a conveyance. Elizabeth can see what Clara is thinking: *That child should walk.* But it's a happy picture nonetheless, and Clara can't sustain her irritation. Instead, her eyes fill with tears.

Suddenly, the child climbs out of the stroller and rushes to Clara. Granny! she cries. Clara stiffens. She holds her hands up and away from the child, a gesture of surrender, or as if she is preparing herself to catch a much larger object.

Granny! the child says. What are you doing here?

The mother looks on for a moment, amused and ashamed both, but she is waiting to see what Clara will do. Clara does not move. Finally, the mother comes forward, gently draws the child away from the table, unpeeling her hands from the shiny buttons on Clara's jacket, explaining that this is not Granny, but a nice woman on holiday.

I'm so sorry, she says. You look like her gran. My mother. You really do.

Clara bows her head. She does not reply.

I hope we didn't upset your mum, the woman whispers to Elizabeth.

The chartered sailboat is the *Sirène,* and her captain is the man who stood beside Elizabeth last night and suggested the jenever. He introduces himself as Dominique. He is Belgian. If he remembers Elizabeth, he gives no sign, except maybe his eyes hold her gaze a bit longer than necessary. He seems to assume that Clara and Elizabeth are mother and daughter. When Clara attempts to climb aboard on her own, he commands Elizabeth in French to help. Clara does not correct him, as Elizabeth expects she will, does not say she's perfectly able. In fact, she looks at him approvingly, as if he is some sort of genius. They behave as if he has not spoken a word—though he has already said a great deal, that he takes on passengers because the fishing is really no good, or he hates fishing, Elizabeth isn't quite sure, but she does hear the word *déteste.* He is much better at farming, he says, *beaucoup mieux fermier,* and Elizabeth wonders why he stays in this place that is too rocky for crops.

He pauses to stare intently at Clara, and Elizabeth feels some sort of fire between them, silent, heated communication. He asks in English where they would like to go.

A little voyage, Clara says. As we discussed.

Dominique nods, casts off the lines, throttles the engine until finally it catches, turns over, about the time Elizabeth begins to wonder if they will ever leave the dock. He stares out to sea with a horrible grimace, scanning the horizon as if he's looking for a hurricane, a white whale, an albatross, or all three. When he assures them there should be something out there—*quelque chose!*—Elizabeth knows he means wind enough for a decent sail, but still the idea of a vague threat unsettles her. A strange notion comes into her head: She is in this small boat with her mother and father, the dead, the bereft, and the failure. But they have been somehow reunited and can take on these trials together. She presses herself into a corner of the cockpit.

When they have motored past the channel marker, Dominique prepares to raise the sail. Before Elizabeth can offer to steer the boat into the wind, Clara steps past her to take the tiller in what appears to be a practiced manner. Dominique climbs up to remove the sail cover, hands it to Clara, and she tosses it down into the cabin. He hoists the sail with five mighty pulls. *Les lignes,* he says, and Elizabeth unwinds the starboard sail lines from the winch, then moves to port. Clara's look is determined, imperious. The ghost of a smile on her face seems to say, *You have underestimated me, my girl.*

Le bôme vive, Dominique calls, unhooking the boom. Clara steers out to sea. France is behind them now.

Dominique says something to Clara in French, points to the tiller and then at Elizabeth.

Though Elizabeth has not asked for any explanation, Clara says, Because he's tired of steering. Just keep on an eastern course.

Clara's voice is rich with sympathy, as if she knows this particular weariness herself. Dominique steps out of the way, and Elizabeth slides left, then realizes she will have to stand in order to look between the boom and the companionway. Dominique watches her for a moment, shakes his head as if to say, *Now we will all drown,* and climbs down into the cabin and disappears. There is no sound from below. It's as if he was never on the boat. Elizabeth looks at Clara.

He is tired of almost everything, Clara says.

Dominique calls up from below.

He's telling you in the first cove, Clara says. There's a stone house with a blue door. A friend lives there. We'll stop to fish.

Then Clara follows Dominique down into the shadows, replacing the boards. Dominique's hand reaches to pull the companionway hatch closed, a gesture like waving. Elizabeth almost waves back.

Well, this is something. She wonders if he will ask Clara how she liked the jenever. Nothing to be done about that now. Sky above, sea all around. The winds are light, the sea is calm. No sound from below. Elizabeth smiles. Why Clara! You minx! Who would ever suspect? The librarian and the sailor—or whatever he is. Elizabeth has to admit she feels a certain envy. The ease with which they can accomplish such things, men and women.

The glide of pelicans is more or less easterly. Might as well follow. Elizabeth tacks, roughly, remembers her passengers below, silently promises them to steer a more even course. A pair of pelicans separates from the rest—the *squadron*—and circles back toward the boat. Elizabeth believes they will fly right through the sail, but one bird banks, turns. The other slows, flaps awkwardly, lands on the prow, arranges itself like a figurehead, completely unconcerned. And profoundly ugly. Scruffy feathers mottled gray and white. Prehistoric, more kin to a dinosaur than anything birdlike. The long bill rummages deep into the breast feathers, under the wings. The pelican does not appear to see Elizabeth. Along for the ride. The boat moves lazily east. What if I turned around and sailed all the way to Wellfleet? Elizabeth muses. The three of us on the open ocean. We could provision in England. Penzance. All that Arthurian magic. And pirates! I think I have had a dream like this, a ship with unknown cargo sealed below.

She wonders suddenly if Clara and Dominique have somehow exited the boat. Or died. Maybe they've made a pact, and they know I'll wait for some minutes, that I'll have to keep steering, that I'll be pre-occupied, and so I won't disturb them for however long . . . whatever form . . . Clara would be thinking of Shakespeare, Romeo and Juliet of course, but mainly of the lovers' failure, not their intent to escape. Clara. No. Clara would never be a suicide. She has too much left to say.

Elizabeth realizes she is making up these small amusements to pass the time. Certainly there is no suicide being enacted below, only awkward, desperate lovemaking. The boat creaks like a bed, the sail flutters like a falling dress, the mast rises . . . obviously. She smiles at her own little pornographic *bons mots*. Louise will enjoy this story. Perhaps Sigrid, too.

Twenty minutes tick by. The pelican preens and shifts but does not fly off. How will the lovers look when they come up for air? she wonders. And what should I be doing? There is nowhere else to go, nowhere to turn away from the closed cabin door. She cannot leave the tiller. She wishes she had not made such a frenzied escape out of Paris. Looking back, she sees there was no need, her hysteria as in-substantial as a hangover. The figurehead pelican looks her in the eye now, just now, with its wise, wild, ancient gaze, mocking. How silly to put human thoughts into the expressions of animals. She's learned this from Marianne Moore. *What is happening here?* she mouths to the bird, which hops to starboard, really an awkward shuffle, not a hop at all. She should write to Miss Moore, Elizabeth decides. Just news. I sailed with the comtesse de Chambrun and a Belgian fisherman. Nothing about this moment, though—she would hardly know how to express this state of affairs to Miss Moore. No, write only about the landscape, the familiarity of the sea, the child in the café.

The pelican lifts suddenly, flies off to the east. Elizabeth follows, tacking carefully, still hugging the shore. She reckons forty minutes have passed, and she's tired of maneuvering the boat by herself. Dominique had said they would fish in the first little cove, and so when the coastline seems to pull open, she sails in. There, as promised, is the stone house with the blue door. She casts the anchor overboard, douses the sail. Fishing poles already set with hooks and bobbers lie at her feet, and she untangles one from the pile, frees the hook, casts toward shore. No bait, but a catch is not really the point, is it? Who really cares to feel a tug, have a little fight, lose the fish or throw it back? The point of fishing is stillness and false purpose, a kind of waking sleep. And not having to steer. Clara and Dominique must have registered the calm of the boat, and this will surely bring them up from below, as soon as they are able.

Onshore, fifty yards away the stone house waits, two stories high, surrounded by tall, bright flowers, maybe something like a zinnia, orange, red, yellow, vivid pink. A vegetable garden to the left, staked tomato plants, beans growing on a fishing net stretched between two poles. A wooden dock reaches out into the cove like a pleading gesture, one armed, odd. A rowboat bobs at the end of the dock. While she looks, the white curtains in the downstairs windows twitch, and two beats later, the front door opens. A figure in dark trousers and a bright green sweater emerges, moves without urgency toward the dock. Elizabeth believes this is a young woman, the balance between arm and hips, the light steps into the rowboat. The woman unties the dock lines, takes up the oars, begins to row slowly toward the *Sirène*. She keeps her eyes fixed on Elizabeth but does not speak. The only sound in the cove is the beat of the oars and the chuff of little waves. As she approaches Elizabeth, the woman seems to grow older. When the boats are a foot apart, and she throws Elizabeth the lines, she's become elderly, the age Elizabeth's grandmother would be. Still, the woman says nothing. Elizabeth pulls the rowboat alongside the *Sirène*, and their faces are so close that Elizabeth can see a faint scar running from the woman's left eye to the middle of her cheek.

Dominique? the woman asks.

Below, Elizabeth says, pointing to the closed cabin door. She ex-

pects to hear, Who are you, and listens hard for the who, the *qui.*
Instead, the woman makes a gesture, slicing the air horizontally. They
stare. The woman is not frightened and not angry. She seems intensely
calm, that paradox of emotion. Again she slices the air and then sets
both hands, palms flat, on the deck railing. Elizabeth realizes this must
mean *Move aside, I'm coming in,* and so she shifts to make room. In a
neat hoist and swivel, the woman is sitting beside her.

Léonie, she says, offering her hand. She stands then, moves ex-
pertly, catlike, around the tiller toward the cabin door. She knocks
loudly, calls Dominique's name. Silence.

Elizabeth wonders if she could possibly explain. French phrases for
love flood her mind, a blue contusion of language. Léonie turns, stares
at Elizabeth. The clear translation is *What have you done with him?*
Elizabeth shakes her head, raises her hands, palms up, widens her eyes,
turns down the corners of her mouth, all the French she has learned
for *I haven't a clue.* The fishing pole, which she had set down, flies off
the boat like a possessed javelin and disappears beneath the swells.

Léonie laughs. Bravo, she says.

They hear shuffling below. A hand slides the hatch open, and
Dominique appears, head and shoulders. Elizabeth is surprised to see
that he is very clearly frightened and then immediately shocked to see
Léonie, the cove, her house.

You told me the first cove, Elizabeth says. The stone house.

He speaks to Léonie in French, too quickly to follow, an argument
that seems as if it will go on and on, until Clara's voice rises out of the
cabin, a piercing *Excusez-moi!*

And then in English: Is Elizabeth all right?

I'm fine, Clara, Elizabeth calls. How are *you?* She cannot keep the
nervous laughter out of her voice.

Nothing is funny, Clara says.

Elizabeth sits down behind the tiller. Mysterious agitation and anger salt the air. Léonie is too old to be Dominique's wife, but really one never knows about such things. His mother? Elizabeth is also terribly sorry about the fishing rod, though that seems to be the least worrisome detail now.

Dominique removes the boards and helps Clara out on deck. Her hair is pinned neatly, her clothes perfectly tidy. Still, there was time to put herself together. She shakes hands with Léonie, who regards Clara with frank curiosity.

Elizabeth, Clara says. *Mon amie.*

Léonie nods as if this is obvious and utterly uninteresting. Then her expression tightens and she turns to Dominique, who shrugs.

You can't help it, Clara says, but Elizabeth can't tell whom she's addressing.

This exchange causes Léonie to shake her head and set her mouth as if she's smelled something disagreeable. She steps closer to Dominique and takes a bunch of his shirtfront in her fist so violently that he stumbles. Then she turns from him, slides past Elizabeth, steps into her boat, unties the line. She takes up an oar and uses it to push off.

Okay, *Bien,* she calls. *Mangez!*

So much happens without the help of language. No, Elizabeth corrects herself, that's not quite right. In spite of language.

Léonie is a friend of Dominique, Clara says, and Dominique is a friend of my brother-in-law Charlie. You remember the incident, Elizabeth, the shooting at Gare du Nord.

Charlie was the ambassador to Italy. He was on his way to see Dominique in Brussels when he was shot by a madwoman who claimed he had poisoned Mussolini against her. Naturally, Dominique was concerned. As soon as Charlie makes a full recovery, Dominique will go home.

The gulls' voices sound like children crying. One of them in particular, directly overhead. You want to do something for the poor thing.

Capture it in your arms, smooth its feathers, feed it. But it's a bird. It's up there, out of your reach. Elizabeth wonders what drama is playing itself out here in front of her. The water distorts and reveals. Sometimes things are inverted but not distorted. Or not much. While the tides work steadily away at everything solid. And if you fall into it, the water, from any height, it's hard as diamonds and just as sharp.

The weak sun catches suddenly in the front windows of Léonie's house, making a flash, a brilliance like explosion. Or more like fire because it doesn't fade. Elizabeth wants to show this to Clara, but Dominique begins to haul in the anchor and Clara tips the fenders overboard. Elizabeth watches helplessly, of course she could do these things, but no one asks. She moves closer to Clara, and when Clara steps up and slides around the mast, Elizabeth follows.

Can I ask who she is? she says. And why we're here?

You can ask, Clara says.

Elizabeth recognizes the arch tone some women take after lovemaking. Louise for example. She tries to laugh but feels frightened.

What do you tell your husband, Clara?

About what?

Traveling. With me. Dominique.

Clara's expression is a confusion of changes, like a sped-up film. Elizabeth can hardly keep track. She waits until Clara's eyes and mouth settle. Behind them, Dominique breathes heavily, winching up the last of the anchor line. Clara turns toward him, then away.

I don't tell him anything, Clara says finally. Anyway, he's too busy with travels of his own. It's not what you think, Elizabeth.

She looks past the mouth of the cove and out to sea. And then she says something very odd.

You are a necessary angel.

She steps past Elizabeth, grasping the lifelines, and climbs the companionway ladder down into the cabin.

The thud and clang of the anchor into the cockpit unsteadies the *Sirène.* Elizabeth reaches for the mast, slides her hand up the weathered wood, worn smooth as glass, gray as clouds. Some days, the mast must be invisible against the sky. Dominique starts the engine, steers to Léonie's dock, reverses to stop just alongside. The fenders do their necessary work, screaming a little, more like a squeal, a barnyard noise.

Mademoiselle, Dominique calls, gesturing to the dock, lifting the line and pretending to throw it. Elizabeth steps over the doused sail to the foredeck and then over the lifelines onto the dock, movements she usually doesn't even have to think about, and yet she does now. It all feels like a dream, in which one can do either more or less than in life, but not the same. Which may be the real purpose of dreams—to instruct, to show us where we're wanting or wrong.

Someone has driven a metal loop, like a croquet wicket, into the dock. Elizabeth sees that Léonie's rowboat is tied to a similar device on the other side. It is a funny, Victorian substitute for a cleat. The simple iron arch reminds Elizabeth of Simone's bed upstairs at Mademoiselle Indira's establishment, a visit that feels like a thousand years ago. The same curve, only these two are smaller, of course, like the head and foot of a mermaid bed, a merchild or some small creature who would sleep here and not die from too much oxygen. Dominique tosses Elizabeth the line and she makes it fast to the loop, a clove hitch. Dominique nods in approval, then glances away, down into the cockpit, and begins to laugh. He moves the remaining fishing rods with his foot.

Je regrette, Elizabeth says. A fish took it. I'm very sorry. I'll buy you another in town.

Tant pis, Dominique says. He calls for Clara to come up and translate.

That fish will have a story, Clara says. Another story. The ones who take the lines have always done it before.

Elizabeth hears a splash and turns to look. There it is, kindly returning the fishing rod. Behind her, she hears Clara let out a little cry. Then she sees it: a long, wet undulation just beyond Léonie's row-boat, the smooth back of a dolphin, but brown.

What in the world? Clara says.

Lion de mer, Dominique tells them.

The sea lion swims and breaches, back and forth, toward shore and then away. On her third pass (Elizabeth has decided this must be a female), the animal turns and looks at them, then slips below the water with a great sigh.

In Douarnenez, Elizabeth says, there was a circus, and one of the seals climbed a stepladder carrying a lighted lamp with a red silk shade and bead fringe on his nose.

That's good luck, Clara says. She's come a long way from Calais. They like singing. I understand they prefer hymns. I only know a few lines. Triumphant gladness. Mighty fortress. *Chantez,* she says to Dominique.

Dominique clears his throat, not theatrically. He begins "Ave Maria." He has a warm tenor. The sky and sea take it willingly up and away out of the cove. Elizabeth hopes the sea lion will walk out of the water on her tail, over the grass and down the dock. Give her a message, handwritten, inside a watertight box, to explain the meaning of *necessary angel.* Then she will bellow like a foghorn and slip back into the sea. It might be alarming, though. She would have to fall over sideways like a creature shot.

What Elizabeth sees first inside Léonie's house is a blizzard of lace: tablecloth and napkins, curtains, wall hangings, doilies, antimacassars on the sofa and chairs. Léonie doesn't seem like the type to want so much in the way of frill. But of course, Brittany is to the west and Belgium to the east, so really what else would she have? And all of it heavily starched, which seems certainly like Léonie, who ties on a lace apron with large openwork, like eyeholes in a mask.

Léonie offers coffee and cider, then puts out a pot and cups, a large brown bottle and thick glass tumblers. Coffee now, Elizabeth decides, but Dominique pours glasses of cider without asking.

The kick is fast and tremendous, a warm whirling through her brain, down her spine.

I might never drink anything else, she whispers to Clara. I might never leave this kitchen.

Léonie is carving a roast chicken, uncovering a bowl of potatoes, mixing green beans with oil and vinegar. Dominique reaches into a cupboard for plates, the drawer below for cutlery. So he has been here before. Which is a clue toward nothing. But the cider is helping her decide to give in to the mystery and stop trying to understand what happened on the boat. Stop trying to know. What a relief!

This cider is a gift, she says, and Clara looks pleased.

They serve themselves, sit and eat without much conversation. When they have finished, Léonie brings out an apple tart, still warm.

Was she expecting us? Elizabeth asks Clara, who shrugs. Not like Clara at all, not to know.

Dominique pats his belly and says something about the boat. Clara translates: We will sink the boat.

Léonie does not smile. *Impossible!* she says, as if she will now explain the physics of flotation.

There is more conversation in brisk French among Dominique, Léonie, and Clara. Elizabeth cannot keep up. She takes small bites of the tart, which tastes like candied apple, and she's reminded of trips to the circus with Miss Moore, an experience from another universe. In her head, she composes the letter she will write tonight and send to Sigrid in the morning. She excuses herself to look for the WC, hoping it's not outside. Léonie points toward the bedroom.

The cider has made walking a bit of a test. The hallway is narrow and dark. Framed pictures line the walls, portraits of men and women and groups. She imagines Léonie's family, only with the faces of her own grandparents, aunts, and uncles, country people who have fished in a cold climate for hundreds of years.

On one side of the bedroom, Elizabeth sees an infant's crib, painted bright turquoise, the same shade as the door of this house. She gasps at the sight, an overwrought, slightly drunken response, but she had not expected anything like it. The smallest shard of a memory breaks loose in her head, a splinter, actually a sting if you touch it too much. The crib is empty, though the bottom sheet is wrinkled and a pair of multi-colored afghans are bunched at one end. A giraffe and another animal of indeterminate species (a bear?), both made of lace, lie nestled in the folds. Elizabeth rests her head on the crib's high rail. She can't recall any talk of a baby, a baby's appearance or departure. Léonie wouldn't have left a child alone when she rowed out to the *Sirène*. She notices now that the crib is really quite wide, larger than usual, certainly big enough for two infants.

She locks herself inside the WC, washes her hands and face in the small sink, reaches for a towel from the stack, and realizes what she holds is a baby's cloth diaper. The proper towel hangs on a hook to the left. She gazes for a long moment at her face in the mirror, wonders whether the children have died, if she should ask. Maybe Léonie is the grandmother and the children live nearby, visit regularly, nap in the crib. A nap would be nice right now. Elizabeth turns to contemplate the adult bed beside the crib, its smooth lace counterpane, the navy blue blanket folded neatly at the foot.

Back in the kitchen, the question surprises her even as she asks it. Is there a child somewhere? *Enfant?*

Dominique and Léonie exchange a glance. Their expressions soften and then mask over. It is astonishing to see, cartoonish, surreal, the flesh seeming to move, adjust into oblivion.

Sometimes, Clara says. Lately about one a week, as I understand it. From Brussels.

Goodness, Elizabeth says. Shock is an actual, physical weight—her legs feel heavy and her shoulders ache. She sits down at the kitchen table.

You're quite right, Clara tells her. Goodness, indeed. They're Jewish. Some are orphans.

But . . . then . . . Where do they go?

To Paris, most of them. To the nuns at the Convent of the Sacred Heart.

Nothing more is said. Forks scrape against plates.

The nuns drinking coffee at Café Varenne. Elizabeth feels as if she's woken with a hangover: overnight the world has become a cubist puzzle. The parts (is it a painting or a sculpture?) seem dislocated, but then the longer one stares, the more one is convinced. The parts make an argument. Normandy, the nuns, travel. Suzanne even. *Help me,* Clara had said. Clara had argued her here, piecemeal, to this place.

Do you like children? Clara had asked.

A sound comes to Elizabeth now: a child crying, a child in a crib, crying, like a gull.

I was one once.

The nuns at Café Varenne were the last piece. She sees them now, at the next table, dark blotches of fabric, sideways, inverted, irregular, the silver coins gleaming like moons in the dish beside their cups of coffee. The nuns had been taking her measure. She was not found wanting.

Elizabeth, Clara says. Come outside with me a moment.

Elizabeth follows Clara through the front door, across the lawn, onto the dock. She hopes to find the sea lion there, waiting for her. Instead there are only gulls, still as decoys, and the late sun making sharp points of light on the water. Ahead of her, Clara strides down the dock as if she plans to reach the end and keep going. Or maybe she will turn suddenly, grab Elizabeth by the collar, and hurl her into the sea. Something about this scene causes Elizabeth's chest and lungs to freeze. Some echo, following a woman in a blue coat, with her hair done up in back—*chignon* is the word—down a wooden peninsula like this one. The panic comes from what she remembers, but also from the sensation of not knowing what will happen when the woman stops and turns.

Suddenly, it is the pier at Economy Point, west of Great Village, and the woman is her mother.

Her mother turns, bends at the waist, catches Elizabeth up into her arms. Aunt Mary, who is sixteen, arrives out of breath. *Gertrude! Don't!* she cries. *Put Elizabeth down.* Then Mary covers her eyes with her hands. Gertrude Bishop has turned away to gaze out into the bay. Not the Bay of Fundy, but the smaller one, whose name is too hard to pronounce. Over her mother's shoulder, Elizabeth watches Mary.

Gertrude Bishop doesn't speak, but she is trembling, so that the chattering of her teeth makes a sound that could have meaning in actual words. Like a typewriter, Elizabeth will think years later the first time she has occasion to use one, *my mother's teeth, when she was cold or confused, sounded like this.*

Being held and being afraid to be held. Horrible, delicious, essential as physical pleasure. *I want this. I could die from this.*

Elizabeth does not believe Clara will touch her. In any case, Clara is probably not strong enough to do any great harm. Still this entire— what is the word for it?—errand here is a kind of madness. Grief appears as a woman in a blue coat, half mad, at the end of a dock, almost twilight, blue-gray water that isn't endless, not very wide.

And something else: words she might have heard all those years ago. *I shouldn't like to lose you.*

But the loss feels inevitable, as madness feels inevitable. A loved one dies, and then you go mad. Clara is an example, a literal embodiment of that causality, that truth. A loved one dies and so you go mad. Elizabeth realizes she has been waiting for it in herself, since she received news of her mother's death right before graduation. Robert's death. It hasn't come. Not yet. Gertrude Bishop driven mad by the death of her husband. Robert by Elizabeth's refusal. Clara driven mad by the death of her daughter. Elizabeth by the death of her mother. Clara and Elizabeth. They make a ragged pair. Léonie appears behind them, having made no sound.

Clara explains: The baby usually arrives on Sunday or Monday. The day workers in the orphanage leave on Friday evenings, carrying their large lunch pails, their weekend shopping in huge canvas market bags, shapeless bundles of nappies to wash at home. It's not difficult to hide a baby. They are handed off twice in Belgium, come into France by car or by boat, and travel west from there. The final destination is Paris, sometimes England, in a few cases America.

The babies are deeply loved, Clara says. A few are sick. Not a single one has died on the way.

They seem to have superhuman strength, an astonishing will to live. They are touched and spoken to constantly. Most have been separated from their mothers for only about a week before they start their travels.

Léonie says something, and Clara translates: they move hand to hand like ten-pound bars of gold.

I was sent that way, Elizabeth wants to tell them. Not secretly, though. My mother went to a kind of prison because people thought her strange and dangerous. Instead of a yellow star, she wore a blue moon, a purple nightshade, a whirling planet. She prayed in a different language, not to God, but to my father.

Elizabeth, Clara says, as if she knows what thoughts have captured and distracted her.

I'm sorry. You were saying . . . ?

We've come, Clara is saying, to bring two infants back to Paris. Two girls.

Had you planned this when I phoned you Thursday? Or before that?

I had not. But last week, I didn't know how I would manage two on my own. And then your call came, and I had my answer.

It's very convenient. Quite a coincidence.

Sometimes that happens, Clara says. Not very often. Not as often as we would like.

Elizabeth understands there is a whole universe moving inside this house. Babies delivered by women who are not their mothers to other, older women who are also not their mothers. It all sounds like a fairy tale or a fable. She could write this. But then she recalls Miss Moore's letter about her stories. *Do you think your calling is to write fables? I can't help wishing you would sometime, in some way, risk some unprotected profundity or experience. Do you think you can see the world by withdrawing from it?* The answer to these last questions is clearly supposed to be no. Elizabeth feels an odd desire to return to the bedroom and lean again on the high side of the wooden crib. What is happening in this house is no fable. *Some characteristic private defiance of the significantly detestable* was how Miss Moore defined substance. This house is substance.

nside, Léonie begins to clear the dishes, but Dominique takes her by the shoulders and steers her toward the parlor. *On y va,* he says, and Clara follows Léonie, who lights a fire in the grate and settles herself in one of the large armchairs. Clara tucks herself into a corner of the sofa, closes her eyes. In a few minutes, her breathing slows to a rhythmic whistle.

Soixante-neuf ans, Dominique says.

He means Léonie. Léonie is sixty-nine. His tone seems to imply that a woman with so many years deserves a nap. He hands Elizabeth a white lace-edged cloth and gestures that she should dry the dishes he is washing. The kitchen window looks out on the sea, a view she can almost remember from childhood—almost. North facing, nearly the same latitude, identical darker and lighter shades of blue and gray, the same west-racing doughy clouds, patches of light beaming through as if a child had poked a hole here and there to expose the blue dish underneath. Storms at sea, probably eight or ten miles out, occasionally a line of silver where the sun has sliced though the cloud cover. The silver line moves west, broadens, thins, disappears.

Je voudrais voir cette scène tous les jours, Elizabeth says.

Regarder, Dominique corrects. *Je voudrais regarder.*

He is telling her not to see, but to look at. There's a difference.

Bien sûr. Merci, Elizabeth says.

What happened to their mothers? Elizabeth asks. *Les mères?* She can't help thinking of the mothers' grief—their separate, then communal, then colossal loss. She doesn't think Dominique will understand the question, but he does.

Mystère, he says.

Are they all Jewish? *Juives?*

Dominique nods.

So, the mothers have done the most reasonable thing: they have tried to save their children. But surely it has brought them anguish. They will not know what's happened to their children. Then, suddenly, she decides this cannot be true. Certainly the orphanages would have asked for an address to send news, to keep track of which babies belonged to which mothers. In case they ever came back.

Léonie's glass tumblers are heavy and large, and Elizabeth struggles to hold on to them inside the lace-edged towel. Such things seem determined to break.

As if he's reading her thoughts, Dominique takes the tumbler from her hands and places it on the shelf beside the sink. His composure calls to mind the sailboat and the three-quarters of an hour he and Clara were occupied belowdecks and how completely unlikely it is that she has come to be in this house with three much older people who seem to be operating a kind of underground railroad for Jewish infants from Germany. Of course, she would be expected not to write to Louise or Margaret or Miss Moore or anyone else about this. Maybe by tomorrow it would all seem like a dream.

No. Tomorrow there will be infants to carry back to Paris. Or if not tomorrow, then the day after. How on earth will they manage it, on a train, with their baggage?

I will have to be the mother, Elizabeth says. Clara is too old. *Je serai la mère.*

Oui, Dominique says. He hands her another plate to dry, and then another.

Will we say they are twins? What is twins? *Deux. La même.*
Oui.

Elizabeth feels afraid, and then angry. I can't do it, she says. I've
never held a baby for more than thirty seconds, and that was long
enough and it was five years ago. *Je ne peux pas.*

C'est simple, Dominique says.

Elizabeth steps away from the sink. She believes Clara must be
out of her mind. They will have to talk it out when they get back
to the hotel in Arromanches. Elizabeth will stand her ground. Clara
should not have put her in this position. She turns to look at Clara
and Léonie, asleep, lit unevenly by the fire. Their faces are stone, like
statues in a graveyard.

That evening, after dinner and a bottle of wine, Elizabeth does not argue
or protest. Annoyance and apprehension sodden into a mild curiosity
that feels familiar. At eight o'clock, the sky goes red then salmon then
pink, hysterical color, a woman trying on shirts: not this but this, not
that, try this. Elizabeth starts toward breathlessness and wonders if she
will need an injection of adrenaline, but she knows it's not really asthma.

After she's paid the bill, Clara suggests they walk down to the marina, crowded tonight with houseboats at the docks and caravans in
the car park, the last vacationers of the season, not quite ready to go
home. Conversations hum, lanterns and cook fires glow, glasses and
bottles chime. They smell charcoal and fermented apples. The *Sirène*
rides in her slip, but Dominique does not seem to be on board. They
sit on a bench at the end of the fishing pier.

I could never live far from the sea, Elizabeth says.

Why is that?

I suppose it's what I'm used to.

All your life?

The important parts.

I imagined you'd have more questions about today.

Elizabeth sighs, feeling a clench in her chest and shoulders. I do, but I hardly know where to begin.

They sit in silence. Elizabeth knows that Clara is waiting, and she wonders at Clara's vast patience, which is not a quality she ordinarily seems to possess in abundance. A woman about Clara's age, carrying a fishing rod and tackle box, walks out of the failing light and positions herself at the railing. She open the tackle box, removes a small jar, unscrews the lid, uses whatever is inside, a slimy inert thing, to bait her hook. She casts in an awkward, sideways movement, as if she's having a seizure, and Elizabeth feels Clara tense, rise halfway off the bench. The woman draws a small flask out of her pocket, thumbs off the stopper, and takes a drink. She wipes her mouth with the back of her hand, sighs deeply.

I know, Elizabeth says quietly, as if this woman could hear her.

What's that, dear?

Dear.

Nothing, Elizabeth says. But what if I were some kind of a spy?

Don't you think I can look into that? You're nothing of the sort.

Of course. But what if I suddenly decide—

You won't, Clara says tartly. You're too busy not writing.

Elizabeth isn't sure who has said the words, Clara or herself. Or maybe the woman fishing spoke. Or something else, the voice of the fishing rod. I know what I know, the fishing rod says. But no—it's her voice, out of her mouth.

It's true. I'm not writing.

That was a guess, but I thought so.

And I have to get back to New York to not write some more. If I manage to get a book under way soon, I'll need to be there.

And your friend will be fine.

For a moment, Elizabeth wonders which friend Clara means. Margaret. The thought gives her a chill. Margaret will never be fine. The sun, huge and blinding, seems to be racing toward the horizon.

What is the name of that color? Clara says.

It would be red, Elizabeth says, except we've smudged it. Pinker than red, redder than salmon.

She doesn't say: like the insides of a fish, a live thing cut open, gutted. The living parts before they fade and stink.

The babies arrive tomorrow night, Elizabeth.

Where will we meet them?

Dieppe.

There is no talk of danger, Elizabeth notices. Which means there must be quite a lot of it.

Are you afraid, Clara?

I can't even think of that, Elizabeth. And when the time comes, you won't think of it either.

I don't know.

When you are my age, you will be lonely and puzzled about your life. You will want it to have had some meaning. Wanting that pushes everything else out of your mind. So.

Clara stands and takes hold of Elizabeth's hand.

There isn't any room for fear, Elizabeth. Dominique will take us back to Léonie's house tomorrow, and we'll go from there.

éonie slides out of the armchair, stands, and crosses the parlor to the desk. From the center drawer, she takes a pad of writing paper, which appears to be handmade, knobby grained and deckle edged, like another visitation of lace. She chooses a pencil from a basket on the desk, returns to her chair, and begins to draw. A house. The pencil's lead is sepia colored, not the ordinary dark gray. Elizabeth wonders where to buy such a pencil—she loves the way it transforms a simple line drawing. Extraordinary what color can do, even a color so mild as this one.

The house, as it is taking shape, looks like Léonie's, the very house they occupy right now. She sketches in the roof, the windows, and an old woman sitting in the window closest to the front door. Then Léonie takes the side of her hand—the right hand, which is curled around the sepia pencil—and drags it over the house, from the roof to the ground.

Hmmm? she says, and turns the sketch so Elizabeth can see it fully. The smeared pencil produces the effect of rain, rain falling on the house, blurring the outline, the sepia a kind of muted sorrow enveloping the house. Léonie draws a winding pathway circling around to the right and disappearing behind the scene. Just before the path runs out of sight, she draws a man—a few quick strokes, but that's what he is, a man wearing a brimmed hat and carrying some sort of long-handled farm tool, a rake or a shovel. Maybe a scythe? No, no curve to it. Behind the house, she draws trees, not very tall, but with many graceful branches.

Apple trees! Elizabeth says, hardly knowing where the idea has come from.

Léonie nods.

The perspective is elegant, perfect: those trees closest to the house are larger, but then they grow smaller, until the trees in the last row are the size of Elizabeth's fingernail.

Léonie stops drawing and looks at her picture, frowning. Her hand comes away from the page, turns downward as if she will smudge the rest, but then she doesn't. The man and the apple orchard remain sharp and clear. Somehow this rain falls only on the house. *Inscrutable* is the word.

Voilà, Léonie says. *Mon père.*

Elizabeth wants to ask Léonie if she can keep the picture. She loves it, the nearly disappearing father.

Et Maupassant, Léonie says.

She tells a story to Clara, who listens, delighted.

Her father, Clara says to Elizabeth, built all the furniture from applewood, even the crib. And do you know who came here once and put his grandchild into this crib? Maupassant! And the story is that his grandchild was a wakeful little monster, but he slept for hours without making a peep!

What a fantastic crib, Elizabeth thinks. Right out of a fairy tale.

Et aussi, Léonie says. She makes a fist with her right hand, as if she will punch something. Then she turns the hand over, opens it, and there in her palm is a small object, also made of applewood, with a hinge and a clasp. *Viens ici,* Léonie says, and Elizabeth leans closer. Léonie whispers and Clara laughs.

She says your hair is unruly, Elizabeth.

I have a friend who says it looks like something to pack china in.

Léonie combs through Elizabeth's hair with her fingers and attaches the clasp.

Voilà, she says, *Maintenant tu peux voir!*

Now you can see!

After the sun sets, Léonie's house turns chilly. She lights a fire in the stove, and they sit together around the kitchen table. Léonie has brought in a huge bushel of apples. She hands out paring knives, and they set to peeling the apples. Elizabeth makes a game of getting the peels off in one piece. It's slow work, and she worries she's falling behind, but then she sees Clara and Léonie are playing the game, too. Léonie is best and Clara is worst. She peels away too much apple flesh, and after a minute, Léonie stops her, demonstrates a technique that involves holding the apple as if it were scalding hot.

Ces pommes, Elizabeth says, holding up an apple. With the other hand, she points at Léonie. *C'est à vous?*

Oui, Léonie says. *Le verger de mon père. Mon grand-père, arrière-grand-père. Et alors, mon frère. Jamais les filles. Comme on dit le proverbe, les fils ont les vergers, les filles ont leurs mères.*

The sons have the orchards and the daughters have their mothers. That is the folk wisdom. What happens, Elizabeth wonders, when the folk wisdom is ignored or denied?

Disorder, suffering, chaos.

Où est votre frère? Elizabeth says, and Léonie makes a sound that's part whistle, part air rushing out of a balloon.

Her brother is a sympathizer, Clara says. He lives in Munich now. He sometimes comes to see about the orchard, but not often. He is not a pleasant person. And as you can imagine, he would not be helpful at the moment.

I n Dieppe, at four o'clock in the morning, there is not much time to waste. Clara leads Elizabeth away from the docks and up a narrow street. Dominique waits in the boat.

A woman takes shape out of the shadows, as if the night air has pulled back, drawn into itself, tightened, the way flesh does when it meets the cold.

The woman whispers something, and Elizabeth steps closer.

The woman turns slightly, reaching back into the retracted darkness. It's a magic trick: suddenly her arms are full of air, squirming breath, two bundles, the babies. Clara takes one infant into her arms, gestures to Elizabeth, *Go on, this one is for you.* The baby is large but strangely weightless, and both asleep and awake. The power to be in this middle consciousness is fascinating, otherworldly. This is what keeps babies alive: our awe.

Va-t-en, the woman says, and she freezes, as if she's heard something. Her eyes go wide, and then she shakes her head. She whispers *Merci* and slips away into the darkness.

Clara starts back down the lane toward the harbor. Elizabeth follows. Moonlight catches in the baby's eyes, disappears, returns, a small beam turned on and off. The baby is still, as if it understands what is happening. Somewhere a dog barks, and the baby startles but does not cry.

Don't trip, Elizabeth tells herself. She cannot see her feet, cannot see ahead, except for the faint outline of Clara's back. She follows Clara's breathing, the skitter of gravel. It's a straight, small alleyway, Elizabeth remembers. There will be lights on the boats in the harbor. They will hand the babies to Dominique, board the *Sirène,* cast off the lines.

Just think about what you have to do next, Clara told her earlier. Just the one next thing.

The lights on the masts might be stars. Dominique reaches for the infants—Elizabeth's first, then Clara's. He holds both babies and steps back so they can climb over the gunwale. Elizabeth's arms, empty now, feel as if they might float upward. Her teeth chatter, so she clamps her jaws shut, but then her whole head trembles.

Dominique hands the infants back, then turns to the motor. Elizabeth worries about the low rattle of the boat's engine, but everywhere in the harbor there is some sort of mechanical purring. Clara climbs below, lights an oil lamp. Clara talks softly as she unwraps the babies' swaddling. Inside this first blanket is another, and inside that, a layer of cloth diapers. Elizabeth watches from the companionway. The babies stare up at Clara. They both have halos of black curly hair. Their silence and stillness are almost alarming, but not quite because it is such a relief to have brought them safely on board. Elizabeth wonders if the babies have been given some kind of drug, a drop or two of brandy on their gums. She recognizes their peaceful state, envies it now.

Clara shows Elizabeth where their names are sewn in one corner of the innermost blanket. She calls them by their names, Rachel and Marta. Maybe there is a flicker of response.

Dominique has rigged a lee cloth above each berth, and Clara settles the babies inside.

Do you think they'd like to be together? Elizabeth says. Are they sisters?

I don't know, Clara says.

They look like twins.

It's possible, but babies at this age . . .

I don't think their hair has ever been cut.

Or combed either.

That would certainly make them cry.

Léonie will do it. She likes to care for them that way.

Don't you? Elizabeth says.

I'm not sure I can remember how to do most parts of it.

And I never learned.

Without comment, Clara moves Rachel from her lee cloth and settles her in with Marta. Their limbs crowd together. Rachel seems to nestle her head into Marta's shoulder.

That's good, Clara says. That's what they want.

Elizabeth can tell the boat has left the harbor and is moving out into open water.

Go up and sit with Dominique awhile, Clara says. So he won't fall asleep.

I can't talk to him very well.

Yes, you can. It doesn't matter if he understands you. And really, puzzling over it will keep him awake.

I guess I can point.

In the cockpit, Dominique smokes and stares out ahead into the velvety night.

Ça va? Elizabeth whispers.

Dominique gestures behind them, back toward Dieppe harbor, and shakes his head. This could mean a great many things. He does not seem agitated or hurried, fearful, furtive, all those words Elizabeth knows only in English. No matter, because he is not any of these. What can she ask him? About the girls—are they twins? That they might be twins? *Sœur* is the word for sister, but out here there is no context. She could point below: The sisters? Dominique is watching the sky, and Elizabeth follows his gaze. The stars are broken pieces of heaven. Of glare. *Les étoiles sont . . .* Time is a star. The night is making her dizzy. The night and that quick walk down the alley with stolen children who are maybe freed now. How can that be possible, to be stolen, hidden, and so to be free? Will they ever be, now that they're taken from their mother?

The hell with it. All this cogitation. What on earth does that mean anyway, free?

Dominique offers Elizabeth a cigarette. Too early, she says, and he laughs. He says a word that sounds like it might be the one that means *never.*

Jamais.

A faint flush appears along the horizon. Clara told Léonie they would return just after sunrise, so here before her is a kind of time-keeping. And then in a few hours, they will take the babies to Paris, to the convent. Maybe Margaret will be better, or at least more accustomed to her hand and its limits. Louise will be ready to go home and then to Key West. It's time.

And yet.

Dominique explains in painfully slow French what she already knows, that the babies will go to Paris. Elizabeth nods. Syllable by excruciating syllable, he asks if she likes Paris. When she nods again, he asks why.

Très belle, Elizabeth begins.

Dominique puffs out air through his pursed lips.

Might as well try in English. The art, she says. The history. Freedom. Clara's apartment. Mrs. Miller's apartment on île Saint-Louis. The light.

Another dismissive *pffft* from Dominique. *Les gens,* he says.

The people. *Oui,* Elizabeth says, *les gens.*

Les femmes, he says then.

Why, Elizabeth wonders, does the word for women catch in his throat like that?

Yes, Elizabeth says, though she wonders if he is talking about herself and Clara or the babies or something entirely different.

Now there is a fine pink line along the horizon, deepening perceptibly.

Les gens qui font le jour comme la nuit, Dominique says.

Elizabeth has heard this phrase before. Sylvia used it to talk about herself and Adrienne Monnier.

People who exchange day for night.

Elizabeth sees Léonie on the dock before she sees them. She waits at the very end, her shoes half over the edge as if she's about to dive or fall, her whole body hanging forward, listening. When the boat rounds the promontory and comes fully into view, she appears to take a step back. Elizabeth wants to bring the babies up from the cabin, raise them into the sky. Then they will all sleep, and afterwards someone—Clara—will explain how the next part is to be managed: babies in their arms and four hours on a train.

The sun breaks through a low cloud, and Elizabeth can see that Léonie is smiling, her feet pattering a little dance of anticipation. The water, illuminated this way, shudders, uncertain, as if the light is asking questions that must be dodged. Then Léonie stops moving. Elizabeth hears Clara on the companionway. She doesn't have to turn around to know that Clara is holding at least one baby and maybe both. They all four stand still as statues—Dominique, too, even as he guides the *Sirène* to Léonie's dock.

They have arrived. The boat meets the dock with a softness, like a kiss or the tail of a shooting star. Léonie asks quietly if all is well.

Presque sans faire tomber l'ancre, Dominique says. Almost without dropping anchor.

Clara calls to Elizabeth and nestles Rachel in her arms, then disappears below, returns with Marta.

Sisters, she says, as she turns toward Léonie, who nods as if she has known this all along.

The babies change hands—it *is* like armfuls of gold—and then they make an orderly, careful procession toward the blue door, the older women ahead, Elizabeth carrying the extra blankets and diapers, Dominique shadowing them.

It is either too early for whiskey, Elizabeth says, or too late.

Nonsense, Clara says. We'll have it in our coffee.

Rachel begins to cry. You're all right, Clara whispers, you're all right. You're all right.

She repeats the words over and over, as if she cannot say them enough, did not say them enough. Her voice is warm and low, a tone Elizabeth has never heard.

Rachel's head lolls as if she will dive backward out of Clara's arms. It might happen. She might think she wants to go back. She might be experiencing a spark of memory, a visitation from her mother. Rachel did not ask to go anywhere. Rachel did not ask to be saved. Clara turns suddenly—it must make the baby dizzy.

I don't know if you can have a story out of this, Elizabeth, she says. In fact, you really ought not to.

I know, Elizabeth says.

The skitter of gravel in Dieppe, the lee cloth, Dominique's cigarette. The streak of white light on the horizon. Without the word *horizon.* Without the word *child.* That is the work to be done.

Not plot but description. Let the scene and the moment make discoveries. Miss Moore said that. The blue door, the silvery wavering light, the women. It's almost as if I'm not here. That's the trick of it, to observe without comment. Not to be tentative or interior. *Risk the unprotected,* Miss Moore says. And then her old refrain: *You can't see the world by withdrawing from it.* The water in this light looks as if it's milling about—the glare is blinding. She can't see Clara, Léonie, or Dominique. A human figure doesn't have to be included to notice a scene or really say any more about it.

Léonie washes the babies one at a time in the large kitchen sink. The warm water delights them, soothes them toward sleep. Léonie cuts their hair. Elizabeth sweeps up the black curls into a dustpan, and Léonie tells her to carry it outside, let the wind take it. Elizabeth stuffs one silky ringlet into her pocket.

For a few minutes, in the applewood crib, the babies fidget and complain, but then settle. Dominique leaves the house. He will rest in the boat, Clara says, and take us back later. One by one, the three of them fall asleep. First Clara, then Léonie, then Elizabeth, who watches the other two, the flutter and giving way of eyelids. She recalls Mrs. Miller telling them one night about watching Margaret fall asleep when she was four or five. Mrs. Miller's pleasure in this moment—why was that?

A mother's pleasure is mysterious, Mrs. Miller said, *even a mystery to me. I don't know why I loved that time with Margaret.*

She described the scene in great detail (Mrs. Miller could wax poetic when she talked about her daughter): the light coming in from the hallway at a bright slant because it reflected off the glass on a photograph on the wall outside Margaret's bedroom. Margaret's profile, the perfect little upturned nose. Mrs. Miller on her side, watching, taking note. The white blanket, the shadow of the wooden mermaid hanging above the bed. And then the eyelids go, closed, then open, closed, then half open. The evening out of breath, a faint whistle, almost singing. Maybe it's that her little mind was finally still, Mrs. Miller said. Maybe because I knew for a while I wouldn't have to worry. A short while. Then I would come up with something new to keep me awake.

Sometimes, if we were at Jennings Beach, the sound of the ocean would fill the house.

Here Mrs. Miller had said something that seemed to shock her: *It felt to me that Margaret's breathing, that whistly song, was keeping the whole world alive.*

Just before falling asleep herself, Elizabeth has the feeling that she can almost—but not quite—understand what Mrs. Miller meant. But then the sense evades her, like a butterfly. Like the Spinoza she'd tried and failed to grasp in college. Ideas floating over her head, but then drifting downward again, closer, almost in reach. Her head, though, too heavy to lift, filled as it was with other barely grasped ideas. Then, this thought, half vision: There is a kind of bird who reaches into her own breast with her own sharp beak and plucks out her own feathers in order to build a nest. The kind of bird who stays with one of her young who is injured or slow to sing or fly.

Elizabeth dreams that she is on a windswept street in Paris, just where another street meets it, and the corner makes a dark cave. There is a kiosk, which no one seems to be tending. The shelves are bare except for a few old newspapers. The giant headlines are indecipherable but terrifying all the same. The wind grows colder and stronger, blowing people back into their apartments, then blowing the doors open again. Suddenly, two angels appear, their faces chalk white (Chinese white, a color she loves). Their open mouths are round black holes. The angels are carrying piles of newspapers. They shout one word, *War!* over and over.

In the dream, Elizabeth turns. She is with someone else, but she can't see who it is. Margaret? Sigrid? Louise? They see a street that stretches all the way to Africa. Lions survey them from the savannah. A bloodred sun is setting, dipping below the horizon. The lions seem to be guarding a fountain. Elizabeth realizes that this is the fountain at the Spanish Steps in Rome, then it is the place de la Concorde. The fountain fills and spills over onto the sand, not with water, but with blood.

The angels continue to cry *War! War! War!* The sound of it wakes her. The babies are hungry.

Rachel and Marta have one more journey by boat, to Port-en-Bessin. This passage is carefully timed for the train to Paris from Caen—complicated maneuvers made easier by money. Elizabeth finally understands. Money is why Clara is necessary, for her money and her connection to Pierre Laval.

It happens at first like a film running backward. Almost exactly as they entered yesterday, Elizabeth and Dominique leave Léonie's house, walk down the dock, board the *Sirène*. Clara follows, carrying Marta. Léonie is last, holding Rachel. Dominique busies himself with lines and fenders, the engine. He is wearing a cap that makes a sort of fleur-de-lis at the top. No one appears to hurry. Clara hands Marta in to Elizabeth. Her blanket spills open to reveal the lace giraffe stolen from the blue crib, clutched in Marta's little fist.

Very clever, Elizabeth whispers. Now you have a souvenir.

She wonders if Rachel has the other animal, the creature of indeterminate species. Clara steps aboard and turns to receive Rachel from Léonie. Then Léonie unties the dock line, throws it into the cockpit. Dominique reverses away from the dock, turns, motors toward the mouth of the cove. Léonie raises her hand high into the air, part wave, part salute.

Before the boat reaches open water, Clara and Elizabeth settle the babies back into the single lee cloth.

I'll stay with them, Clara says. You can go up.

On deck, Elizabeth sees that Léonie is still standing at the end of the dock. Again, from this distance, she looks very young, a girl, as if time were receding with the *Sirène*. Elizabeth tries to think how to ask Dominique when the next baby will arrive, but she can't puzzle it out. Anyway, he is probably not allowed to tell her. Or perhaps he doesn't know until he's summoned—and how does the summons arrive? She settles into the cockpit and watches him steer. Beyond him, the world is divided into pieces by the line of the mast: two-thirds sky, one-third sea. The mast itself rises like a marble pillar. The geometry is stark and odd, almost flat, since the sail is furled and the boat runs level. The sun splinters on the surface of the water, the clouds skein out above and behind. *I miss the slant perspective of a heeling boat,* Margaret said once, and Elizabeth had said, *Yes, like the view from the bed when you first wake up and you don't quite remember how you got there.*

How did I get here? What series of accidents? And the hardest part is still to come.

Dominique and the *Sirène* are a monument to stillness, to steadiness, discretion, valor, secrecy, sleight of hand. To something that hasn't happened yet but is contained inside her, in her galley-belly. The opposite of a gravestone but curiously the same, marking what is below, sheltering what's not intended to be seen.

Elizabeth feels a quietly rising terror, a heaviness gathering in her body, like the morning after drinking too much Pernod. *Mal aux cheveux.* My hairs ache. It would be very difficult now to stand up and stay standing. Time takes on the same weight. Did they leave Léonie's dock five minutes ago, or twenty-five? The mouth of the cove appears no closer.

And then, a moment later, they come through, into open sea. Léonie on the dock is a speck, the blue door slightly larger, a lozenge. Suddenly, it's as if the sound has been turned on, the volume turned up. Gulls cry from behind, from the rocks at the mouth of the cove. Some riddle of acoustics: the narrow opening of the cove must have muted the birds before. The motor chugs along, steady, healthy, sounding relieved. The gulls' cries change, as if they've flown closer, down inside the boat. It's Rachel or Marta, wanting something. Wanting someone. How does the baby sense that Clara is not her mother? Would it be by touch, by smell, the same way animals know when humans are afraid?

The only movement in Dominique's entire body: his eyes, scanning the horizon. His hands stay still, as if the tiller is moving them and not the other way around.

Elizabeth, come down here, Clara calls. I want to give you a holding lesson.

Dominique nods. He says the word that may mean sea or may mean mother.

Not holding really, Clara says as Elizabeth climbs through the companionway. You've had enough of that. It's time to learn carrying. It's a question of balance. No better place to learn than a ship at sea.

All right, Elizabeth says.

But first, the lifting. Slide your hands under her head and bottom. Like so. You have to look as though you've been doing it for some long time.

The plan is this, Clara says the next morning. Elizabeth and Dominique will stay on the boat in the harbor at Port-en-Bessin while Clara walks up to the hotel. She will go to their rooms, where the luggage has already been assembled, take a last look, then call for a porter. Downstairs, she will arrange to have their things sent ahead to Caen, to the train station, deposited there with baggage for the one o'clock train to Paris. Then she will have the hotel staff call a taxi to the harbor. The taxi will take them to the train station in Caen, where they will board the one o'clock train, on which Clara has reserved two seats, one for herself, and one for a friend who is the young mother of twin girls. The woman's name is Mme Évêque.

Évêque? Elizabeth says. How did you come up with that?

Check your Larousse, Clara says.

It's in my suitcase.

When you get back to Paris.

Elizabeth wonders for a moment why Clara doesn't just tell her, but then she is too preoccupied with holding and carrying Marta and following Clara off the boat. She almost forgets to say goodbye to Dominique. She hears him wish her good luck, and even though she is afraid to turn around, she manages. Clara, she sees, has already handed Rachel to the surprised taxi driver.

What the Man-Moth fears most he must do.

Yes. I wrote that before I had any idea, Elizabeth thinks. And then I wrote that he failed.

On the train, Clara has given Elizabeth the seat that faces the wrong direction, and Elizabeth wonders what it will be like for Marta, whose gaze is caught by the scenery rushing away from her.

The train ride—the train itself—is more dream than real. Their car moves from shadow to shadow. Massive trees hang over the tracks, elm, poplar, sycamore, walnut, maybe all of these or maybe none. Traveling at this rate, it's too hard to tell. It's evening all afternoon. Just a few passengers board at each stop. Women passengers notice Rachel and Marta, the two women holding them, the difference in their ages, taking it in all at once, inventing the story as quickly and naturally as drawing in a breath and letting it go. The conductor reads their tickets, addresses Elizabeth as Madame, and this sustains the dream, props it up with matchstick architecture that's still utterly convincing, the bold-faced lies of dreams. He clucks over the babies and says something in French to Clara that makes her smile and seem to swell with pride.

She is a very good actress, Elizabeth thinks. Not for nothing has she studied all that Shakespeare.

He said, Clara whispers, that Rachel has your eyes.

It's evening all afternoon. That line . . . Elizabeth begins to doze and has to shake herself awake. Don't let go of her, a voice says. Not Clara's voice. Not her own. It's the same voice that sometimes says *Elizabeth!* when she's drifting off to sleep, a warning, or a call to attention, or maybe just a reminder that she exists. The voice says, I grow but to divide your heart again. She wrote that, too, a long time ago, it seems. Does everybody live such divided lives, Elizabeth wonders: one self moving about the world like all the other million selves, and another that's stuck somewhere behind?

I wonder if they will remember any of this, Elizabeth says to Clara.

I expect not, Clara says. She lifts Rachel, holds her close, kisses the top of her head.

I'd like to know, though, if one day when they're seven or eight, and they're on a sailboat . . .

If what? Clara says.

If something about the motor or the motion will remind them.

Maybe. It could be any sort of ship. Or a train.

Elizabeth leans across the space between their seats. Do you think they'll keep them together? she whispers.

I don't know. I hope so.

They're such beautiful babies. I can imagine a person would say that and want two.

Yes, Clara says. And they're girls, so the nuns could—

She stops abruptly, sits back in her seat in a way Elizabeth understands to mean they ought not to be talking this way.

Every few miles, the tunnel of shade bursts open onto squares of fields, orderly, quiet, domestic as tablecloths. A few cows make a postcard tableau. Elizabeth noticed this just before the car accident, and just after, how the landscape's clarity comes from tasks performed there. The farmer moves in rows. The cows follow nose to tail in a line from barn to pasture and back again. Maybe Marta should see this, the calm order of things, to balance the vertigo in her past few days. She reaches her little hand toward the window as if to stop it sliding past. But it's too fast, dizzying, like being passed from hand to hand, house to house, father to mother to granny to aunt to cousin.

The familiarity of this sort of passage comes like an electric shock.

Oh! Elizabeth says.

What is it?

Nothing. I just remembered—

Did we forget something? Clara looks over at Marta, then down at Rachel, asleep in her lap.

No, no, Elizabeth says. It's all right.

This baby could be me, she thinks. Or I could be her. Which is it? Life and the memory of life. So close in this moment they have become each other. A child given up, let go, kidnapped. A little girl with just one name. But no. That's the mystery and the danger of these twins. They have two names, just like everyone else.

Clara, she says. Does anyone know their surname?

Clara puts her finger to her lips, quickly, as if she's blowing a kiss.

Évêque, Clara says. Same as you.

The train slows at Domfront, and there's the station, a hunched building made of gray stone that looks soft to the touch, worn by departures and arrivals. A wall of windows, for looking, for waving. At this hour, the sunlight seems to sit on the glass like paint, as if someone had wanted the blue-milky color of water at seven in the morning. A trick of light, a miracle: water hanging in the air like a curtain. Marta notices it, too, with a baby's useless concentration. It doesn't surprise her, water hanging that way. She takes note, then she looks at something else. Or does she even take note?

A few passengers rise, gather their bags, wait for the train to come to a stop and the doors to be opened by the stationmaster. Then they're gone. A brief stillness, and then the bustle of new passengers, footsteps and calling out of seat numbers. The far door to their car slides open with a metallic bang, and two German soldiers step in. The eagle emblem on the jacket is unmistakable, the small swastika pin like a red eye staring out from the collar. They seem very large, too tall for the passageway, where they stop to remove their hats. Elizabeth freezes, looks at Clara, who does not meet her eyes. Her head trembles slightly. Marta wakes suddenly, begins to cry.

The bottle, Clara says. Quickly.

But Marta does not want to drink. Clara reaches for her, and in an awkward exchange, Elizabeth takes Rachel, who looks up at her and at the luggage rack above as if she finds this shift of perspective deeply interesting. Marta's cries are piercing, shrill, an alarm.

Why are they here? Elizabeth whispers.

I'm sure they're just on their way to Paris for the exposition, Clara replies.

They make a strange pair, one olive skinned, with dark, curly hair, who looks a bit like vom Rath's friend Hermann. The other is unusually fair, with golden hair and light eyes.

The train begins to move, and the Germans shoulder their large packs and struggle their way forward awkwardly, catching hold of seat backs. They are looking for two seats together. They stop near the middle of the car. Elizabeth believes they must be asking a man seated on the aisle if he will move. The man does not—or pretends not to—understand the question or their gestures toward an empty seat across the aisle. Marta continues to wail. Other passengers stare at Clara and shake their heads, though no one seems to be angry. The dark-haired soldier grows agitated. He lifts his arm as if he will strike the man or lift him bodily out of the seat, but his companion says no, and shakes his head, lifts his chin, indicating that they should move on.

The blond German scans the rows ahead. Elizabeth understands that Marta's crying is like a beacon, distracting, distressing. They stop again, three rows away, and confer quietly. Elizabeth cannot hear what they are saying. She doubts she could understand anyway. She glances at Clara, who appears to have fixed her attention on Marta. Rachel makes a tiny sound, like a dove. Then she smiles at Elizabeth and grasps her finger. She feel Clara's body tense and looks up. The Germans are right there, both frowning.

Was ist mit dem Kind los?

She is tired, Clara says, then collects herself. *Das Kind ist müde.*

Ach du unglückliches kleines Kind. Bitte geben Sie es mir.

Es wird in Ordnung sein. Danke. Entschuldigung, Sie zu belästigen.

Ich habe auch einen Sohn. Meine Frau sagt, ich bin sehr gut Umgang mit ihm.

Clara's smile is forced. She looks at Elizabeth.

He is asking you if it's all right for him to comfort the baby, she says.

Yes, Elizabeth says as carefully as she can. She is afraid she might weep or be sick.

Rachel has closed her eyes. She is sleeping.

Clara lifts Marta out of her lap and gently places her in the German's open hands. As she's in midair, Marta begins to quiet. She coughs. Clara hands up the bottle, and the German runs the nipple along Marta's bottom lip. She drinks.

Die beiden sind Zwillinge, the dark-haired German says suddenly. He looks at Elizabeth, shakes his head in amazement. *Die Kinder müssen wie ihr Vater aussehen.*

Ja, ja, Clara says, smiling. She puts her arm around Elizabeth, draws her close. They look exactly like their father, she says.

Marta drinks hungrily. She reaches one tiny hand toward the German's face. His companion continues to stare at Rachel. Elizabeth hopes he will not ask to hold her. The train is so quiet that she wonders if she's gone deaf, except that she hears her heart pounding, echoed in the wheels of the train running over the tracks. She watches Rachel sleep. What a good thing to have a baby to look at, to divert one's attention.

Perhaps half a minute later, the German hands Marta back to Clara.

Es scheint, meine Frau hatte Recht, he says, smiling. *Es hat sich be-ruhigt. Es war mir eine Freude.* They take up their packs again and move away, looking for seats. The door between the cars wheezes open.

Danke, Clara calls after them, faintly, as if she really doesn't want to be heard. *Sie haben ein Leben gerettet.*

Elizabeth recognizes the important words as she hears them, recalls them stamped across the life-saving equipment aboard the S.S. *König-stein.* The orange jackets, the rubber rings, the inflatable dinghies hung in glass cases along the narrow passageways as if they were art. *To save a life.*

The babies are quiet. Clara's right hand on the bottle trembles. Elizabeth listens to their breathing, the four of them, the uneven rhythm, as if they were taking turns.

Though it's really you I should thank, Elizabeth, Clara says. A thousand times over.

In Gare Saint-Lazare, Clara tells Elizabeth they have one more taxi ride, not very far, a mile perhaps, to the convent. It's half past five o'clock. Not anywhere close to dark. The station is oddly silent, so that Rachel's crying echoes. She needs her diaper changed (Léonie has sent a dozen, ironed and neatly folded), so Clara takes her to the lounge while Elizabeth waits in the domed arrivals hall. Light filters in from the east. Monet painted this in 1877, this same train arriving from Normandy, over and over, twelve versions, his portrayal increasingly accurate, progressively *real.* Elizabeth and Margaret learned this in art history class. The meaning, the interpretation of the paintings came later: Monet was painting the chaos of modern life. A dirty, gritty place made beautiful, but not by the artist, not really. He's entirely forgotten. Margaret had said, Let that be a lesson to you, Elizabeth. He painted what he saw, and it's so real that it becomes abstract. Coal-burning steam engines dissolve under the light, as if light were water.

A train arriving. How ordinary. Even now. Now while the modern world slips into chaos again.

I am standing here, Elizabeth thinks, holding a child, as if it were the most ordinary thing in the world. I'm waiting. That's what everyone will think. Whether to arrive or to depart, no can really tell. No one will really care.

Clara is taking a long time, but this glacial passage of minutes is somehow comforting. For a moment, Elizabeth forgets the truth of what they're doing here. How preposterous: not that she, Elizabeth, should be carrying a child to safety, but that safety is even possible. She knows she must try not to look lost, but now Marta is squirming in her arms and beginning to whimper. She steps a little way away from their baggage, lowers herself to a bench, talking to Marta, *Now, now, there, there.* Marta starts to cry.

Elizabeth does not know what to do. She's heard both Clara and Léonie singing to the babies.

What song would you like? she whispers. I know some opera. I know some Billie Holiday. I know two different national anthems by heart. I know a few hymns. If Dominique were here, he would sing "Ave Maria."

A gendarme appears, points to the baggage, asks in French what Elizabeth assumes to be a questions about ownership. She nods, and so the gendarme busies himself carrying the bags closer to the bench. *Trop de bagages!* he says, and Elizabeth wonders how it might be possible to explain this much luggage: my friend, this child's twin. Marta is crying in earnest now, and the gendarme frowns, perhaps in sympathy, but it's hard to tell. He might have children at home. But it could also be that he is angry. It could be that he sees a different picture, how *preposterous* it is that Elizabeth could be this child's mother. He steps closer, kneels, reaches to move the blanket from Marta's face.

Très belle, he says. *Très adorable.*

He looks up at Elizabeth. He asks if she speaks French.

A little, she says. *Un peu.*

Elle a faim, he says. He speaks very slowly, a bit too loud, as if Elizabeth might be deaf. He raises his right hand, presses the tips of his fingers together, and brings them to his lips. He moves his jaw as if chewing. Eating, hungry, yes, yes.

Elizabeth points toward the baggage with an awkward jutting of her left elbow. She doesn't dare loosen her grip on Marta. The gendarme stands, lifts the bags one by one, until Elizabeth nods to show he's found the one with the bottles. He brings over the small satchel, sets it on the bench beside her, begins to undo the snaps. Elizabeth tries to think what else, what damning item, might be in this bag. The bottle of jenever. A notebook. She tries to recall what's written on the first page. Or on the last. If anyone opened a notebook, that's what they would read, the start and the finish. Unless they're looking for something specific, something incriminating, some words they can bend to suit their suspicions.

Ah, the gendarme says. He draws Marta's bottle out of the bag, raises the bottle to the light, as if it were wine in a glass. He frowns at the bottle, at Elizabeth.

Pas de lait? he says.

Elizabeth shakes her head. A long journey, she says. Milk might spoil. *Acide. Très mal.*

Ah, he says again. He hands her the bottle. He waits.

Now, surely, he will see she is not this child's mother, an imposter. Marta's crying grows louder. She can see the bottle, but it isn't close enough. Elizabeth tries to remember how to do it, touch the nipple to Marta's lower lip, gently, so that she will think it's her own idea to drink. That's what Clara said: you have to make them believe it's all their doing. That's how they learn, by thinking they already know what they want.

The gendarme is still watching. Marta's mouth is closed in a tight, angry line. Talk to her, too, Clara had said. Tell her what a good girl she is, how smart, how beautiful, how sweet.

Elizabeth begins to say these things. At first she doesn't recognize the voice that comes out of her mouth. She listens to the words even as she's saying them. It's a little like falling out of one's own body (imagine that, but not now).

Sweet child, beautiful girl.

The sound of her voice seems to create more sound, but it is really that the station is beginning to fill with people leaving work, everyone rushing to catch a train, going home.

Elizabeth doesn't look at the gendarme. She couldn't see him if she wanted to. She's gone from here, from Gare Saint-Lazare, gone from time. No, she's inside time, Elizabeth and Marta alone inside a giant clock. Marta's blue eyes fixed on, fallen into Elizabeth's. She seems to forget about crying. She opens her mouth, as if to smile, and takes the bottle. She drinks as if she will never get enough

Elizabeth is still talking. The words come in a stream, like the sugar water into Marta's mouth. Sweet girl, beautiful child.

That voice. Thirsty, thirsty.

Then she's seized by a memory so vivid, she nearly lets go of the baby. Another voice, harsh and sudden as thunder. *No, Elizabeth. Don't touch that.*

She is very thirsty. There is a fire in Great Village. Many people have lost their homes. She wants something she cannot have. She is three years old.

Oh, Elizabeth says, Mama.

The word feels pressed up from her lungs, into her throat.

Mama.

Then to Marta she says, Mama's here.

Marta is drinking happily, and Elizabeth finds the courage to look up at the gendarme, who smiles, speaks gently. Elizabeth believes he must be talking about his own children. She listens intently, trying to get a few words. His children have children—that's it. His wistful expression would match that statement. He is, she sees now, of grandfatherly age and disposition. He has the prominent French nose, like de Gaulle, large ears that do not lie flat against his skull. She likes this face. It has come to be a comfort. The uniform, too, the fringed epaulets.

The gendarme is asking a question now. Where? Where are you going?

Into Paris, Elizabeth says.

He is puzzled, she knows, because of course she is already in Paris.

I have need of a taxi, Elizabeth says in slow, painful French, thinking he will leave to find a taxi and never come back. Clara will return, and they will gather the bags and go. Instead, he calls for a porter, who brings a cart and begins to load the luggage. This might take a long time, but of course the porter is an expert. The bags are quickly loaded, and the porter directs the cart toward the taxi stand. The gendarme steps closer, slides his hand under Elizabeth's elbow. His breath and his jacket smell of peppermint and tobacco. He is large—she has not really noticed this before—and strong. He might lift her, with Marta, into the air, hold them aloft over the heads of all the travelers in the station. She can almost feel her feet rise off the floor.

Elizabeth! Clara says. What are you doing?

A taxi, Elizabeth says. It's been arranged. The baggage is waiting.

The gendarme turns, takes in Clara with Rachel in her arms. He begins to laugh.

Deux! he says. He understands the situation immediately, just as Léonie had imagined. *Venez, Madame,* he says to Clara, *on y va!*

Behind him suddenly, there is a flash of color, an enormous bouquet of flowers, a man carrying them, two men, their separate angular darknesses broken by splashes of pink and yellow and purple. The man carrying the bouquet looks at her—Elizabeth feels as if she's waking from a dream; here is Ernst vom Rath and the Polish boy beside him. Vom Rath stops, stands perfectly still, trying to get the meaning of it, Elizabeth in Gare Saint-Lazare, feeding an infant while a gendarme looks on. Now I am done for, Elizabeth thinks. She knows she should bow her head, hide her face somehow. But she can't. She finds it impossible to look away from these two men and all the flowers.

The longer she stares at vom Rath, the more completely he will understand that they are two people who find themselves in a moment that has outrun them, engulfed them, that they are moving pieces in a frightening, hideous game, and they must keep moving, silently, or else everyone, many people they do not even know, will be undone, betrayed, and killed. Vom Rath is the only person who might talk about what Elizabeth is doing, but in this moment, they reach some agreement. He points at something on the other side of the arrivals hall, and the Polish boy turns that way, and vom Rath follows.

Vom Rath will never talk about what he has seen, and fourteen months later, he will never talk about anything because he is dead.

This taxi is a fortress. It is warm, slightly musty, like the house of an elderly relative. The seat covers a bit frayed, but really quite soft. The faint smell of food—Sunday dinner. The gendarme from the station watches them go, a misty-eyed grandfather.

Will we take them to your apartment? Elizabeth asks.

Of course not, Clara says.

She has, Elizabeth notes, resumed her old persona: tart, dismissive, Parisian Clara.

If you take them home, Elizabeth, you will fall in love with them. And then no one will be safe.

I think maybe I already have.

You must not do that. You must turn your feelings off this instant. It's a spigot, Elizabeth. Twist it to the right. Hard.

Marta has dropped the lace giraffe. Elizabeth wants to give it back, but the child does not seem to want it. She slides the toy into her coat pocket.

Inside the convent, the exchange goes very fast: quite suddenly, Elizabeth's arms are empty, and Clara's, too, and half their bags, swept away by three older nuns who seem to have been waiting just inside the door when they ring the bell.

A young nun, perhaps a novice, leads them to a sitting room and leaves them. Clara stands very close to Elizabeth, as if she will maneuver them into an embrace

Very well done, Elizabeth, she says.

Thank you. What will happen now?

She said we should wait here. I don't know. Perhaps someone wants to speak to us.

The room is comfortably furnished with chintz-covered armchairs, a green sofa, two low tables. A fire burns in the fireplace, though it's summer. Across the room is a small cabinet that in any other place would hold liquor and glasses. Above it, a mirror framed by happy cherubs. Directly across, the nuns have placed another mirror, so the effect is telescoping endlessness, maybe meant to signify eternity. The other walls are decorated with pastoral scenes and still lifes. In fact, Elizabeth notices the only religious artifact is a small crucifix above the door, the Christ's feet dangling below the door frame.

This is where the girls tell their families goodbye, Clara says suddenly. This room has seen a thousand tears.

I didn't think of that. I almost wish I didn't know.

I'm sorry.

From far away, deep in the center of the house, they hear the wail of an infant.

I think that's Marta, Elizabeth says.

I don't know, Clara says. There might be other children, too.

But Elizabeth is sure.

And suddenly then the memory from the station is complete. She is three years old, in Great Village. She is standing in her crib. She is very thirsty. She is crying for her mother, whom she can see out the window, walking across the lawn below, back and forth, handing out coffee and water to people who have fled the fire. Elizabeth can't understand why her mother won't look up at the window, won't leave those people on the lawn, rush upstairs, lift Elizabeth into her arms, give her something to drink. She doesn't understand. She will never understand. Who is this *she*? Elizabeth? Or her distracted mother?

And then the end of the memory: the scolding voice. The next day, out on the trampled lawn, a woman's silk stocking glitters, gossamer with dew, as if a fairy queen had left her leg behind (somehow not awful or frightening, this lost limb). Elizabeth picks up the toe, expecting the leg to amplify and make an entire shining body. The anticipation is delicious.

From across the yard, her mother screams.

No! Elizabeth! No! Put that down!

The voice is cruel. Elizabeth hears that now. She knows her mother couldn't help herself. Deranged by grief, made vicious and desperate, like a wounded animal. Frightened. That voice kept her away: *No, Elizabeth!* As if the question were always, May I come to you? May I see you?

No, Elizabeth! No!

Something has broken, Clara says. She steps between the sofa and the table, bends to pick a small piece of glass out of the rug.

Oh! Elizabeth says.

You don't want to know the story of that, Clara says.

Elizabeth closes her eyes. No, she tells herself. If you knew, you would never stop thinking about it. It would never leave you alone.

When I traveled in Spain, I learned a word for this. For what we are doing. *Criado*. It means brought up in the family. The English is nicer: daughter of creation.

That is nice. Daughter of creation. A child created.

Exactly, Clara says.

Maybe that's what we all are.

Perhaps, Clara says. I'll send you home now, Elizabeth. Wherever that may be.

GEOGRAPHY IV

≥≡ 1937 ≡≤

E lizabeth feels as if she's been away from Paris for a lifetime, a century. Margaret, Louise, Mrs. Miller, all ask the usual questions: *What did you do? Where did you stay? Whom did you see?* She is very careful about the answers.

We sailed.

We stayed in Arromanches.

I saw perhaps too much of Clara.

The unsaid catches in her throat. One particular phrase that comes out of nowhere: *I saw the dark ajar.* The alley in Dieppe where Rachel and Marta were put into their arms. The unlit streets with their treacherous, uneven cobblestones. That gutting, wordless fear. She would say she saw a door cracked open and just inside, the cruelty of the Germans, the black heart of their intentions. She would say this. Not all Germans, of course. Not Sigrid, though she is a puzzle, will never be completely known. Elizabeth sees her now with clear eyes— this feels literally true—as if Sigrid has stepped from behind a veil, as if Elizabeth has scrubbed her own vision clean. This is what the nuns must believe: that mystery is a fact.

Elizabeth lifts her suitcase onto the bed in the Millers' apartment and begins to unpack. Louise comes to stand in the doorway, and Elizabeth worries that some small strange trinket will fly up out of the contents. She knows this is foolish, but still she angles herself so that

Louise can't see what she's unfolding, sorting. Her clothes still have the bitter tang of marine air.

You were missed, Louise says. But we went to Versailles without you. It was dusty.

Then it's just as well, Elizabeth says.

Josephine Baker is back. She got married to a businessman.

Are you heartbroken?

I'll get over it.

I'm sure you will, Elizabeth says. She tries to look Louise in the eye and smile, but she feels not quite in full control of her expression.

I met someone interesting, Louise says. Natalie Barney. Remember? The Friday salon on rue Jacob? The countess said she would make an introduction.

Elizabeth feels as if the countess and Clara cannot possibly be the same person.

I remember.

She's speaking next week at Sylvia's. We should go.

All right.

Elizabeth, what's wrong?

I think I'm just tired. You can imagine what it's like keeping up with Clara.

Did she make you do all the sailing?

Not all of it.

Louise sits down on the bed, then stretches out beside the open suitcase. She crosses her arms behind her head, glances down into the suitcase, frowns. Elizabeth wonders what she sees.

You need some new clothes, Louise says. I swear you had these the year I met you.

I probably did.

Louise sighs. Margaret seems better, she says. Her mother found a new surgeon. They all feel hopeful. Margaret actually went with us to the opening ceremonies for the International Exposition. She said she thought the fireworks were a bit too operatic.

That sounds like the old Margaret, Elizabeth says. She stops rummaging in her suitcase. She's come across no evidence to suggest she and Clara did anything besides sail and fish and take in the sea views. She smiles at Louise, considers all that is unspoken between them, years now of assumptions and omissions, averted gazes, privacy.

You know me so well, she says.

Do I? Louise asks.

Sigrid telephones to welcome Elizabeth home. She uses the exact word, *home,* as though Elizabeth lives in Paris now and always will. Her voice is warm, confiding, intimate. She does not ask the usual questions about Elizabeth's trip. This is a both a relief and a puzzle, almost a physical sensation.

How did you know I was back? she asks.

A photographer from Berlin was in the embassy, Sigrid says. She knows Americans. It is like a web connecting all of you.

I'm not sure I like the idea, Elizabeth says. She feels powerfully the need to see Sigrid, to read her expression as she talks about this photographer.

A film has just opened at the Marivaux, Sigrid tells her then. Near the Opéra Garnier. *La Grande Illusion.* Everyone is raving about it, but the German ambassador has forbidden his staff to go. German soldiers are depicted as cruel. Jews are good. It has been viciously denounced by the Nazis. Vom Rath has said it is brilliant.

Would you like to come with me? she asks.

That seems reckless, Elizabeth says. What if someone sees you?

I will think about that. Meet me there, please. Outside. Maybe I won't go in.

All right, Elizabeth says.

There is a show at six o'clock.

Elizabeth replaces the receiver in its cradle and gazes at her reflection in the hallway mirror. Impassive. She recalls using that word to describe her first conversation with Miss Moore. No. *Impersonal.* She's noticed this in photographs—detachment, the impression that's she's just about to turn her head away from the camera, walk out of its range. Except now there's something else in the face looking back at her, some worry, some plea that has not been there before.

Even though the crowds have spilled east from the exposition, and the boulevard des Italiens is roiling with people, Elizabeth cannot imagine Sigrid wouldn't be observed. She is wearing a dark blue suit, which makes her hair appear brighter, a fiery burnt orange. She is one of the only women on the street without a hat. They shake hands.

You would be foolish to go into the theater, Elizabeth says.

You look at me too hard, Sigrid replies.

I think when he comes to Paris, Hitler will be afraid of you and change his mind.

About what?

About everything.

He is incapable of changing his mind.

It's too late now, Elizabeth says. The film will have already started.

You arrived late on purpose.

What if I did?

It's good of you to save me from myself.

Behind the Marivaux there are benches in a small, shady park. Sigrid suggests they sit for a half hour before she makes her way north to Saint-Denis.

The photographer is called Gisèle Freund, Sigrid says. She fled to

France with Bertolt Brecht and Walter Benjamin when Berlin became too dangerous for Jews. There is a story that she left Berlin with her negatives strapped to her body, under her clothes, so that she would not have to surrender them to the Nazis.

Elizabeth imagines the slick negatives pressed against the skin, their edges like razors. Suddenly, blood through one's clothes, betrayal like stigmata.

Americans have helped her make a marriage of convenience, Sigrid says. The man is very sympathetic, very friendly.

How odd to do that, Elizabeth says.

But necessary. I heard she is interested in making photographs of writers, so I told her about you.

Elizabeth does not want to be photographed, especially not by someone so serious.

I don't think so, she says.

I can take you there, Sigrid says. But I suspect you know the way yourself. She lives above Sylvia Beach's bookshop.

How interesting, Elizabeth says. I'm going there anyway, when Sylvia returns from America. She is going to lend me a typewriter.

Sigrid smiles, pats Elizabeth on the knee.

You already knew that, didn't you?

As I told you, Sigrid says, you're in a web.

The idea makes Elizabeth go cold all over. Her bones feel as if they've frozen. She can almost see them, long white icebergs floating beneath her skin.

f one stands at the Palais de Chaillot facing south, the view of the Paris Exposition is terrifying: the German Pavilion to the east, the Soviet Union's to the west, and the Eiffel Tower just below, or so it seems from this perspective. Really the Eiffel Tower is *beyond,* cast away, half forgotten. The two pavilions appear to glare at each other. The Eiffel Tower looks on, helpless.

But there's something else, Margaret says. Look. It's as if the Soviets are trying to capture the Nazi eagle. And the eagle wants to devour them, or at least claw their eyes out.

And what will the Eiffel Tower do? Elizabeth asks.

It's very formal, Louise says. Very upright. Stiff.

It's a nightmare, Margaret says.

But how terribly French, Louise says. The Eiffel Tower is what gets you out of the nightmare.

What do you mean? Margaret says.

She means Paris is unfailingly heroic, Elizabeth says. They join the crowds wandering through the Trocadéro.

I don't want to see either of those two pavilions, Louise says. I don't really want to see Spain and that hideous Picasso.

Of course you do, Margaret says.

But in the end, they can't stay away from the Spanish Pavilion. Or it may be they have just let the crowd push them along, up the inclined ramp, through the steel doors, past the photograph montage, which is frame after frame of dead children, and upstairs to the second floor and to *Guernica*. In some ways the painting makes more physical sense than the photographs: humans bent sideways, deformed and broken, rather than dead in one piece. It's certainly more horrifying. Elizabeth has to look away, turn her back for a moment. Just beyond is Mr. Calder's fountain. Right there, so people would have something to turn to from *Guernica,* a reprieve, an object of beauty.

A guide explains that the piece protests the mistreatment of workers in the mercury mines at Almadén, Spain, but Elizabeth has to put that out of her mind.

In one hundred years, Elizabeth says to Louise, this fountain will still be beautiful. That—she tips her head backward to indicate the *Guernica*—will not.

It will, though, Margaret says. It's supposed to disturb you.

This doesn't disturb me, though, Elizabeth says. They stare at the Mercury Fountain, the plod of its fluid mechanics.

The difference is the location of the violence, Margaret says. That's all. In the painting it's already there. In Calder's fountain, violence is waiting just outside.

It makes you prefer mercury to water, Louise says. Which seems dangerous.

The fountain is made mostly of glass and polished steel, because mercury would corrode any other material. Elizabeth thinks about Miss Moore and her fascination with tattoos, the idea of something under your skin that could poison you but somehow does not. Pipes from the pump and reservoir run under the paving stones to the ground floor. The fountain's basin is concrete lined with pitch, making a flat black surface that contrasts with the sheen of the mercury, a better balance than the glass or the polished steel.

Pitch will not corrode, the guide says.

I wonder, Louise says, why nature made that so.

The mercury spews onto a warped plate, then pours out of a weir onto a second plate, a smoother surface, so that it appears to be flowing into a sort of lagoon. The third plate is actually a chute and a dam, forming a pool into which the mercury spills. From there, it's returned to the center of the basin. The flat pooling surfaces are balanced by two rods attached to the plates so that they sway when the mercury hits them. A red disc hangs from one of the rods. The metaphor is obvious: spilled blood.

The name of the mine, *Almadén,* fashioned from twisted wire, hangs from the other. A line of poetry begins to take shape in Elizabeth's head, even as she refuses it: no, no, not another one about some Parisian mechanical oddity.

Guides tell the tale of the mercury's arrival, in English, in French, in German and Spanish, a fugue of a story. The driver got lost navigating around the pavilions, and so the truck was late. Calder and Sert the architect began to believe that the mercury had been lost or stolen, and the exhibit would be a disaster. But finally they saw the truck in the distance, making its tortured way through the Trocadéro. The driver emerged from the cab, cursing them, cursing Parisians, cursing whatever was in the two hundred tiny cylinders, demanding twice the promised fee. He refused to unlock the rear door of his truck. Picasso's wife, Olga, led the driver into a nearby café and bought him glasses of wine until he agreed to give up his keys. Olga arranged with the waiter that the driver should eat and drink all he wanted, and if he fell asleep, he should be tucked into the banquette and allowed to stay.

Now watch, the guides say in their cacophony of languages. Everyone in the room turns toward the fountain, one group at a time, a dance, a ballet, perfectly choreographed. Tourists continue to stream through the doorway, admire *Guernica,* then the fountain. Some visitors seem not to understand or to care that the flowing element is mercury and not water, and they toss coins into the silvery pool.

For the children of Spain, the guide whispers, the little ones poisoned by mercury, we collect three hundred francs a day.

If we keep an open mind, Natalie Barney says, too much is likely to fall into it.

The crowd in Sylvia Beach's bookshop stills for a moment, then laughs somewhat uncertainly. From the large green velvet armchair at the front of the room, Miss Barney looks pleased. She spies Louise in the doorway, waves to her. Then she folds her hands in her lap and waits. She looks, Elizabeth realizes, like middle-aged Oscar Wilde. There was a story that he had saved her, when she was five, from a gang of marauding boys.

Miss Barney, Sylvia says, surely you don't really believe that?

I mean it in a certain way. Sometimes it's all right for the mind to be closed. To have one's mind made up. But you didn't ask me here to talk about that, Sylvia. You said I should talk about the modern world. And so I shall.

Miss Barney stops talking, gazes at the ceiling. I believe, she says, that we will have a war with Germany. Another one. Not tomorrow. Maybe not next year. But soon enough.

Clara, Elizabeth thinks, should be here. She looks at the backs of women's heads. She counts ten rows and ten heads in each. She does not believe any one of them belongs to Clara, and that is a relief. She wonders what she would say to Clara—how she could possibly act as if they had simply gone on holiday together.

And I have had an odd realization, Natalie Barney continues. Women are simply not interested in the war effort.

An uncomfortable silence settles into the room, like fog. Heads bow as if in prayer.

If women are not heart and soul, as well as bodily, in this war, as they were in the former one, why don't they speak up, instead of letting it be forced upon them? Violent death, rotting corpses, cold rain, mud inside your shoes, in your hair, in your nose—the men can write about that. But this war—the one that's inevitable, why aren't women talking about it? The government asks for our services, but not for our opinions. English women have got the vote, but it's symbolic rather than functional. I don't understand why men want to wage war and kill. Look at that Nazi bird. That's what I mean. *Reichsadler.* What kind of animal is that?

There must be female eagles, Elizabeth says quietly.

Liberty is a woman, Miss Barney says. Wisdom is a woman. Love is a woman.

Hunting is a woman, Louise whispers.

Amazons, Elizabeth whispers back.

Obviously, Miss Barney is saying, there is some satisfaction in fighting that women have never enjoyed.

Elizabeth can't quite get the eagle image out of her head—its cruel feet, the glare of its stupid eyes, all anger and no depth. Is there a male bird that is always male? A bird without a female of the species who's simply less colorful? With a completely different name? She can't think of any. Miss Moore would know. And then it comes to her: a rooster. So much arrogance over a cockscomb and a wattle. And the poor hen's life: courted when necessary, then despised and stuffed in a henhouse.

Why this horrible insistence on bloodshed? Miss Barney says. And senseless orders telling us we have to get up and stop dreaming. And for what? To be flung on a pile of stinking bodies and forgotten. Fighting is worse than whoring, some people say, so why is one against the law and not the other? How, pray, is fighting worse? Whores don't kill anyone.

At least not on purpose, Louise says.

We women can't hide behind the wallpaper, Miss Barney continues. There will be fighting there, too. I mean fighting at home. The war will come into the home. Women will not be safe. Women's frivolity, my own included, disappoints me. Do not let this war be forced upon you.

Elizabeth turns and makes her way back into the bookstore proper, the orderly shelves, the reverent hush of reading. She feels shaken, ill, desperately in need of air. She hears Louise call her name, but she does not stop until she's outside, on rue de l'Odéon.

You're not well, Louise says. I'll find a taxi.

No, Elizabeth says. Thank you. I need to walk.

As far as that café, Louise says, pointing up the street. Not a step farther. We'll have something to drink. See if that helps.

I don't know, Elizabeth says.

What she fears most is that she will have one drink and then another, and then she will lose her resolve and begin to talk about Clara and the babies, the train ride, the soldiers, all of it. At Le Comptoir, Elizabeth insists they sit inside, at the far end of the bar, where there is some privacy. The bartender serves their beers—the large ones called *formidables*—with a disapproving shake of her head. Elizabeth tries to drink slowly.

What Natalie Barney said, she begins. About frivolity. I wish I were writing.

Have you thought about psychoanalysis? Louise says. I've heard it can work wonders. You'll write better and more easily.

If I wrote more easily, Elizabeth says, I wouldn't recognize myself.

And as for *better*. Well, I would like that very much, but I'm not sure it's possible.

Maybe you need to go home?

I need a typewriter, Elizabeth says. Sylvia wrote to me about it. I can have hers. Now that she's back from America. I meant to say something to her tonight, but well . . .

Drink got to you first, Louise says, tapping the side of Elizabeth's glass.

Elizabeth raises the glass. It's empty. The urge to talk about Clara passes. She can feel it drain away incrementally, as if it were an ache driven out by medicine.

Elizabeth and Sigrid stand outside Sylvia's apartment on rue de l'Odéon. They hear shouting, then loud weeping, then silence. Elizabeth lifts her hand to press the bell. The ringing drowns under the splinter and splash of glass shattering.

No typewriter today, Sigrid says.

But I need it, Elizabeth says.

A tall woman with a small, ironic mouth and wild black hair lets herself out of the building. She carries a large box camera, a Leica. Elizabeth understands that this must be Gisèle. She speaks to Sigrid in German. She seems to be laughing, but then there are tears in her eyes.

Gisèle asks if she can take your photograph instead, Sigrid says. Instead of Sylvia's. Instead of the typewriter.

The last thing Elizabeth expected today was to be photographed. Still, she has come all the way here from Mrs. Miller's apartment, trusting that tomorrow she would start writing again, the typewriter her mechanical muse, as Louise put it.

Gisèle says, Sigrid continues, you have a face like a heart. Like a child also.

Gisèle steps between them, links her arms through theirs.

On y va, she says, leading them across the street to Sylvia's bookstore. Inside, she roams from one end of the room to the other, like a great lioness, calculating the strength and angle of the sunlight. She poses Elizabeth by the front window so that the afternoon light falls on the right side of her face. Elizabeth cannot see the effect, but she can tell from Sigrid's expression, a gaze of horror and interest, that something alarming is about to happen.

Is it that bad? Elizabeth says.

Sigrid says nothing.

Gut, Gisèle says.

Behind Gisèle, Elizabeth notices a silver frame, and in it what she at first believes to be a picture of a corpse, a chalk-white face, eyes startled open by death, a shadow looming off to the left. The picture is familiar, her cousin Arthur, or her father, though she couldn't really remember that face, those peeled-open eyes. It's as if she's gone into time and gotten stuck there. The image blinks, and then she understands—she's looking into a mirror. Elizabeth cannot feel her own eyes in her head: the mirror has stolen her away. Or that old trick: two mirrors facing each other make an infinity of images. That's what she feels—infinitely away—even surrounded by these two beautiful Germans. Or maybe because of that, because their beauty makes her feel invisible.

Sylvie est triste? Elizabeth says. Sigrid translates, and Gisèle shrugs. Elizabeth listens patiently to another exchange in ricocheting German between Sigrid and Gisèle.

Gisèle thinks Sylvia was away too long, Sigrid says.

But she was ill, Elizabeth says. And before that, her father was ill. And then he died.

Gisèle is behind her camera, where no illness can reach her. Elizabeth remembers that Sylvia and Adrienne said this: as a photographer, Gisèle was very powerful. She could get her subjects to do whatever she asked, beyond reason and decorum. They would embrace strangers, take off their clothes, strike shocking and erotic poses. Gisèle could make them become symbols, Sylvia had said, but Adrienne had corrected her. *Ironique,* she had insisted.

Elizabeth wonders if she is becoming ironic right now, her face half in shadow.

As if summoned by this thought, Sylvia steps out of the building across the street, into the sun, and shields her eyes, even though she is wearing dark glasses. She grips a suitcase. She glances down at her wristwatch, then stares, drops the suitcase, and taps furiously on the face of the watch with the first two fingers of her right hand.

Vater Armbanduhr, Gisèle says.

Sigrid translates: her father's watch.

And it decides to stop now, Elizabeth says quietly. She looks away from Gisèle and Sigrid, watches Sylvia remove her sunglasses and fasten her gaze on Elizabeth. Gisèle snaps the picture.

The photograph that will come out of this moment is one of the few Elizabeth likes of herself. She looks different, older. Thinner and fearless. Changed.

Sylvia lifts the suitcase again and starts across the street. Gisèle lowers the camera and watches her approach with great apprehension. At the last minute, she raises the camera to cover her face, as if expecting to be slapped or punched. Sylvia pushes open the door, shoves her suitcase inside.

There's an apartment upstairs, Sylvia says, but no kitchen. May I come over sometimes for dinner?

Mais oui, Gisèle says. And lunch, she adds, in English.

I'll be at work then, Sylvia says.

Elizabeth hears this exchange, but she's also studying Gisèle and Sigrid, the way they fill the shadow in the room, fill it in really, so that the two of them, in their dark jackets, seem to be joined, the space between them elided, run together, made whole. She feels cold. These tall, beautiful women from that dangerous country. They understand each other perfectly. Nothing new to learn. She can almost see them, alone with each other, an upstairs room, light pouring over their bodies.

Be careful, Sylvia says, as if to everyone. She begins to climb the stairs, then stops.

Ça va? Gisèle says.

Elizabeth, Sylvia says. The typewriter. I have it for you up here. Come take a look. Your friend can come, too.

Elizabeth breaks from the pose, steps out of the mirror's frame, and follows Sylvia. At the foot of the stairs, she turns to wait for Sigrid.

A moment, Sigrid says. She and Gisèle have not moved.

The apartment upstairs is one room, a sink, a folding screen in front of the toilet.

I wouldn't want a kitchen anyway, Sylvia says. What if something caught fire? All the books.

Adrienne has a kitchen above her shop, Elizabeth says.

Adrienne prefers to take chances. Isn't that obvious?

There's no sound from below. Sylvia and Elizabeth exchange a long look. Then downstairs, the shop door opens. Elizabeth walks to the window, watches as Gisèle crosses back to Adrienne's apartment building and disappears inside.

Sylvia rubs her eyes with the heels of her hands. She lets out a sob that's as piercing as a siren.

She's gone to Adrienne, Sylvia says, because she's afraid. And Adrienne is afraid. I can go back to America, but Adrienne has to stay here. She knows what's coming. Gisèle has already been through it, with the Nazis, when she got out of Berlin. They think I'm lucky. Or they think I'll betray them. They think Americans can't keep secrets, that under the least pressure, we'll tell anybody anything they want to hear.

Elizabeth would like to put her arms around Sylvia, but she finds she cannot move.

Do you think that's true, Elizabeth?

I hope not, Elizabeth says. But I hope I'm never tested.

In Le Boeuf sur le Toit, there is loud music and frenetic dancing, and, in the corner farthest from the door, André Gide presides over a table of men in evening dress. Vom Rath guides Elizabeth and Sigrid to a table halfway into the room. He orders a bottle of champagne. He gazes steadily at Elizabeth, but not in any meaningful way, and she wonders if he even recognized her in the Gare du Nord. The doe-eyed Polish boy materializes out of the noise and cigarette smoke and takes the fourth seat, beside vom Rath, who does not seem to notice. Vom Rath is waiting for something, not the champagne, and Elizabeth realizes he is waiting to be seen. And then he is observed, recognized, like a kind of percussive burst. Men rise from their chairs, step away from the bar, helplessly, drawn to the table. They kiss vom Rath on both cheeks and then again, they offer cigarettes, a few set down sweating glasses. They have been waiting for him, these drinks clutched in their hands for some time, hours maybe. Vom Rath introduces some— Jean-Luc, Matthieu, Pierre, Victor—but not others. The champagne arrives, and the waiter fills their glasses.

Racontez-moi, vom Rath says in a theatrical whisper, *les cancans!*

Magda Fontanges, Victor says. He tells the story in French and then translates for Elizabeth. She shot the French ambassador, the count de Chambrun.

Oh! Elizabeth says. That's Clara's brother-in-law!

You know him? Victor says. He grips Elizabeth's hand.

Not really.

Victor's grip relaxes. Magda was Mussolini's lover, he says, but the count warned him against her. Her lawyer reads from her diary. Mussolini tells her she is better than Ethiopia.

Vom Rath places his right hand over his heart. Magda, *la belle pute,* he says.

Monsieur! S'il vous plaît! Sigrid says, gesturing toward Elizabeth.

Pardon, vom Rath says. He lifts the champagne bottle from the bucket, refills Elizabeth's glass, speaks to Sigrid in German.

He says he's very sorry, Sigrid tells Elizabeth. He forgot you were here. *Il y a poli de chinois.* The men laugh wildly and Sigrid looks pleased with herself.

I don't think I want to know what that means, Elizabeth says.

Sigrid promises to tell her later.

To be taken by storm, to be kissed on the throat, to have her undone hair falling around us like a curtain, to lie on top of her, to feel her skin is mine, to feel her body shake, the pulsing at her very core, to believe she is fighting me, to believe she is both close and far, far away, to kiss her eyelids, to shock her into ecstasy, to remove her clothes without unbuttoning, her hands inside my blouse, the cool of the sheets, the fiery rub of blankets, the tick of a fan keeping time with our bodies, the rest of the world silenced as if we were underwater, except for her breathing, the sighs that break into sound from her belly to her chest to her throat and out into the air between us, the moment just before and just after. Her shoes across the room, one on its side, the inner sole lolling like a tongue. Her tongue, pointed like the head of a snake, and relentless. Clothes pooled on the floor, a painter's palette, daubs of clothes, all over the room. Don't pick them up yet. Don't pick them up ever.

*   *   *

They are cruel, Sigrid says, the führer and Mussolini. In all the photographs, they hold a stick or a riding crop. To beat someone. This gives them pleasure. I think sometimes what they want is not about the country, really. They want to violate. It is like sex. They want to shove everyone up against a wall in a dark room. They want this very badly, no matter the consequences. And certain sorts of people make them very nervous. People who have unusual magic.

Who? says Elizabeth, fascinated by the idea. Who has unusual magic?

You do, Sigrid says. I do. Gisèle does. Gypsies. The insane. Hitler would have killed your mother right away.

Don't, Elizabeth says.

All right, Sigrid says. Twins. Twins have the magic. They are two of the same thing. How can you tell which is which? The question is too distracting. Too philosophical. Yes, twins are the worst. The rest of us are dirty, disgusting creatures living in slime. Twins are not dirty. They are a living puzzle. They are a surprise. They are surreal.

I know that, Elizabeth says.

She does not say: That is why they must be saved.

After typing all morning, happily, a delicious sense of promise, Elizabeth walks aimlessly down boulevard Saint-Michel. Clamoring tourists appear to anger the Parisian shopkeepers. The sunlight seems hysterically bright. Objects gleam sharply from storefronts. A flash in the front window of a bridal shop catches her eye, and there is Sigrid, running her hand over the white confection of a dress. Elizabeth stops, dumbfounded. Sigrid is speaking to someone who stands half hidden behind the mannequin. Elizabeth observes animated happiness in Sigrid's expression, but as she stares, this joy becomes too much, overacting, a parody, and for this reason alone she does not want to reveal herself or even be observed by chance. Still, there is a distinctly proprietary air in the way Sigrid lifts and drops the folds of the voluminous white skirt. Against the taffeta, Sigrid's hand appears to be quite large and oddly dark. She runs her index finger up the bodice slowly, so that Elizabeth notes the uneven ride of the finger's path over the sequins and seed pearls, a broken road, and she remembers the moment in the car when Louise lost control of the wheel. With her hand on the dress's bosom, Sigrid appears to be listening to the hidden figure—this attitude of attention is obvious, almost stylized, the cocked head, the raised eyebrows, the eye rolling—as if Sigrid knows she has an audience. Then her expression darkens, her brows knit. She looks almost pained.

Vom Rath emerges from behind the mannequin and gazes out the window. Elizabeth wonders if she is dreaming. He wears his usual suit and tie, but he is carrying an enormous bouquet of lilies, white lilies against his black suit—as if he is on his way to a grand funeral, as if this bridal shop would be precisely the place one would stop before attending to the graver business of the grave. It's as if he has concocted this scene and now must get a look at his audience.

Elizabeth steps back, almost into the street. Her heels hang off the curb, over the gutter. She believes vom Rath would be more likely to see her. His eyes move restlessly, as always, beyond Sigrid. He turns his back to the window, then peers over his own shoulder, out into the passing crowds.

From this farther distance details are somehow more arresting. Sigrid's fingernails are painted a dark red, like blood fresh from a large wound. This, Elizabeth now realizes, is exactly what makes her hands appear gigantic, disturbing against the white dress. She sees, too, that Sigrid is wearing gaudy diamond earrings that drip like chandeliers, and a necklace of similar design. The jewelry is not meant to complement Sigrid's clothing—her black suit is the twin of vom Rath's. She's quite sure Sigrid did not leave the apartment in Saint-Denis this morning with these jewels—and clearly they are paste—in her ears and at her throat.

What I've never understood, Elizabeth whispers to no one, to herself, what I've always wanted to know, is why women pay so much attention to the bride's dress.

She's had this thought a hundred times in her life. All those girls at Vassar: the dress, *my mother's dress, my grandmother's dress.* But Miss Rose Peebles said you can wear any old thing to get married, and it's cheaper, too, in the long run. Although sometimes the dress might be free. Elizabeth's own mother wore a suit borrowed from her aunt. She's been told it was dark blue, but in all the photographs it looks black, as if her mother was anticipating the events to follow, the need for this other costume: her husband's untimely death and burial. So maybe a white dress would have been better, less of an omen or a curse.

There is, of course, no way to be sure, no way to make any of it turn out differently.

Now vom Rath turns toward Sigrid. She lets go of the dress, he takes her in his arms, and they begin a slow waltz, back and forth behind the three headless mannequins. No one enters or leaves the bridal shop. No one else appears in the window, amused (or otherwise) by these antics. They seem to be enjoying complete privacy, and Elizabeth wonders if this is what she envies, this privacy, rather than vom Rath's hand on Sigrid's back. Boulevard Saint-Michel seems by contrast to grow more crowded, as if to regulate some imbalance, the vacuum of this scene. Some people here in the street stop to watch. They laugh, but their laughter sounds cruel.

Vom Rath gazes out at them over Sigrid's shoulder and smiles. He has an audience. He nods as if acknowledging applause. If he sees Elizabeth in the crowd, he pretends not to recognize her. She realizes she does not want Sigrid to know she was watching. Sigrid's privacy is somehow frightening, full of terrifying possibility.

The next day, Elizabeth walks from île Saint-Louis to the *boulangerie,* the best one, on rue Saint-Paul. She wants to buy bread for the party she will give for Sigrid, Ann, and Marie. A baguette, a boule, and on impulse, a half-dozen croissants for the morning. She's had a wild idea: what if the dinner turns into a breakfast? What if everyone brings an excellent bottle of wine and demands it be opened? What if there is so much food that the eating never stops until everyone drops off to sleep or into a stupor of epic proportions, and it's too late to call for a taxi or take the Métro to Saint-Denis? Where will they all sleep? Elizabeth will give up her bed to Ann and Marie. Margaret and Louise will keep their own rooms, of course. Elizabeth and Sigrid will negotiate for the couch or make themselves a cozy nest on the rug in front of the fire.

So when she sees Sigrid twined in an embrace with a man, she cannot remember where she is and what she is supposed to be doing. She notices quite outside her own consciousness that she is meant to be buying bread. Automatic pilot they call it, one of those trains whose wheels are locked onto the track beneath it. Full speed ahead. She enters the bakery, waits her turn in line. She speaks pleasantly to the woman behind the counter, orders what she needs, pays with correct change and an extra centime for the baker. She waits while the box is tied up with pale blue twine. She leaves the shop. In the street, she thinks about throwing the box away, but she doesn't. She holds it carefully as if the contents were glass, retraces her steps, lets herself into the apartment. She sets the box on the counter in the kitchen and crosses the hallway to check on Margaret, who is quite motionless, taken by the profound sleep of the massively sedated.

For a moment, Elizabeth listens to Margaret's breathing. She finds herself counting.

Then she closes the door, crosses the living room into the kitchen. She reaches into the low cupboard for the yellow gratin dish from Dehillerin. She steps up onto one of the kitchen chairs, raises the dish high over her head, and throws it to the slate floor. The dish cracks neatly, perfectly, into four pieces.

No more gratin, she says to the kitchen.

The rest of the crockery must be nervous.

She climbs down from the chair, takes a glass from the sideboard and the bottle of Armorik from the top of the icebox, pours three fingers. She leaves the broken dish splayed on the floor. In the living room, she sips the whiskey and stares out the window at the great squatting hulk of Notre-Dame. When the glass is empty, she lets herself quietly into Margaret's room, eases herself onto the bed, and tucks her face into Margaret's shoulder until the tears running into her nose and mouth make breathing a little difficult.

The mismatched towers of Saint-Sulpice. Six architects, one hundred years, a place that could never crumble to dust, no matter what awful secrets are confessed inside. The light heavy as mist, as fog. Elizabeth waits for Sigrid, as instructed, in the last row on the north side of the nave. She is late, as usual. She's not very German that way, Louise has said. Elizabeth doesn't mind. She's walked down from the apartment on île Saint-Louis after a bad night's sleep, a long day worrying about Margaret, about Sigrid outside the bakery, about what it is that Sigrid wants to tell her in the back of this fortress of a church. She is alone here except for seven schoolgirls in uniform who seem to have escaped one sort of captivity and not yet surrendered to the next. Elizabeth glances at her watch—a quarter after four. They have likely just been sitting quietly behind their desks, a teacher's voice counting or reciting or admonishing, and now they are here, now rising as if to sing hymns a cappella, climbing onto the chairs six rows ahead, balancing, not laughing, not even a giggle. Then after some invisible signal, they step across the row as if it were a bridge over a small flood, a somewhat dangerous but still mostly rather delightful undertaking. Each girl seems to be lifting the next out of a sort of drowning in the center aisle, and then they move quickly down the row, holding hands, dancing lightly on the balls of their feet. Their white shirts glow in the gloom, red neckties flash in a beam of late sunlight from the window above. In the middle of the row, the leader loses her balance momentarily but is saved when the girl beside her lets go of her hand and grasps her shoulder. The line of girls stops, teeters, each girl saving the next in a chain reaction so perfectly graceful it might have been choreographed and rehearsed.

At the end of the row, each girl steps off the last chair, and they leave soundlessly. What was that? Elizabeth wonders. A dare? A game? A lark? She turns to watch their departure and sees Sigrid in the doorway, patting each child on the head, once, a solid but gentle tap, as if counting them, keeping track. When they have disappeared, Sigrid turns and touches her lips, blows them a kiss. She enters the church, acknowledges Elizabeth with a wave, but walks away toward the racks of offertory votives. She drops a coin in the box, and the metal *yawp* flies up into the air and away. She lights the candle, peering into the red glass, staring at the flame. Then she joins Elizabeth, but leaves two chairs empty in between.

They look straight ahead at the altar, as though something will happen up there now that Sigrid has arrived. Elizabeth waits. She tries to prepare herself for the disappointment the two empty seats suggest she is about to endure. *Oh well,* a little bird chirps in her chest, *oh well, oh well, oh well.*

Leezabet, Sigrid begins, Marie and Ann say the only way I can stay in France is to make a marriage. *Mariage de raison.*

Elizabeth nods. The little bird stops its insane chirp.

Let's walk, Sigrid says.

Hours later, after supper, they stand on the sidewalk outside the café.

It's not that bad, Sigrid says.

Elizabeth tries to smile, fails. No, she says, it's worse.

No.

What does he think about it?

Think?

Elizabeth wonders if she knows the words in German.

Sigrid seems to understand. He believes, she says.

I feel sorry for him then.

Sigrid shakes her head, meaning *Don't*.

Certain scenarios present themselves in Elizabeth's imagination.

What will he expect? she asks.

Sigrid slides her right arm under Elizabeth's left and grasps her elbow. He will get what he wants, she says. Now, come with me. We have a thing to do.

Rue des Canettes and then the alley. The pavement shines, dark and wet.

Streets are women, Elizabeth says.

Perhaps Sigrid will understand. What a silly idea anyway. Sigrid nods and keeps walking, taking Elizabeth somewhere, fierce intent in her stride, in her grip on Elizabeth's arm.

Elizabeth realizes they are walking in the direction of the German embassy. We can go to my work, Sigrid says.

Despite the clutch of Sigrid's hand, Elizabeth notes the tenderness in her voice. The falling darkness makes all shapes equal: trash bins and bicycles, a metal chair someone has left outside, a case of empty wine bottles, a man wearing an apron, smoking a cigarette, staring past them.

A small voice in Elizabeth's head says, *Expect nothing. Wait without waiting.*

Two military police guard the embassy gate. Sigrid shows them her identification cards, speaking in polite, sprightly German, as if she is happy to see them. The police let Sigrid through the gate but close it before Elizabeth can enter.

Bitte, Sigrid says. A brief exchange follows, and the police laugh, open the gate, motion to Elizabeth to follow.

You are my sister, Sigrid whispers.

Another guard steps in front of them, unlocks the front door. He stands at attention in the entry. He will wait.

Sigrid leads Elizabeth upstairs to the private quarters, still in readiness for the führer who will never arrive. Fruit piled in bowls, white wicks on the candles, fresh flowers in the vases, the large dining room set with linens, plates, silver cutlery, glassware. Sigrid walks through the apartment, turning on lights, turning them off again. Elizabeth listens to the click and sizzle of the lamps, waiting for Sigrid to make a discovery. The führer in his pajamas, a glass of whiskey in his hand. But no. No one.

Back in the sitting room, Sigrid pauses in front of a gigantic arrangement of lilies and roses, peonies, baby's breath and statice.

Too much, she says. Too much for *him*.

She begins to pull smaller stems from the vase, laying them on the low table. She moves next to the arrangement across the room and performs the same subtractions, the smallest flowers with the longest stems. Elizabeth follows her to the dining room, the bedroom, observes the same cull, Sigrid carrying fistfuls of flowers to the table in front of the sofa. She instructs Elizabeth to sit down, to watch. She quickly and carefully begins to braid the flowers together. She bends the stems nearly to the breaking point but seems to know the limit of each. Her hands move constantly between the pile of stems and the construction in her lap, machinelike.

In a few minutes, Sigrid has fashioned a wreath, seven or eight inches in diameter, which she sets gently on the table.

My mother taught me to do this, she says.

She begins another braid. When this one finished, she slips both wreaths over her arm, takes Elizabeth's hand, and leads her into the bedroom. She closes the door. She positions Elizabeth in front of the full-length mirror and places one of the wreaths on her head. She wears the other. They stand for a minute, gazing at themselves. Elizabeth cannot think what to say except that to say anything would ruin it all. Then Sigrid removes her wreath and Elizabeth's and settles them carefully into the top dresser drawer.

Tomorrow I will bring a larger bag, she says. To take them back to Saint-Denis. Tonight they would be crushed.

The next day is Saturday. Sigrid telephones at noon and suggests they meet by the river.

Elizabeth walks from the apartment. It's not far, but her breathing grows ragged. By the time Sigrid finds her, she is wheezing.

What do you need? Sigrid asks. What can I do?

I'll be all right in a minute, Elizabeth says. I just have to sit.

They find a bench below the quai Saint-Michel.

What is happening?

Asthma, Elizabeth tells her. It came on years ago, when I was a little girl.

How old?

Five or six. Lately cities seem to bring on the attacks. I seem to need water or a coast.

Now the countess will take you to Normandy again. You are her little pet.

It's not like that.

They watch the light on the Seine. Eerie, uncanny, the boundary between reality and what's reflected in the water. Mirrored, silvery surfaces, the shadow of a bridge like a deeper, secret bridge, or the loneliness of a bridge when no one crosses it for hours. The wake boats leave behind. So many actual things—wake, shadow, smoke—that can't be held or put to use. Reflection. Reflection, which is specific and also insubstantial.

Sigrid holds the tips of her fingers against Elizabeth's temple. In here, she says, you have already gone. The countess has already stolen you. In here—she reaches lower, taps Elizabeth's breastbone—you are trying to catch your breath. She withdraws her hand.

Louise wants to buy a house in Florida, Elizabeth says. Key West. Water on all sides. Practically nothing but coast.

It's very far away.

Ships go there.

I have never been on a ship at sea. A sailboat, yes, but always in sight of land.

How did you get to Paris?

On the train. It was terrible, though, all the stopping. Showing your papers all the time. Ann was very good, very charming. Guards fell in love with her.

Not just guards.

Sigrid throws back her head, laughs for a long time. True, she says finally. But I think a ship would have been easier.

Yes, Elizabeth says.

No stopping. No borders to cross. From Le Havre, you would pass the Azores, but the captain might be the sort who, once the land is behind him, hardens his heart and will not stop. Because his heart is an iceberg anyway, undissolving. He hates the land that tries to melt it with all its human heat and warmth. Away wife! Keep away! For the entire journey, he stands watch, facing west, the wheel in his grip as hard and steady as his heart. You could pack your passport and identity papers away and never look at them for days.

When I get to Florida, she says, I want you to come there. Right away. You and Ann and Marie. Louise will want that, too.

It's not going to be safe for us here?

No. Not even here. Clara believes that nothing will stop it. She believes the Germans will be in Paris.

When? Soon?

She can't say when. But she's sure.

Tears gather in the corners of Sigrid's eyes. She leans her head back, Elizabeth imagines to keep them from spilling over.

I'm sorry I frightened you, Elizabeth says.

It's all right, Sigrid tells her, pressing the heels of her hands against her eyes. I would rather know. I'm ashamed to cry. Don't tell anyone.

Of course not, Elizabeth says. She reaches into her pocket and finds a handkerchief, hands it to Sigrid. Let's be happy before I go.

Yes, Sigrid says. I want to give you something for bon voyage. Come with me.

They cross the little bridge and the Pont Notre-Dame to the quai de Gesvres. Outside a café, Sigrid tells Elizabeth to wait. She goes into the café and returns with a bottle wrapped in brown paper.

I will take you somewhere beautiful, Sigrid says.

They walk, rounding three corners, so that Elizabeth has the sense that they have made a perfect square, but she allows herself to be led. Sigrid stops at a small gray door on rue Brisemiche. The sign reads Hôtel Colombe.

In the small reception room, Sigrid asks Elizabeth to sit in one of the blue armchairs. The wallpaper looks as though it might have come from a painting by Vuillard, the one called *Misia at the Piano.* Sigrid speaks to the clerk in German. No money appears to change hands. Elizabeth marvels somewhere outside herself. Her mind stays completely blank except for curiosity about the wrapped bottle, curiosity so mild it's a ghost of itself or curiosity belonging to someone else. The clerk gestures, pointing above her head. Sigrid turns toward Elizabeth. She's holding a silver key attached to a wooden bird. Of course it is a dove, *colombe.* They climb two flights of stairs in silence. Sigrid unlocks the door of number 4.

It's a lovely small room: a bed, a dresser, a sink, a pot of violets on the low bedside table. The bottle turns out to be champagne.

I know you like scotch, Sigrid says, and she gives a small shrug.

I like this, too, Elizabeth says. I think maybe I like it better.

Glasses for juice, Sigrid says, pointing to the tumblers on the edge of the sink. The champagne cork releases like a gunshot.

I hope she doesn't think there's a murder being committed up here, Elizabeth says.

Sigrid raises her glass. Bon voyage, my Leezabet.

When they've finished, Sigrid takes their empty glasses and sets them on the dresser. She bends to remove Elizabeth's shoes and then her stockings, reaching slowly up under her skirt. How can you stand to wear these? she asks, rolling the stockings down and slipping them off. She places the rolls neatly inside Elizabeth's shoes.

You never wear them? Elizabeth says.

Only in winter.

Sigrid is still completely clothed. I want to do it this way, she says. She pins Elizabeth's body beneath her own, holding her arms above her head. The feel of Sigrid's flesh and bones through the layers of cotton and silk is a delicious tease, Sigrid's lips on hers, on her cheeks and chin and throat, opening the buttons of Elizabeth's blouse with her teeth. Elizabeth hears her own voice but far away and small.

Sounds like doves, Sigrid says. Where the name comes from. Or like little girls calling.

Yes, Elizabeth says. Yes.

They receive a handwritten invitation: Miss Barney will be at home two Fridays hence. Perhaps Miss Bishop would do us the honor . . .

She likes the poem about Paris and the clocks, Louise says. She told me that.

Too many clocks, Elizabeth says. Why do so many of my poems begin with some assertion about what time it is?

Time is of the essence?

I wonder if Clara will be there.

It's odd that we haven't seen her. She seems to have disappeared.

Elizabeth wants to change the subject.

I don't think I'm brave enough to read a poem, she says. They're so terribly slight.

Suit yourself, Louise says. I won't beg. Though Miss Barney may.

Rue Jacob is an impressive address, the last private expanse in the heart of Paris, but quite unassuming from the front. The man at the door is Chinese with black lacquered hair, painted on. Beside him, doves startle in their cages. The walls inside are papered red, textured to feel like velvet. *Flocked* is the word. The rest of the downstairs appears dingy, drafts rushing in at the windows. The garden is the miracle, though, a long lawn and woods beyond, tucked away behind the most crowded street in Saint-Germain.

In the dining room, one could not see to eat. No matter: the Chinaman passes chocolates on a tarnished tray and teacups filled with wine or sherry. Difficult to know which one is choosing.

Miss Barney is a small woman but somehow much larger in her own house. Her blue eyes see through a person's skull, read her thoughts.

She's old enough to be your mother, Louise says.

Sigrid must not meet her, Elizabeth decides. Or is it the other way around?

Imitations of Rockefeller's unicorn tapestries hang on the walls. The six sofas are covered in velvet, shades of burgundy and brown. No chair matches any other.

We've fallen into the storage closet at the Metropolitan Museum, Louise says.

On top of the tapestries are portraits. Upon closer examination, Elizabeth sees they are all of the same person, a child, a girl, a woman who looks very like Miss Barney. Close up, one understands that the sofas are really beds, piled with pillows and furs. Mirrors to gaze into and out of, hung so that a person might watch what is happening across the room. A grand piano in need of a polishing and perhaps in need of tuning. Though the room is dark, all these furnishings cast light as if they're lit from inside, though when one looks away, turns one's attention to some other object, they seem to fade, to forget themselves.

Dust has gathered on every surface. Elizabeth is finding it a little hard to breathe. She wonders how she will ever be able to read a poem.

Someone turns on a light in the dining room to reveal a new table setting: fresh fruit, sandwiches, and cakes made by Miss Barney's famous cook, Berthe. Gin and whiskey on the sideboard.

Look at the bottles, Louise says. I'll bet you'll be able to read a poem.

Outside the garden runs all the way to the Seine, the lawn and then a forest cut through with paths mostly leading nowhere but occasionally to a single iron chair, rusted, askew, but oddly welcoming. The marble fountain is just a basin full of leaves, the temple a kind of theater, the stage already set to look like a sitting room—or is it really just another place to sit? And be watched. And to that end, Elizabeth discovers, the back side of the house is one gigantic mirror.

The sun can never get past the tops of trees, so gloom drenches the garden, but it makes one thoughtful.

If Clara were here, Elizabeth thinks, this is where she'd be waiting for us.

You feel old here, Elizabeth says. You take on the ages.

I think the opposite, Louise says. Unborn. It's sort of dark and womby.

I like it. But we should go back inside. People are saying Miss Barney is about to give a speech.

Natalie Barney holds court in the dining room. I think the truth is this, she is saying, men have skin, but women have flesh, which gives and takes light.

What does she mean? Elizabeth asks Louise.

I have been told, Louise says, that we should see her bedroom.

They leave the crowded parlor and follow a velvet rope to the staircase and up the steps.

The bedroom is dim on purpose, curtains half drawn, a pattern of gray and white stars on all the upholstery and linens. The brightest light is a tiara glittering from inside the open armoire, which is heavy, dark, hulking, from another world. Elizabeth can't help thinking it's as if a man is in the room, pointedly occupying the space, belligerent, vaguely threatening. It's hard to believe Miss Barney would not have seen this for herself. Perhaps she notices individuals more than effect, although her parlor would seem to disprove that notion.

Someone has left a pile of old letters on the low dresser, a walking stick; a life-size china swan sits in front of a mirror. Three photographs of a woman in a top hat, in embellished frames, arranged like a triptych of icons.

Wouldn't you like to lie down and go to sleep? Louise says.

It's too gloomy. I'd be afraid I might never wake up.

They hear footsteps on the stairs. The Chinaman appears in the doorway.

Miss Barney is looking for you, Miss Bishop, he whispers.

There you are, Miss Barney says. She takes both of Elizabeth's hands and leads her toward the piano. It's a kind of odd two-step, but Miss Barney is very graceful, so that their procession, all the way across the room, is not the least bit awkward. At the last minute, Elizabeth wonders if Miss Barney has made a terrible mistake—she believes Elizabeth is a singer, and that is why a musician introduced as Monsieur Poulenc is settling himself at the piano.

But no, she is calling Elizabeth a poet, a protegée of Miss Marianne Moore, but a new and distinctive voice in her own right. Evidently, Miss Barney has looked into things. The older poet, she says, tells us this younger one has a methodically oblique, intent way of working. She is not like the vegetable shredder that cuts into the life of a thing. Miss Barney says this in both English and French. Elizabeth is interested and somewhat horrified to realize that the French word for shredder is *râpe*.

She has decided to read "Paris, 7 A.M." as Louise suggested. As soon as she begins, however, the words sound dull and flat—a series of sheep bleats is how the French will hear it, or anyone who doesn't know English and maybe some who do. The rhymes occur in the oddest places. Some people will surely go mad waiting for rhyming words when there is no real pattern. Weathers and feathers, high, die, below and snow. What does it all mean anyway? She hopes no one will ask because she will not be able to answer the question.

Extraordinary that she can say the words of the poem and listen to herself at the same time. She scans the sea of faces for Clara's.

Then it's over. The word *snow* followed by silence. The audience politely waits for more. Elizabeth thinks she might drown in the horrible awkward moment of judgment that follows.

Miss Barney begins the applause. It's astonishing, the racket her two tiny hands can make. Louise joins in, nods her head decisively, mouthing the word *triumph*. Elizabeth rolls her eyes. One poem does not a triumph make.

Miss Barney is sixty years old, almost exactly her mother's age, Clara's age, so the attraction Elizabeth feels is very strange. Clara is a few years older but seems more like a governess or a nursemaid. Miss Barney, though. Elizabeth would like to stay in the beam of her attention forever—though she suspects no one does for very long. She would like to sit very close to Miss Barney, on one of the velvet sofas, Miss Barney's arm around her shoulder, Miss Barney whispering in her ear that Elizabeth is a good girl, smart and pretty and soon to make something extraordinary of herself. She would like to lie in bed with Miss Barney and talk about the day's events and plan for the next day. Then Miss Barney would put her arms around Elizabeth and hold her for a full minute, kiss her on her cheek or her forehead or both, get up, turn out the light, step out of the room, close the door, whisper something necessary from the other side.

Necessary? Now where did that word come from? *Necessary angel.*

But Miss Barney bestows her attention, her concentrated gaze, on everyone. That is why the Friday salons are such a success.

It's interesting, Louise says now, what she chooses not to see.

What? Elizabeth says. Louise points discreetly to the staircase, two women ascending, arms and hips touching, not accidentally.

That looks like fun, Louise says.

Elizabeth feels the electricity of her reading drain away, and gravity, that mundane force, take its place. She knows what's happening in her expression, and that Louise is watching the change, the fade.

Don't worry, Elizabeth. I won't leave you.

Elizabeth moves closer to Louise.

And there's always Sigrid.

I don't know about always.

I don't think she's leaving Paris anytime soon.

No, I don't suppose she is.

Do you want another whiskey?

I do, but let's go before I can get it. I want to use my typewriter.

And not be the monkey typing Shakespeare?

They search for Miss Barney to say goodbye, but she does not appear to be in the house.

Try the Temple, Berthe tells them.

They wind through the crowd outside, to the Temple de l'Amitié. Miss Barney is indeed inside, with a dozen other guests, listening to a young singer. The singer is nervous to the point of trembling, a full-body vibrato, but her voice lacks color and depth. Next to Miss Barney is a woman whose frozen smile suggests she must be the girl's mother. Elizabeth and Louise stop in the doorway to listen. Poulenc accompanies her on the piano. A woman beside them whispers that it's his newest composition, incidental music for a poem by Paul Éluard. Everyone in the room wears the same look of confusion, including Poulenc. Only Miss Barney is rapt. The sight of her rapture causes Elizabeth to wonder about her poem and the depth of Miss Barney's appreciation. She tries to drive the thought away.

Can you follow the words? she asks Louise.

He's a surrealist, Louise says. Don't worry.

When the young singer is finished, she begins to weep. She drops onto the piano bench and buries her face in Poulenc's sleeve, clutching the folds of his coat in her hands. This almost seems like a part of the performance. Poulenc stares straight ahead, his expression now devoid of any emotion. He is absent.

He is someone, Elizabeth can tell, who has mastered the art of listening, and so must also have a deep understanding of silence, things unsaid and unheard. Elizabeth watches Poulenc and learns something. He has found a way to be anonymous, invisible. Even while he was playing—his music absorbs or intuits Éluard's poems but doesn't feel them. It is like living close to a graveyard in which no one you know is buried: the grief is far, far way. Like pain a half hour after the analgesic. All this seems to Elizabeth like the kind of poem she wants to write. Fear and panic finally calmed, lying quietly underneath the words. Poems like Poulenc's silence, his stare. He will not comment on the singer and her mortification. No. His silence *is* the comment.

Elizabeth remembers: a boat going to save somebody, to save children. The boat carries out this very great task, but the boat doesn't feel anything at all.

The *Sirène,* in fact, bobs once again at Léonie's dock without comment, a pool of bilge on the floor of the cabin, an oil rainbow spreading below the lee cloth that held the babies. There is a sort of boat called *tender.* Elizabeth remembers the stars that guided them back from Dieppe. The Dipper, itself a kind of boat, swings overhead. You want to climb up into it, be safe above the fray, be tended. Such pleasure. A real boat could never be that. The heeling, the bilge, the torn sail, the broken mast. It may be stars are the only pleasure boats we have.

ELSEWHERE

1938

At the Murray Hill Hotel in New York, there is a letter for Elizabeth, from Sigrid.

Your ghost is everywhere: Hotel Colombe, the underground rooms at Dehillerin, which I cause myself to pass every day, and where I have no purpose but to think of us there. Ann and Marie do not allow me to cook—have I told you this? They say I will have many years to do the cooking for someone who will not appreciate it, and so I should stay away from stoves and pots and knives for as long as I can. I ask them if I will have to cook when I am married, and they explained everything. So it will be all right. I will tell you when you return. And when will that be? I hope it will be soon because there is something in Paris now that frightens me. I sense danger all over. The führer writes or telephones to say that he will visit, and we prepare again. Flowers mostly. The rest of it stays upstairs without comment, as if it had known what was to be.

Elizabeth likes this turn of phrase, as if all the tables and chairs, the dresser, the bed with its fat pillows might speak of their ambition and dashed hopes.

And then we wait. And then there is a telegram saying he is not coming this week. Then E takes the flowers out of the rooms. You should see it when he gets into the taxi and I hand him the bouquets, pack them in as if he would be preserved in flowers. He says his apartment is like a florist's shop, the most terrible florist in Paris, who never sells a single stem.

E is worrisome. I wish he might stay at work in the evenings. I am afraid he will cause trouble, for himself and for other people. The Polish boy waits for him in the street most days. Once the police told him to go away. If loitering is a crime in Paris, he will soon be arrested. I am afraid for that, too, because now we have met him and he knows our names.

Most evenings, I travel right back to Saint-Denis after work, but yesterday, I stayed in the city. I do not really know why. I felt quite lost, and I began to walk. Though I managed to put one foot ahead of the other, I did not know where I was going. It was as if I were asleep, Paris hung with soft, gray fog, which turned to rain and then back to mist. I found myself in front of Sylvia's bookshop—I had walked all the way in the damp to this very spot without any plan to do so.

I stepped inside intending to ask for a drink of water. The shop seemed nearly empty, and silent. I stood, shivering, trying to understand. Then I heard, faintly, from the back room, the sound of a woman's voice. I could not make out the words or even the language, but I became convinced that the voice was yours. You had returned to Paris but had not told me—or you had never really left. I wanted to go toward your voice, but I did not want to discover or embarrass you. I turned away, went back out into the street to look for a taxi.

I tried not to write to you, but I could not help it. I think I should not bother you—you who have so many important things to do. I am sure New York is keeping you busy and entertained. And yet, somehow writing to you makes me think you are here. For a few minutes, you are standing beside me or sitting across a table. There is a bottle of wine between us. We are holding hands around it.

But in the end, when I try to stop writing the letter and sign my name, I find I can't do it, and I think of more to tell you.

Such as this: Marie returned from Seville disgusted by the fascists and how they have destroyed the monuments and beautiful places. A chapel she saw was saved from fire but ruined all the same, the ceiling black with smoke, everything drenched. She is furious and frightened. Ann was angry that she went. But Marie said it was her research. And Ann said, your research could kill us. So now I think we will all be staying home. I must say I do not really know what that means. The English word is not sufficient.

1940

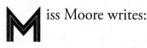iss Moore writes:

Though we would very much enjoy traveling with you, Mother and I are entangled beyond ingenuity. Our illness has made us like snakes in alcohol, and that is abhorrent. You must come back and help us by example to have leisurely habits and better health.

From Key West, Miss Moore requests snake fangs, a rattlesnake rattle, and alligator teeth. After Elizabeth wraps the parcel, she worries that it will arouse suspicion—already it sounds broken inside—and be torn open by some diligent postal clerk in Brooklyn, who will now have further cause to wonder about the eccentricities of the Moore household. But the package arrives safely, unbreached.

I have always wanted to see the hypodermic opening in a snake fang, but could not have anticipated what a treatise on specialization the entire implement is—with that swirling taper and high polish. To think of your sending two fangs and two alligator teeth. The rattle in nine or ten ways is a mechanism of inexhaustible interest. . . . I felt a slight shudder of superstition as I first held it up, as if I were touching the bones of Osiris.

Who traveled, Elizabeth knows, out to sea in the boat of his own coffin.

&

Miss Moore continues:

Thank you for the descriptions of chameleons, ostrich, and the bathing grackles. One of an animal's more endearing savageries— her habit of carrying things with her and keeping guard over them.

&

The owl is perhaps my favorite—nothing it seems to me can rival the look of remoteness in its eyes.

&

I have always wanted to see cork trees like those under which Sancho Panza and Don Quixote rested; the Hispanic Museum catalogue of locks, grilles, and weapons made me imagine that wrought iron is one of my hobbies.

When Miss Moore's mother dies, her handwriting in these letters suddenly appears as child's scrawl, oversized, slanting downward across the page. *I'm trying to be peaceable about things, Elizabeth; and not aggrieved that life is just nothing like what life should be.*

༄

But in time, she recovers her good sense:

> *In connection with traveling, you must leave out everything you*
> *can and must not think of answering letters if anyone writes to*
> *ask what you are doing.*

1949

What Elizabeth believes first is that Louise has stopped drinking. She looks well-preserved but mirthless. Like something that has been entombed here in the Library of Congress, in the closet behind the poetry consultant's office or under a drop cloth in a storage room, an unloved and forgotten sheaf of thin pages, bound still, but stiffened. There's a creak and a splitting of the spine when you touch it.

You didn't tell me you were coming to Washington, Elizabeth says.

That's not much of a greeting, Louise says. You look tired.

I'm not, though. Not tired. Just citified.

You've lost weight. It's nice.

Thank you. How's Victoria?

Will you ask me to come in?

Elizabeth steps back into her office, motions to the chair. A battered typewriter sits on her desk, surrounded by piles of paper.

I have a lovely view, she says. The Capitol dome. Do you know you can get a ten percent discount on pens at the House of Representatives? Good thing since I keep losing pens. I've lost the black-and-gold one I've had since Paris.

Louise falls heavily into the chair, as if she's walked a long way. Elizabeth crosses the room, sits down behind her desk.

You look rich, Elizabeth, Louise says. Successful. You never did before. You were always such a church mouse.

I'm not rich. But people treat me as if I were. Or might become rich. Or make *them* rich.

You wear it well, that treatment. It's alluring.

And I've become an expert filler of forms. Before I came here I was wretched at it. I'm going to the zoo this week to see the two new baby elephants and the baby leopard, who chases his tail constantly, everyone says, because he knows he's in Washington and that's what they do here.

I hope you will forgive me, Louise says suddenly.

That was ten years ago. I wish I could believe in free love, but I can't. Anyway, I've nearly forgotten it.

Well, I haven't.

You should try. Really, Louise, we were so young. Traveling like we knew what we were doing. Rushing to the next excitement. Then Margaret's arm. It made us all strange, I think. How is she? She doesn't speak to me anymore.

She's all right. She doesn't drive, but hardly anyone in New York drives. She talks about you.

She does?

Would you like to go get a cup of coffee? I'm chilled to the bone.

In the Library of Congress snack bar, Elizabeth watches a small, dark-haired woman, about forty, who is eating her lunch alone. There is something about her stillness—and then Elizabeth realizes this woman is the only person in the entire room who isn't talking. She's the only person by herself. And she's not tucked away into a corner or against a wall or facing away from the rest of the tables. She's not distracting herself by reading or writing in a notebook. She takes small teeth-baring bites of her sandwich, tears at a ruffle of lettuce. She stares into space or watches other diners with a sort of brazen attention.

Louise follows Elizabeth's gaze. That one? she says. She's probably your age. Isn't that too old for you?

Don't even joke. I could lose my job. They're already firing one a day.

One what?

Louise. Don't be dense.

You mean us.

Elizabeth nods. Anyway, that's not it. I'm jealous of how peaceful she looks. Here they'd say she was *comfortable in her skin.* In Canada, you would say she was *in her skirt.*

Too bad about that. She's lovely.

Louise.

And you do have power.

Elizabeth stirs her coffee. Not really. I'm terribly ill-suited for this job. And for this town. The way people assume you'll do favors. Writers mostly, but regular people, too.

And can you do favors if you're asked? Louise says.

I'm glad you didn't say *do you.* Most people don't even ask. It's rather cold and calculating that way.

And just plain cold.

Winter in Washington is so damp. It's rather like Paris. Without the compensations.

So you don't do favors for other people? Louise says. Not ever?

Suddenly, Elizabeth feels a weight in her arms—the ghostly memory of a weight, carrying a small, living bundle. The coffee in her cup is as dark as the streets of Dieppe, as the back of Clara's coat hurrying ahead toward the port.

Apparently, she says, if someone asks, I'll do just about anything.

1953

Elizabeth recognizes the woman standing on the platform in Grand Central Station, but for an instant, the name will not come. All she remembers—or envisions really—is a photograph held up to the light. Light flooding in through the windows on her left, and a fresh tinge in the air, the lightened air, the promise of trees nearby but not quite visible. The photograph, who was it? A young woman, somber, some injury about her face, causing a kind of squint, as if she had just been hit and believed she would be again, very soon. Elizabeth doesn't know where this comes from, the bone-deep memory, not only of having seen the face but having felt it in some way, as if *she* had been the woman struck. Or, less possible, the man—she thought it must have been a man—behind the camera, the one who had just raised his hand to the woman and caused her to flinch that way, inwardly, a flinching of the soul.

Suzanne. From the photograph, the awful one meant to show Suzanne how she looked. How awful she looked.

Clara, Elizabeth says.

Elizabeth. How strange to see you here.

Isn't it? But really, where else would we have met?

A train station of course, Clara says.

Clara and Elizabeth look at each other for a long minute. Each waits for the other to speak, but then the politeness passes, and in its place a kind of stubbornness grows. Elizabeth sees that Clara's coat is warm and expensive, certainly too hot for New York in June. Clara seems to shrivel inside it, dry out to an essential self. It's as if Elizabeth is seeing her really for the first time, this innermost Clara, a hot, hard, brittle, wounded thing in a chinchilla coat.

I want to thank you, Clara says.

I have never spoken of it, Elizabeth says. I was glad to help.

And I was glad to buy you a bottle of jenever.

And a fountain pen (Elizabeth does not admit she's lost the pen).

That, too, Clara says.

What did you do after?

My husband and I had to leave, though the library was allowed to remain open. You know this, I expect.

I didn't. I heard some things. I think I hoped the Paris I knew just . . . went to sleep.

Like the fairy tale? Well, it didn't.

Clara stops talking. She looks down at her beautiful leather shoes. She seems to collapse into her coat like a fallen marionette. Then she rights herself and begins again.

You'd be standing in line behind a woman and marveling that she had silk stockings. Where did she get them? Whom did she know? And then you'd see her legs were bare and she'd drawn a line like a seam up the back of her calf.

Oh, Elizabeth says.

Dorothy was a marvel. She ran a kind of underground lending service for people who couldn't get books. Soldiers and Jews. Even after the library was closed to the public, she came to work every day.

We heard your Vichy connection—

Yes. It was useful. We don't speak of it now.

Certainly not.

That is Clara, Elizabeth thinks. Enthusiasm and then withdrawal. Warm wind and then a cloud passes over the sun. Still, that gigantic, unseen force, the magnetic pull of the past, keeps us rooted here. Elizabeth thinks she might miss her train. The idea is completely neutral, neither a hope nor a worry.

You must have a train to catch, she says.

Perhaps it will miss me.

Did you ever see them, Clara?

Léonie and Dominique died in the war.

Clara bows her head. Another train departure is announced with bells.

The babies? Elizabeth says. Did you see them?

No, I never did. Anyway, not that I knew. But so often in Paris, I would see little dark-haired girls, and sometimes I would be quite certain. But that isn't the same as really seeing, is it?

It's not.

Clara reaches into her coat pocket, extracts a ticket. She turns and surveys the tracks, but Elizabeth notices she is looking in the wrong direction, southbound.

I don't much follow the poetry scene, Clara says, but I have followed you.

There's not much to follow.

Not yet maybe, but I shall keep a lookout.

The 1:42 from Philadelphia arrives without, it seems, any announcement. Disgorged passengers swarm around and between them, and Clara lets herself or causes herself to be swept away into the crowd. Elizabeth thinks she sees the back of the chinchilla coat climbing the stairs slowly, like a tired, misunderstood beast resigned to move among humans.

1964

Elizabeth wants the owls because she believes after she and Lota return to Brazil, they will remind her of Italy, where she could always breathe better than any other place in Europe, where she was farthest from Margaret's mother, and the daily horror of the accident, where Louise was away from all her lovers, Mademoiselle Indira and maybe Ann and who knows who else. And, too, there was all the mythological, fantastical nonsense about owls. She believes in that, too, though it's somewhat embarrassing to talk about. Also, the owls look like little girls—Elizabeth doesn't really understand this part, or doesn't want to—like tiny girls bundled up against the snow. Girls she might have seen or grown up with. The girl she might have been, at four or five, before her mother went away for good. Girls safe in a cage.

But Lota insists she leave the owls behind in Genoa. The customs official promises to write and let her know what has become of them. He looks to be very young, barely out of school, she guesses, but he wears a wedding band, a rarity for Italian men. He is shy to the point of nervous collapse. She believes he might weep when he has to remove the owls' cage from her baggage cart.

Sorry, he whispers in English and then in Italian, *mi dispiace,* quietly, as if to speak his own language pains him more.

Lota, Elizabeth knows, is not at all dismayed.

I don't know what we would do with them in a rough crossing, she says.

Just like a windy branch, Elizabeth tells her. They'd know how to hang on.

Lota rolls her eyes. I expect your Miss Marianne Moore would say that, too.

No, Marianne would actually be clever.

At the last minute, the young customs official asks if the owls have names. Archimedes, Elizabeth tells him, and Helen. Octavian. And the little one is Dante. This makes the young man smile—a gorgeous light washing across his face as if he's thinking, *An Italian owl! The most profound and prolific of all Italians!*

He'll take good care of *that* one, Lota says.

Don't, Elizabeth says, don't even joke.

She gives the young man their address in Ouro Preto and tries to forget about the owls.

Who do you know in the Italian civil service? Lota asks, waving the envelope just out of Elizabeth's reach (a gesture she's lately adopted).

Elizabeth turns and starts toward her room, knowing Lota will eventually tire of the taunt. She hears the letter fall onto the tray that holds the day's mail.

The handwriting is shockingly graceful, the kind of script you might see on a wedding invitation. *Miss Bishop.* Elizabeth swears the seal has been perfumed.

I am dictating this to my sister who studies English. I want to tell you of your owls. They are well and very gentle. My son has taken a friendship with them. He likes to wear them on his body and head to believe he is a tree. Dante sleeps in his hair. My son is also gentle. He does not rush around like some boys. He is blind from his birth. Most animals are a danger but not your owls. He says they take care of him, just as he takes care of them. They give him wise ideas about the things he cannot see. He says they are his invisible babies.

Later, Elizabeth shows the letter to Lilli.

It's funny, she says, that notion that if you can't see something, it must be invisible.

1966

I *am sorry you are not well,* Elizabeth writes to Margaret.

I am sending the name and address of my analyst who has been a great help to me over the years. Please come to see Lota and me in Rio. The best art here is quite primitive, as I'm sure you know, but I think I can convince you to like at least some of it.

I am working on a book about Brazil. The first chapter is to be called "Brazil: A Warm and Reasonable People." It begins with a story I know.

In Rio de Janeiro, one of those "human interest" dramas took place, the same small drama that takes place every so often . . . a newborn baby kidnapped from a maternity hospital. The hospital staff was questioned. A feebleminded woman feeding an infant in the train station was questioned . . .

Even today, one occasionally sees an elegant lady out walking leaning on the arm of a little, dressed-up dark girl, or taking tea or orangeade with her in a tearoom; the little girl is her "daughter of creation," whom she is bringing up as if she were her own.

This next part, she crossed out:

I once had this experience for a few days in France, after the car accident, a daughter of creation. And then I had to let her go.

And this part, too:

For many years, I would wake up thinking of you and a great knot would tie itself in my chest. Then one day, the knot was gone, extinguished itself by itself, like a wave, a wake. The sea that was always so desperate for your attention: wave after wave. That was me.

But not this:

I think we will be friends now, for the rest of our lives.

1970

Elizabeth dreams that her mother is walking ahead of her, down the beach at Wellfleet. She recognizes—even though this is not possible—her mother's back, the fall of her shoulders, the color of her hair, which is the same as the sky, flat gray shot with white: waves in skeins, cirrus clouds. In the dream, she thinks she has just spoken, called out to her mother. She is waiting for a response, but none comes. Her mother keeps walking, toward nothing. Sand and sea and sky into infinity.

This beach at Wellfleet is endless. Elizabeth feels she can move forever toward some unknown, unseen horizon. Suddenly, her mother is gone, and a tall, rangy man is with her and talking a blue streak. This is literal: the sky behind his head flashes azure as he speaks. The face appears and dissolves, like the Cheshire Cat. Then the dark tortoise-shell glasses frames materialize: Robert Lowell. In the dream, Elizabeth wishes he was her mother. The wish is so strong as to be pungent, like the salt air. She wishes her dead, disturbed mother was her living, disturbed friend. She wishes this with all her heart. Maybe if she says it, the name everyone calls him, *Cal*, her mother will turn and walk back to her, and some staggering imbalance in the universe would be repaired.

She opens her mouth to speak, but of course dreams have their specific and cruel peripheries. She cannot push the words into the air, and her mother keeps going. The distance between them amplifies, as if it were sound. Sand flashes into the air behind her mother's feet as she moves. Elizabeth thinks, If I were closer, I would be blinded and weeping for days.

☙

When she wakes, Elizabeth knows she must leave Roxanne to her own darkening madness. She tries to think how she can rescue Roxanne's baby. It's too awful and familiar a picture (the mother taken away, the endangered child packed off to relatives). She scans the roil and indifference of Puget Sound, but the necessary sailboat and its Belgian captain do not, of course, appear.

1972

I don't know why I remember the look of Robert's hand on the tiller.

I don't know why I remember that Robert was fascinated by the idea of the Quabbin.

Elizabeth and Cal Lowell (the second Robert, she calls him privately) drive out to the Quabbin Reservoir to sail.

She has been told the story many times, how four towns, called Dana, Prescott, Enfield, and Greenwich, had been flooded to make the Quabbin Reservoir, how the stone foundations sat on the bottom, home now only to fish and other such watery life. She sees it in her mind's eye, the ruin, the whole empty towns lost, so heavy with water they couldn't even crumble.

It is a perfectly lovely morning, though it would be hot later. Cal has phoned for permission to walk through the reserve. The officials are well-disposed toward the old families from the four towns. They felt sorriest for the children, of whom Cal's mother was one of the oldest, who had lost their homes. Cal had said something else to them, romantic and mysterious, something about showing a brilliant poet what his family had lost.

They hoist the canoe and walk in from the parking lot—not very far—to where the old town center of Dana had once stood—very near the water, but not in it. In the long grass, Cal shows Elizabeth a hitching post and a mile marker.

I know these, he says, but I don't remember them. They're so lost. There was a hotel here, and the town hall. The church was just over there. He crosses to the place and stands, staring at the ground. Isn't it odd, he says finally, to lose a whole town?

I have been thinking of that, Elizabeth says.

But at least no one died here, Cal says. And there are no dead. The graves were all moved. Very carefully, though it was unpleasant business. Mother said it felt like going to the same funerals twice.

They find a flattened spot in the grass at the water's edge—it appears someone else had launched a boat there, too, or lain close to the water.

My father was terribly frightened by water, Cal says, or so my mother told me. All his life, he believed he would drown. But no. It was still a horrible death. I would not wish it on my worst enemy.

They wade in to their ankles. Cal helps Elizabeth into the canoe.

I'm going to take you on a tour first, Cal says, and then we'll try to find the house.

I have to get to just the right place, he says, and then we can look down and see the cellar holes.

How can you tell them apart?

I have to see the hills a certain way. For a while, I came every year, on my mother's birthday. But then once, I didn't come, and it was as if a spell had been broken.

Spell?

The way boys love their mothers. He smiles as he says this.

Cal stops talking and looks up at the line of the hills, then shakes his head. He moves slowly, turning in a lazy circle, not fast enough to make them dizzy. After a few minutes, he begins to look down into the water, as well as up to the hills, taking off his sunglasses and putting them on again, counting silently.

That's it, he says at last. Look down, Elizabeth. Here, this side, about three feet out.

She sees it, a short stack of stones, like a chimney or a ruined wall. They're all over here. Ours was a bit tilted, canted to the left. It's got a sort of drunken look to it.

They find the angle of the sun has to be just right, or else they can't see them clearly, make out the individual stones. Without light upon them, the cellar holes resemble dark beasts, or men crouched and hiding, ready to shoot to the surface of the water. Elizabeth does not like the look of them.

That may be the one. A little to the west. There, Cal whispers. That's it. The stack of squared-off stones that someone had tried to push over. Just on top of those stones. They were the stairs to the cellar.

It's not very deep, Elizabeth says.

No, he says. The deepest water then was Sunk Pond. He points to the west. There. But now it's all the same water.

That's true.

I want to bring Harriet out here, but her mother says she's too young. I think Lizzie is really afraid I'll get distracted and Harriet will go overboard and drown.

A baby on a boat, Elizabeth says. It's a terrifying idea.

1974

Louise sent the newspaper clipping from New York. *My mother kept this. I thought you would want it.*

Clara Longworth de Chambrun Dies in Paris.

Twenty years ago. They must all be gone now. So there is no one left to say what really happened.

છ

Elizabeth loses a watch, three continents, North America, South America, and Europe. Write it.

Elizabeth loses a fountain pen that she bought in Paris. That Clara bought for her.

Elizabeth loses the keys to a steamer trunk. Elizabeth loses a photograph of George Sand's statue in the Luxembourg Gardens.

Elizabeth loses all the fish off all the lines on all the Atlantic coasts.

Elizabeth loses everything she might bargain with.

Elizabeth loses ground—all the land beneath the plane, where the wing shades it from view.

Elizabeth loses the legend to the map.

Elizabeth loses too many kites. What to do with all that string?

Elizabeth loses an empty wasp's nest.

Elizabeth loses three houses (but gains a condominium!).

Elizabeth never loses the key to the liquor cabinet.

Elizabeth loses a card on which she had written Clara's telephone number. Even though she's memorized the number, the card seems important evidence that she'd known Clara or had called Clara, or could have called her. The card is a very light gray, just a squint past white, really. She keeps it in her coat pocket. It is embossed, and the ridges and grooves of the letters settle her, calm her when she touches the card. Like Braille. This is the blindness with which she approached and then understood Clara. Clara was a thing mostly unseen. *The thing unseen, buried, its grave never marked.* But under Elizabeth's worrying fingers, Clara becomes known, visible.

The card, like Clara, is both attractive and frightening, but now it is lost.

Write it. Write it. Write it. *Write it.*

No. Never.

1979

Number 437 Lewis Wharf. The yellow gratin dish sits in pieces on Elizabeth's bedside table. It was for some years an assemblage of vessels, for jewelry: one quadrant each for rings, earrings, necklaces, and bracelets. Now it keeps lipstick (Chanel #87 Rendez-Vous), a train ticket (Paris to Caen), Sigrid's left glove, blond leather. Two photographs, one of Robert Seaver and one of her mother as a child. Her mother's broken wristwatch, which wasn't lost after all. A spoon from Clara's apartment and a key she never returned. A lock of black hair in an applewood clip. A small animal made entirely of lace. An origami sailboat.

ACKNOWLEDGMENTS

I am indebted to the work of Peter Brazeau, Bonnie Costello, Joanne Feit Diehl, Jonathan Ellis, Gary Fountain, David Kalstone, Megan Marshall, Brett Miller, George Monteiro, Andrew Motion, Camille Roman, and Colm Tóibín, as well as conversations with Philip Levine, Mark Strand, and Chris Castiglia.

Thank you, Kerry D'Agostino, Ira Silverberg, Julianna Haubner, Lashanda Anakwah, Marysue Ricci, Carina Guiterman, Samantha Hoback, Catherine Casalino, Carly Loman, Brigid Black, and the wonderful team at Simon & Schuster. Suzanne Guiod for your generosity, and Solveig Bosse for help with the German translations.

Mary Katherine Kinniburgh at the New York Public Library, and Dean Rogers at Vassar College Library Special Collections.

So many dear friends whose support and kindness during the writing of this book was essential.

My family, especially Georgia.

ABOUT THE AUTHOR

Liza Wieland is the author of seven works of fiction and a volume of poems. She graduated from Harvard College and Columbia University and is the winner of the Robert Penn Warren Award, the Michigan Literary Fiction Award, and a Bridgeport Prize. She lives in North Carolina.